THE
DRIFT

CHRIS THRALL

SERF
BOOKS

The Drift

First published in Great Britain by Serf Books Ltd
in 2016.

www.serfbooks.com

ISBN: 978-0-9935439-0-6

A catalogue record for this book is available from
the British Library.

Design by www.golden-rivet.co.uk

1 3 5 7 9 10 8 6 4 2

For Harry

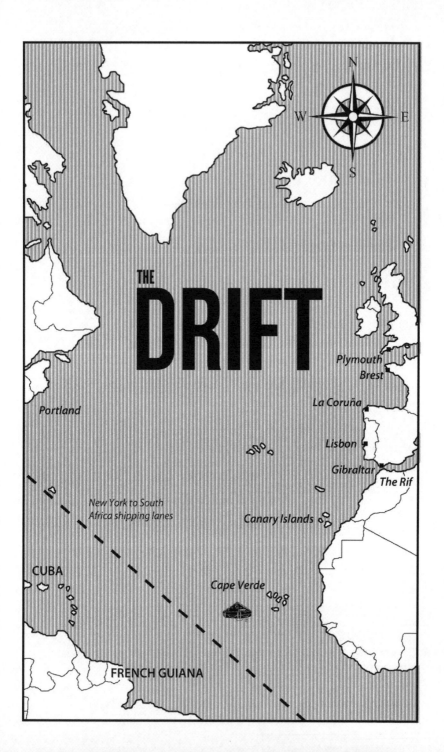

The man stirred, believing he was aboard the yacht. As he opened his eyes, orange gloom brought reality crashing home.

No!

What happened to his little girl? He lifted his head.

Thank God . . .

She lay at rest, an arm outside the sleeping bag, a damp lock stuck to her brow.

The trip had seemed a good idea after what happened, a chance to bond and rebuild life after loss. Now, seeing her infant face, acquiescent and trusting, he felt guilty they ever set sail.

The raft was awash, but it did not matter. The yacht sat on the bottom of the Atlantic, but he did not care so long as he had her.

He fumbled with the zipper in the canopy's thin fabric, needing light to check the ditch kit for the emergency radio and beacon. He'd searched for them last night, until shock and exhaustion overcame him.

The seascape should have been something to behold. Ruffled by the breeze, the aqua-green plane spilled lazily to the horizon under a deep-blue sky touched with delicate sprays of white. A lone gull circled in the salt air, mewing in anticipation of any bounty this orange dot might bequeath. Something to behold from the safety of a yacht perhaps, but from the flimsy cocoon, not a sight any sailor wished to see.

"Can we go back now?" she asked, rubbing sleep from her eyes.

"Huh?"

"Can we go back on *Future*?"

"No. Not now."

"When?"

"Not ever."

The man pulled the ditch kit toward him, an unwelcome wave of salt water accompanying it across the rippling rubber floor. He'd packed it himself, putting in all that is necessary to survive lost at sea. Most importantly, it contained a handheld radio and emergency beacon.

He unzipped the bag and rummaging through its contents but found neither. He gave the girl a look. "Have you been playing with this?"

She gave him a look back. It said everything but nothing.

The man stared out across nature's glassy face. They truly were adrift.

Leaning out, he half expected to see the upturned hull of *Future* floating nearby. Perhaps he could lash the life raft to it, making a bigger target for search and rescue. Maybe he could dive below, holding his breath long enough to swim into the cabin and locate the lost equipment and other vital survival stores.

Then *there* she was! Their beautiful yacht!

Bursting to the surface like a submarine, looking as splendid as the day he bought her, sleek lines and powerful rigging, buoyant as a cork atop the shimmering ocean.

Chris Thrall

Salvation!

Then she vanished, a wet wilderness replacing her.

- 2 -

Three months earlier

As the 747 climbed out of LaGuardia, the North Atlantic edged into view. Hans Larsson couldn't quite believe that in a few days' time he would begin sailing back across this vast gray tract. Stranger still, it would be in a boat he did not yet own and with seven-year-old Jessica by his side.

The original plan had been to make a double crossing of the Pond, stopping at the Azores en route to England and returning via Cape Verde, the Caribbean and then north on to Maine. Jessica's brother, JJ, would have been great company for her as they explored the open ocean as a family, and Mom could have taken turns at the helm and shared the schooling.

Only now it was just two of them, Hans felt it inappropriate for Jessica to spend such a long time at sea. He was determined, though, to see at least a part of the Larsson dream through, opting to fly to England with his daughter, purchase a yacht and sail the southerly passage home. It would be their special time. One he would treasure forever.

"Would you like a drink, sir?" whispered the female flight attendant, smiling at Jessica curled up asleep hugging her teddy. Since the incident, she and Bear had

4

been inseparable, something which brought tears to Hans' eyes if he dwelt too long on it.

"A Budweiser please." He smiled, settling into his seat to take in the great ocean below.

Hans had not had the easiest of upbringings, which resulted in him being unable to concentrate in class. The one escape he had as a youth was the sea, his grandfather treating him to an aging wooden daysailer for his twelfth birthday. In the final year of high school, Hans would give his name for the morning register and then disappear to spend the day exploring the inlets around Misty Port.

Local fishermen befriended him, giving advice on bait and tackle and the best locations to drop his line. He would reel in cod, bluefish and striped bass, selling them to fishmongers in the market and putting the money toward repairs to his boat. When fishing proved futile, he would anchor in a cove and get lost in books – anything to do with the sea or stories of adventure.

Other times he would don a mask and snorkel and dive down holding his breath for minutes at a time, like the pearl divers in the South Pacific islands he read about, to hook lobster and crab from rocky hidey-holes with a homemade gaff. Grilling them on an oilcan barbeque was a real treat, particularly in the winter, when he would huddle close to the embers and rewarm his shivering self after a dip in the bitter Atlantic.

One afternoon, as Hans cruised a mile offshore he saw a Cessna returning to the local airport with its wings rolling from side to side and its engine sputtering. Forced to accept fate, the pilot eased back the stick, flaring the aircraft into an attitude best suited for impact. Its undercarriage raked through the wave crests at speed before shunting into a roller. For a moment it looked as if the plane would flip forwards, like an ungainly seabird, before settling back onto its fuselage.

Hans brought *Bella* sharp about and, tacking into a stiff headwind, fought to reach the downed plane's occupants before it was too late. By the time he got there, the pilot and his wife were in shock, both with deep gashes to the head pumping out rivers of blood as they clung to the sinking airframe.

Although hailed a hero by many in the community, Hans received a thrashing from his stepfather and a six-month grounding. The after-school detentions he could have dealt with. Foregoing his beloved sailing he could not. It came as no surprise when he joined the US Navy at seventeen, serving as a radar operator aboard USS *Nimitz* before a thirst for adventure saw him volunteer for "other" operations.

From London Heathrow they took a black cab across town to Paddington Station. Hans pointed out the capital's landmark edifices to Jessica – the short, squat Gherkin building, clad in iconic green-and-black-mirrored whorls; Canary Wharf's metallic towers of commerce; and a gigantic space-age Ferris wheel, the London Eye. They boarded a southbound train to Plymouth, the English countryside prevailing as quaint red phone booths, roads not wide enough for golf karts, and aging stone farmhouses whizzed by. Hans felt he was doing a great job of keeping his little girl occupied, although in truth the Old Country fascinated him a lot more.

In three short hours the carriages hugged the Devon coastline, carving around towering sandstone cliffs, the sea pounding against rocks just feet below the tracks. Further south the scenery morphed into a rich tapestry of agriculture, fringed by deciduous trees, before becoming slowly grayer as Plymouth's urban spread took hold.

"You okay, funny face?" Hans prodded Jessica.

"I have *not* gotta funny face, Papa!"

"You have. You gotta funny face, you gotta funny nose, and your ears look like smelly frogs!"

"No, *you* have!"

"I have what?"

"You have ears!"

"Everybody's got ears."

"No! Smelly froggy!"

"Ha, you're the froggy!"

Hans chuckled and tickled Jessica's tummy. He loved the fact his daughter could take a joke and her cute attempts at defense.

"Come on, funny face. Let's go grab a cab to our hotel."

The Trapthorn Plaza did not look as inviting up close as it did on its website – "Eastern Bloc" might better describe the weathered-concrete beast – but as Hans booked in at the front desk, he wasn't bothered. Crossing the Atlantic occupied his mind.

"So, Jessie. Now we're unpacked, we need to have a crew briefing."

"What is it?"

"It's where the people who are gonna be on this boat – that's me and you – get told what they need to do. I think we should have a crew briefing over a Coca-Cola in the bar. What do you think?"

"Yay!"

"No, not *yay*. You gotta say, 'Aye aye, skipper!'"

"Aye aye, skippa!"

"Aye aye, First Mate!" Hans threw up a comical salute. "See, I'm the skipper, because the skipper is the captain of the boat. You're the first mate, because you're the first person the captain asks for help when there's a problem."

"I'm the first mate."

"Aye aye, honey. You're the first mate."

The plan was simple. Hans had arranged to view some of the boats for sale in a local marina. Having bought one, he would sort out any repairs and upgrades and recruit an additional crew member to help with the sailing. He hoped that together with provisioning the yacht, this would take no more than a week, allowing them time to explore the historic port of Plymouth before departure.

"So, do you think you can help me choose a boat, First Mate?"

"Aye aye, skippa!"

*F*uture.

The name of the yacht appealed as much to Hans as her ability to engage open water. He knew there and then he would buy her.

The Atlantic was not a new challenge for the teardrop-hulled cruiser, her previous owner making the crossing several times before the tumors took hold. A single mast, roller-furling mainsail and electric winch made for ease of handling, and a salon-style cockpit, modern galley and spacious lounge additional comfort – an important consideration with a seven-year-old aboard. To her builders – Marine Projects of Plymouth, England – *Future* represented the leading edge of sail power. To Hans Larsson, from Portland, USA, she meant a whole lot more.

It had been a difficult time. Family and friends felt uncomfortable discussing the murders, preferring to ask, "Are you okay?" and "How's Jessica doing?" Had he been young and single – he *was* single – he could have drowned the pain in alcohol and self-pity. But there wasn't only him to consider. He'd never say it, but Jessica had always been the special child. Two years older than her brother, she exuded that innocence only a daughter can. He had to be strong now for her sake and put the horror behind them.

"What do you think, Jessie?' he asked, as *Future* bobbed beneath their feet in the marina. "Do you like this boat?"

"Uh-huh."

"Would you like to go see some places in her?"

"Can Bear come?"

"Of course. Bear can help sail her."

"I like it!"

"I'll take her," he told the agent.

Afterwards, father and daughter sat dangling their legs over the dock, the emerald water lapping against the marina's wooden posts. A school of mullet cruised by, torpedoes shimmering in the sunlight. With their blunt heads and prominent scales, they looked like the carp of the sea.

Hans smiled and pointed. "Look!"

"Fish, Papa!"

"And you know what, sweet pea?"

"What, Papa?"

"We're gonna catch a lot of fish on our trip!"

"Yay!" She thrust her arms in the air awkwardly, as youngsters do, with palms upwards and fingers bent and splayed. "Will Mommy and JJ be coming with us, Pa—?"

She fell silent, staring into the water.

"Don't you remember what we said, Jessie, when we sprinkled them in the sea?"

"That the sea will always be around us."

"So *who* will always be around us?"

"Mommy and JJ!" She grinned.

"That's right."

"I miss Mommy and JJ."

"Me too, sweetie. But do you know what I do?"

"What, Papa?"

"Sometimes, when I feel the sun on my face I close my eyes and imagine we are walking along a soft sandy beach by a beautiful blue sea – you, me, Mommy and JJ – and it's sunny and warm . . . and the seagulls are squawking . . . and the air tastes fresh and salty . . . and we're smiling, sweet pea . . . We'll always be together . . . and we're smiling, my darling. We're smiling."

- 4 -

"TV, Papa!" Jessica rushed into the yacht's saloon.

Hans smiled. The twelve-volt flat-screen with built-in DVD player wouldn't place too much demand on the yacht's batteries, and, seeing Jessica's face light up, he knew it would serve a purpose in the coming weeks.

Another item Hans was pleased to have aboard was a compressor for filling scuba tanks. Diving was in his blood and had played a central role in his military career. He had introduced Jessica to the sport at a young age – not that she needed encouragement. In their twelve-meter pool in Portland, she swam without aid by the age of two, paddling like fury facedown in the water and rolling on her back every few seconds to grab air. At three she could swim a length, often underwater on a single breath.

With her aquatic ability, scuba diving came naturally to Jessica. Hans had introduced her to the equipment in the shallow end of the pool, and before her fifth birthday they were diving together in open water off Maine. Hans had altered the smallest buoyancy jacket available on the market to fit her, and she only needed two pounds of lead to submerge. He was glad they had brought their gear with them, including Jessica's three-liter cylinder, though it cost a small fortune in extra baggage charges.

When it came to sea survival, the previous owner had

12

relied on *Future*'s inflatable tender for abandoning ship. Hans shook his head and sought directions for the nearest chandlery.

Old Bill looked the sort to have sunk a few boats in his time – along with a good amount of grog. Standing amongst the dusty merchandise packing his dated premises, the archetypal sea dog was pleased to meet an American who put the safety of his crew first.

"So, me hearty, you need a life raft?" He looked at Jessica, his weathered lines curling skyward.

"Aye aye, skippa," she replied to his delight.

"Well, let's just see what we've got then, 'ey?"

The four-person OceanTech Emergency Pod catered for every sailor's worst nightmare, the company's smaller model far too cramped for even a minute adrift. At £2,700, Hans felt it was worth every penny. The instruction manual listed its onboard equipment but, leaving nothing to chance, Hans put together an accompanying ditch kit – a waterproof bag containing additional survival essentials. Most important of all, he bought a hand-cranked desalinator, handheld VHF radio and emergency position-indicating radio beacon, although where to place the latter item presented something of a problem.

When activated by contact with water, the EPIRB would broadcast a global-positioning signal on frequencies monitored by commercial aircraft and satellite. Search and rescue services could then locate them should they have to board the life raft. The instructions said to protect the device from outside interferences, listing every hazard existing on a boat, and that it should be accessible at all times. The dilemma posed to Hans was, would they have time to retrieve the beacon as the boat sank beneath their feet? In the end he resorted to packing it in the ditch kit. He would make sure to grab the bag should the worst-case scenario unfold.

- 5 -

Despite the friendly nature of the Trapthorn Plaza's staff, it was a relief for Hans to finally check out and move on board *Future*. The adventure suddenly seemed so real.

After unpacking their gear, Hans and Jessica took the yacht for her first sea trial under their command. As they motored away from the dock, Hans pointed to a sea lion happily porpoising in the opposite direction.

"Look, Jessie!"

"*Yeeeee!*" She clenched her tiny teeth.

Once clear of the marina, Hans showed Jessica how to cut the engine and unfurl the mainsail. Unlike the SAS – the Saturday and Sunday brigade – he never relied on auxiliary power longer than necessary.

Under a cerulean sky they cruised into the picturesque bay. Behind them, crowning the city's seafront cliffs, the historic esplanade of Plymouth Hoe grew distant and a small tree-crested island rose out of the inky depths ahead. Nestled in the island's contours were a number of fortifications and outbuildings.

"That's Drake's Island, sweet pea." Hans had done his homework. "A long, long time ago a man called Sir Francis Drake was the queen of England's favorite sailor. He sailed around the world and found out about people living in places like the jungle, and he discovered plants and animals that nobody knew about before."

"Did he live on the island, Papa?"

"No, the people of Plymouth just named it after him because he was such a good sailor."

"Did he have a boat like *Future*?"

"He had an even bigger boat, called a galleon. It had lots of guns, and he needed a hundred men to sail her."

"Why did it have guns, Papa?"

"Because in those days the English were at war with a country called Spain, a long way over there." Hans pointed to the horizon. "If the English sailors saw a Spanish ship, they would fire their guns and stop her. Then they would jump aboard and steal all the treasure."

Hans chose not to reveal the darker aspect of Drake's career.

"And, hey, you'll never guess what."

"What, Papa?"

"One time Sir Francis was playing a game of bowls – you know, like the bowling we play at home sometimes."

"Uh-huh."

"Well, he was playing a game of bowling right up there on the grass" – Hans pointed to the long flat stretch of Plymouth Hoe – "and a messenger ran up to him and said, 'Sir Francis, quick, quick, the Spanish fleet is coming to attack us. You must take our ships to sea and stop them!' And do you know what he said?"

She shook her head, eyes fixed on her father.

"He said, 'Okay, I will stop them. But first I'm going to finish my game'!"

"And will people shoot guns at us, Papa?" She looked at him in earnest.

"No! Don't worry, sweet pea. I'd never let that

happen."

Guarding the entrance to Plymouth's harbor stood a mile-long breakwater, built by French prisoners captured during the Napoleonic Wars. Four million tons of locally quarried limestone ferried out and dropped to the seafloor. Standing ten feet proud of the water at high tide and capped with dovetailed granite, it was an impressive sight – remarkable still that some of its five-hundred-ton blocks simply disappeared when Neptune threw a tantrum.

Leading up to the bulwark the sea was calm, but no sooner had they passed its protective lee then the swell angered. No problem for *Future*, though. She sliced stoically on through with hardly a roll.

"What's the most important rule at sea, First Mate?"

"Life jacket and safety line, Pap— er, skippa."

She'd put on both and G-clipped herself to the guardrail without prompting.

"Well done!"

Seeing Jessica take responsibility for her welfare reassured Hans. Even for experienced crews it was nigh on impossible to rescue someone who fell overboard in heavy seas. Hans intended to avoid such an emergency and would drum the drill home at every opportunity.

They circuited the bay with Jessica at the helm, Hans giving systematic instruction in the art of yachting. Despite her short years, she caught on fast. Hans beamed with pride.

"You up for a challenge, froggy face?"

"Yes!" Jessica nodded enthusiastically but kept her eyes dead ahead.

"It's called the keelhaul challenge."

"What is it?"

"In the olden days, when Sir Francis was a captain, if one of his men was naughty – like he stole something or didn't do his job properly – the ship's crew would tie a rope around his waist, throw him in the sea and then haul him under the keel – that's the bottom of the boat."

"Why, Papa?"

"It was a type of punishment. The boats were big, so it was a long time to be underwater and very frightening, and the keels were covered in sharp barnacles, so if the sailor got pulled really fast he would get badly cut and wouldn't be naughty again. But don't worry: we won't use a rope, and *Future* hasn't got any barnacles. We'll just swim under her for a bit of fun, right?"

"You go first, *froggy*!"

"Ooh, you're *definitely* gonna get a keelhaul!"

With *Future* drifting under bare poles, Hans stripped to his shorts, and Jessica put on her wetsuit.

"Monster backflip?" he suggested.

"*Heeeee!*"

Jessica was the master of the monster backflip – or any other execution involving her father lobbing her into a body of water with flagrant disregard for health and safety protocol.

Standing on the upper deck, Hans cupped his hands around her foot. "Okay . . . seven . . . three . . . eight . . . four . . . two . . . *go!*" He launched her into the air, his protégée rotating one and a half times before piercing the surface with hardly a splash.

"Ha-ha! Nice dive, Jess!" Hans passed her a mask and

snorkel and a set of fins. "Best dive of the century from Daddy?"

"No, you're *stupid*!"

"Oh, stupid, am I?" His mouth fell open as he looked to the sky. "I suppose you think I'm not even the best diver in the whole wide world and I look like a big hairy elephant."

"No, stupid froggy. Hee-hee!"

"We'll see about that then, won't we? I'm gonna do a forward somersault, then I'm gonna do a back somersault. Then I'm gonna fly around the boat *three* times, and then I'm gonna hit the water perfect like . . . like an angel, and then I'm gonna eat you all up like a big ugly shark!"

"Froggy shark!" Jessica giggled, having gotten used to her papa's idiocy.

"Okay, coming in . . ." Hans concentrated intently, ready to pull off the stunt of all stunts. "You better tell everyone we're gonna make history here!"

"There's no one else here, stupid froggy."

"Yeah, but there's a whole lotta fish, and they probably wanna know there's an amazing thing about to happen."

"Little fish, Papa is a stupid froggy face, and he's just gonna fall in like he always does."

"Oh, that is *so* cruel! You don't believe this is the dive of the century?"

"Ut-*uhh*." She gave a definitive shake of her head.

"Well, watch this . . . *Yeeee-hah*!"

Hans leapt high in the air . . . to land with the worst belly flop Plymouth had ever seen.

"Did you see that!" he shrieked, his chest turning red.

"Terrible! Daddy's very terrible!"

"I'll give you terrible!"

Hans sunk below the surface. Jessica screamed and tried to make a break for it, but even wearing fins she was no match for her father's powerful strokes. Hans zeroed in from below like a great white shark targeting a seal and lifted her clear out of the water.

"*Arrrrrh*! Gonna eat you all up!"

Jessica squealed in a mixture of torture and delight, Hans smothering her with kisses. Since Mom's and JJ's death, the bond between them had reached a new level, and now, holding her tight, Hans felt something special again, something inexplicable. He started to cry silently, the water masking his tears.

Jessica wasn't blind to these episodes, though, her mind ascribing them to the "thing" that happened to her mother and brother, too young to understand her father's outpouring of emotion was an expression of the love he felt for her.

"Right, time to swim under the boat." Hans rallied himself. "Who's going first?"

"You are." Jessica prodded him in the chest.

"No, I think *you* should."

"No, silly froggy goes first."

"How about handsome froggy and monkey butt go together?"

"O-*kay*."

They duck-dove and swam down. With the late-spring sunshine penetrating the surface at slack tide, visibility wasn't too bad, but the water was by no means warm. Hans held the family record for holding a breath – four and a half minutes – Jessica once managing an impressive two minutes twenty.

Future's draft was deeper than Hans had imagined, but fortunately they were able to swim around her bulbous T-shaped keel instead of under it. He was pleased to see the agent was good to his word and the hull was free from algae and other gunk. He felt a pang of pride: their new boat looked as smart below the waterline as she did above it.

Surfacing on the port side, Jessica had plenty of breath left.

"Reckon you can do it without fins, sweet pea?"

"Uh-huh."

"Pass them here then."

Jessica pulled the rubber flippers off one at a time and handed them to her father, who threw them on deck. On the count of three they ducked under once more, Jessica's feet kicking ten to the dozen as Hans followed close behind. The little girl would quite happily have gone for it again, only *Future* had drifted too near the rocks for comfort. Hans congratulated Jessica on passing the keelhaul challenge, and they climbed the stern ladder.

On the return journey the yacht's engine decided not to play, so Hans entered the marina under sail, to the delight and applause of the Saturday and Sunday brigade, who sat sipping Sundowners while waiting for barbecues to heat. Hans aimed *Future* at the pontoon at quite some speed, furling in the remaining sailcloth at the last moment and sluing her around to step onto the dock, mooring line in hand, as if it were the order of the day.

"Whey-hey!" came a voice, English and female.

Hans looked over to see a young woman, late twenties, reading a book on the adjacent yacht.

"Good read?"

"*A Manual of Yacht and Boat Sailing*," she replied, scrambling up to help him. "It's a reprint of Kemp's original 1923 text."

"Oh!" said Hans, marveling at the speed with which she secured *Future*'s front line.

- 6 -

In the morning Hans and Jessica set about getting *Future* "shipshape and Bristol fashion," as the Brits liked to say. She was already well equipped to cross the Atlantic, but Hans always erred on the side of caution, a trait carried over from his military service. For repairs at sea, *Future* carried spares of all essential items, along with an ample tool kit and materials for constructing a jury rig and shoring a damaged hull.

On the next trip to Old Bill's chandlery, they bought additional fire extinguishers, a fire blanket and a heat shield that Hans fitted behind the stove in the galley. To secure the life raft to the deck, Hans opted for a hydrostatic release unit and a weak-link painter. Should *Future* sink, water pressure would activate the HRU, allowing the capsule to float free, the weak-link painter triggering a carbon dioxide inflation cylinder before snapping under tension to prevent the yacht dragging the raft into the deep. Hans did not want to be preoccupied with launching the inflatable should his daughter be struggling to escape a flooded cabin.

Foul-weather gear was also on the list, Jessie looking so cute parading up and down the store in hers that both men chuckled.

Having figured out why the engine would not fire, Hans replaced the brushes in the starter motor. He also gave the backup generator a thorough check over. In the event of further engine trouble, the machine would supply onboard electricity and, in conjunction with solar panels and a wind turbine, charge *Future*'s batteries. It ran on regular gas, so Hans filled up eight two-gallon plastic cans at the pump on the marina. He then hired a specialist to test all the electrical equipment. Their final purchase from Old Bill was a high-power flare gun and twenty cartridges to send a distress signal in an emergency.

Just as they were about to leave the cramped store, the door burst open. It was the young woman who had helped Hans tie up the yacht the previous day.

"Hey, Bill! Mind if I stick this in the window?" She held up a postcard note.

"The finest skipper on the 'igh seas don't need Old Bill's permission to do that, Cap'n Penny." Bill grinned. "You put it where you want, my girl. So you be looking for a new command?"

"Yeah. I just got in from the Med, crewing for a local family. So this job ends here unfortunately. I'm looking to reach Cape Verde before—"

"Cape Verde?" Hans interrupted.

"Oh! Hello again!" The woman's face lit up. "Yeah, I need to reach there by autumn."

"Cape Verde's on our route," Hans tendered, turning to Old Bill, seeking guidance.

"Listen," said Bill, "if you need an extra pair of hands, then you can't go wrong with Penny Masters. She'll see you around the Cape, Antarctica and back again." He winked.

"And where are you guys heading from there?" asked

Penny.

"Across to the Caribbean and up the East Coast home to Maine."

"Excellent! When are you leaving?"

"As soon as possible," said Hans. "If you've got time later, I can show you our plans . . . over a bite to eat perhaps."

"Sure! That'll be great!"

- 7 -

Penny was delightful, a real free spirit. She and Jessica hit it off immediately, the little girl insisting her new friend tuck her into bed with a story that evening.

Sitting in *Future*'s cockpit enjoying red wine and a takeout in the warm air, Penny listened intently to Hans as he explained the reasoning behind taking his daughter to sea.

"My parents had a few issues – kinda strict too – so I've always given Jessica and J—" Hans stopped abruptly and reached for the second bottle of Merlot.

"I've always given Jessica free rein. Tried to treat her as an equal and support her to make her own choices. I thought the trip would be good for both of us."

"I couldn't agree more." Penny passed the corkscrew. "I was born into the sailing community. My parents are what you might call bohemian."

"So you've crossed the Atlantic a few times."

"The Atlantic, the Pacific, the Indian . . ." She smiled. "All the Seven Seas, and most of them more than I can remember."

Hans filled two coffee mugs to brimming with the fruity Californian tipple, making a mental note to put wineglasses on the shopping list.

"And what's happening in Cape Verde in fall?"

"All being well, I'm skippering a Parisian millionaire

and his wife across to French Guiana."

Penny reached in her bag and handed Hans an impressive résumé with a gold-lettered business card clipped to the front.

"Perfect!" said Hans, having heard enough. "Cape Verde's on our route – if we can employ your services, that is."

"Sounds like a deal!"

"*Arrhk-arrhk.*"

The noise startled them.

Leaning over the coaming, they spotted the sea lion Hans and Jessica saw earlier. Swimming on its back and clapping its flippers, the pinniped looked to be applauding Penny's decision.

"Hee-hee!" Her face lit up. "That's Guz."

"Guz?"

"Yeah, Golf Uniform Zulu – Plymouth's call sign during the war. He's kind of been adopted by the yachties and fishermen around here. Tame as anything. Look." She picked a king prawn from her stir-fry and tossed it over the side. Guz plucked it from the water with ease.

Hans smiled. There was something about this girl.

- 8 -

While Penny moved her belongings aboard *Future* and took care of last-minute business, Hans, Jessica and Bear explored the city, starting with the old town district surrounding the marina. This was the historic Barbican Quay, where Tudor buildings framed in oaken timbers flanked tiny cobbled streets, many of them former Elizabethan merchant houses now trading in cream teas.

Below the high-water mark, seaweed tendrils lagged the basin's block-stone walls, its edge stones polished smooth by centuries of mooring lines. Hefty iron cleats the size of blacksmiths' anvils studded the quayside, interspersed with bollards made from antique cannons cut in half, upended and sunk into the stonework.

Along with pleasure craft, the picturesque port sheltered a large number of commercial vessels. Scuba enthusiasts busied themselves aboard dive boats, setting up regulators and buoyancy vests and zipping each other into dry suits. Trawlers reeking of sea fare off-loaded plastic tubs brimming with catch onto the wharf, from which excited youngsters dangled crab lines. With so many tourists buzzing around, sightseeing and visiting souvenir stores and restaurants, and locals going about their business, the place was a hive of activity. Ambling along the dock, Hans could just imagine Sir Francis spending an evening of debauchery in one of the

Barbican's raucous taverns before staggering back aboard the *Golden Hind*.

"Look, sweet pea!"

Hans sighted the legendary Mayflower Steps leading down to the water's edge. A pompous Greek portico marked the spot where in 1620 the Pilgrim Fathers boarded the *Mayflower* and sailed for the New World in search of religious freedom and civil liberty. They reached North America in sixty-six days and laid the foundations of the New England States. Hans' lineage was Swedish, but his late wife's ancestors were English.

"You see these steps, Jessie?"

"Uh-huh."

She eyed the chiseled granite slabs descending through a flotilla of seaweed, beer and soda cans, bottles and candy wrappers into the murky green water.

"This is where your great-great-great-grandparents got on a big ship and sailed all the way to America."

"Why, Papa?"

"Because back then they were very poor, and people were horrible to them. So they said, 'Hey, let's sail to America and build a house and a church and have a new life.'"

"We're sailing to America, Papa."

"We are, sweet pea."

Hans neglected to mention that, according to a chuckling Old Bill, no one actually knew the exact location the pilgrims set sail from. However, the portico, with its ludicrous Doric columns and commemorative plaques, kept the tourists happy.

From the doorway of a takeout, a blast of warm air

flavored with battered fish and vinegar blindsided them. Hans went inside and ordered cod and fries at Jessica's request and a traditional Cornish pasty for himself. They sat on the harbor's edge enjoying their lunch and spotting fish swimming beneath the flotsam on the water below.

"What's a pasty, Papa?" Jessica eyed his half-moon-shaped meat-and-potato pie, the recipe for which dated back centuries.

"Pasties were the staple diet of local miners who lived two hundred years ago, Jessie. You know about mining, right?"

"We did it in school. It's called a *gold* rush."

"Good girl! Well, here in Devon they mined a metal called tin. On Sunday evenings the men would walk twenty miles from Plymouth up to their mine workings in the Dartmoor highlands—"

"Where the little horses are." Jessica remembered seeing postcards in the tourist office depicting the rugged landscape and its wild roaming ponies.

"That's right. The miners' wives would cook their husbands enough pasties to last them the week, before they walked all the way home again. And you see this thick crimped piece?"

"The crust?"

"Well done. The miners would throw this bit away, so if any poisons from the rocks in the mine, like arsenic, got on their fingers they wouldn't get sick. Do you wanna try a bit?"

"Mmm, please, Papa."

As Jessica turned to take the offering, a piercing screeching broke out. Two seagulls dove out of nowhere and engulfed her in a blaze of white feathers. One snatched the entire fillet of fish from her Styrofoam tray with its fat yellow bill and swallowed it whole before its wings flapped twice. The other, in a moment of confusion, plucked Bear from her lap.

"*Nooooo!*"

She lunged to grab him back but toppled headlong into the sea.

Without pause Hans leapt from the dock.

When Jessica surfaced through the oil, weed and scum, he put his arm out to stabilize her.

"It's okay, honey. Daddy's gotcha."

Treading water, Hans put on a broad grin to dispel the drama.

"*Bear*, Papa!"

"It's all right. He's over there." Hans nodded in the direction of her teddy, floating nearby with his ass in the air. It was a sign of her remarkable maturity that a cold plunge from a height of eight feet didn't faze her, only the possibility of losing her beloved companion. "You okay to go and rescue him?"

"Uh-huh." She nodded, peeling away using breaststroke.

A crowd gathered on the quayside.

"You all right, mate?" A man handed his wallet and Nokia to the woman next to him.

"Yeah, we're fine, buddy. Thank you."

Hans was glad he left his cell phone on board.

Holding Bear, Jessica struggled to keep her head above water, so Hans took him, and they struck out for a rusting iron ladder bolted to the quay wall.

"You've a right one on yer 'ands there, me 'andsome

boy!" a fisherman remarked, grinning broadly as he passed by, surrounded by mesh pots at the tiller of his crab boat.

"Er . . . yeah!" Hans replied, sensing the man meant well.

"You guys having fun?"

The voice came from above. Hans and Jessica looked up to see Penny's effervescent presence shining down on them.

"Penny – *phuh*." Jessica swallowed a mouthful of harbor. "Bear fell in the water!"

"I can see that."

Just then the thunderous clap of unsilenced Harley-Davidson engines broke out around them. Two burly bikers in grease-smeared jeans, worn leather jackets and denim vests, tattoos and bandanas had watched the episode unfold from an open-air burger joint named Captain Jasper's. Stepping off their impressive custom-builds, they reached down and hauled Jessica onto the dockside.

"You all right, me bird?" one of them asked.

"I'm not a bird!" She giggled.

"You're a beautiful bird to me, mate!" He grinned, kissing her on the cheek and displaying a row of nicotine-stained tombstones.

Hans received the same treatment – without the endearment.

"Where you staying to?" the other petrol head inquired.

"On a yacht in the marina."

"Jump on."

The man straddled his chromed beast and kicked up

its stylish skeleton foot stand with his booted heel.

Hans sat behind him and planted Jessica in between them, noting the black eagle patch on the man's denim vest and the badges "Aquila" and "Devon" above and below it.

Hell, these dudes are serious! Hans thought, Penny riding pillion on the other chopper as they sped the wrong way down a one-way street.

"Say, aren't you guys supposed to wear helmets?" Hans yelled above the din. "Isn't it law here?"

"Ha!" the biker scoffed as traffic veered from their path. "We *are* the law."

After a shower, Hans and Jessica drank a mug of hot chocolate and ate buttery scrambled eggs cooked by Penny. Then the two of them set off to do some more sightseeing, with Jessica reluctantly agreeing to leave Bear pegged to the backstay.

Hans figured the central district would be as charming as the seafront but was unaware of the enormous damage Hitler's bomber crews did during the Blitz, for attempting to neutralize Plymouth's maritime infrastructure the Luftwaffe had leveled the city, destroying historic buildings and thousands of homes.

The charred stone ruins of an ancient church sat in the middle of a busy roundabout, surrounded by modern office blocks and a shopping mall. Gutted by German firebombs, the church was an eerie sight and testament to the Plymouthians' indomitable spirit and the horror of war.

Plymouth's postwar reconstruction looked like some sort of socialist experiment, the buildings – gray, concrete and austere – reminding Hans of the crass, sixties and seventies town planning he had seen in the north of Sweden. Every so often they came across a halfhearted attempt to revitalize the dreary architecture with a garish postmodern design, like sprucing up an out-of-fashion suit with a loud tie.

"Look, Papa!"

Jessica caught sight of a colossal sundial, the city's avant-garde centerpiece, its twenty-foot-high chrome gnomon rising out of a gently cascading fountain to cast a shadow onto marble-block hour markers, which at this time doubled as seats for weary shoppers. She dragged her father up the five concentric tiers of neat brown bricks forming the sundial's base.

Upon reaching the top, Hans chuckled. Despite the obvious investment involved in commissioning the sculpture . . . it ran two hours slow.

Hans did not know what to make of Plymouth. He knew not to expect cap-doffing peasants and tea-drinking gentry, as in Hollywood's portrayal of Little England, but what he witnessed surprised him nonetheless. The city had a distinct element of behind-the-times naivety bordering on bizarre. They passed a motorbike dealership named Not 4 Girlz and a sports car showroom called Boyz Toyz. It was as if the struggle for equality had simply bypassed this place. Hans would teach Jessica to ride a motorcycle and drive a car as good as any man – if she chose to, that was. No fool would pigeonhole her with their bigoted designs.

In the city center's pedestrianized shopping area, an adult store, Good Vibrations, featured lingerie-clad mannequins in provocative poses in its window display, along with a sale sign designed to look like an oral sex act. In the front of another store, Homeward Bound, the dummies were a gimp-suited man whipping a woman in a latex bikini.

"Has she been naughty, Papa?" Jessica's eyes screwed up.

"Er . . . no, honey. It's a grown-up thing."

In no way prudish, Hans wondered how local parents felt about the message these prominent outlets gave to impressionable youngsters. The city seemed to go out of its way to objectify women.

Am I getting cynical?

Hans tried to think back to his younger self. Such issues certainly didn't bother him when sitting in the hold of a C-130 armed to the teeth, ready to parachute out with his team and unleash hell on complete strangers. Was it something to do with all the lies, double standards and corruption he had witnessed over the years, the hubris and greed of yellow-streaked suits born into privilege and hiding behind the bastions of power? Could it be fatherhood and the responsibility of looking out for someone else's welfare and not just his own? On the other hand, perhaps he was just sick to the back teeth of the whole goddamn show.

Just when Hans thought they had seen it all, he spotted a recently opened wine bar with the sign "Hawkins House" above the door. He shook his head, having read in the guidebook that Sir John Hawkins had been Britain's most prolific slave trader.

Who in their right mind would name a pub after this guy?

In the States, such a lack of consideration would

cause protests, even riots. It all came as something of a shock to the American, who believed the British to be a cultured people with a history of fighting oppression.

Keen to get out of the area, "Fancy a walk along Plymouth Hoe?" he asked the first mate.

"Okay, Papa."

"How's the legs?"

"They're fine."

Jessica gave a nonchalant shrug to cover her fib – anything to spend more time exploring with her father.

- 9 -

Hans and Jessica went in search of Plymouth Hoe, the four-hundred-year-old esplanade atop the city's cliff front.

In reality "cliff front" proved somewhat misleading, since over the years a number of now-decadent-looking oddities – belvederes, sunbathing plinths, a high-diving platform, an art deco lido – as well as café bars and sailing clubs had been built amongst the limestone's craggy contours, giving the impression of a hedonist's playground. Interconnecting the eclectic mix of old and new, and in synergy with the rock, an elaborate network of steps, colonnades and walkways gave the impression of the interlinking staircases you see in optical illusions – the ones angling up and down at the same time.

The Larssons hiked up a hilly backstreet lined with grand townhouses to find themselves in the center of the Hoe's mile-long stretch. A visual banquet greeted them, the view rolling out over the oily blue water of the English Channel, taking in the fairy-tale image of Drake's Island, the colossal stone breakwater and lush shades of forest sprouting from the headland guarding the bay.

Hans bent down and kissed his daughter. "It's so beautiful up here, honey."

"It's a magic place, Papa."

"And do you know what?"

She shook her head.

"I'm happy we're exploring it together."

Jessica wrapped her arms around her father and they hugged awhile in silence.

Hans unfolded the tourist map and began pointing out features of interest. At the far left of the plateau stood the Royal Citadel, a sprawling fortress built in 1660 during the Anglo-Dutch Wars, now garrisoning an elite artillery unit. Hans recalled serving on joint operations with the commandos stationed behind the imposing Baroque gateway.

Strangely, a number of the citadel's gun emplacements faced the city as opposed to the ocean, apparently a warning to locals in days of old not to rise against the Crown.

Hans began to chuckle.

"What, Papa?" Jessica tugged his shirt.

The idea of a fort facing backwards reminded Hans of *Monty Python and the Holy Grail* in their DVD collection at home. To Jessica's delight, he began mimicking the Black Knight, hopping around on one leg with his arms behind his back.

"*Just* a flesh wound!"

To the rear of the esplanade stood a row of stately hotels with striking white façades, prominent chimney stacks and spectacular seaward vistas. In front lay an undulating carpet of neatly mown grass stretching to the cliff edge, at this time packed with picnickers relaxing on treat-laden blankets and office workers taking a break to soak up the sun's rays.

No one does lawns like the Brits, thought Hans.

"What's that, Papa?" Jessica spotted a tall, round tower painted in red and white stripes like a barbershop pole.

"It's a lighthouse, Jess. Wanna take a look?"

He needn't have asked.

Walking toward the structure, they passed a number of monuments honoring fallen military personnel and notable seafarers.

Hans paused. "Hey, Jess. Do you know who this is?"

Atop a granite plinth, a bronze casting depicted a portly gent sporting a sea captain's beard and wearing an ornate leather doublet and breeches. Staring expectantly out over the sound, he carried a rapier in a scabbard by his side and stood next to a world globe, the kind employed by navigators and explorers.

"Sir Fran— "

"–cis . . ."

"Drake."

"Well done, sweet pea. And can you read what the plaque says?"

As Jessica narrated the challenges Drake faced in his 1577 circumnavigation of the planet – violent storms, mutiny, tropical disease and skirmishes with tribesmen – Hans' interest in the queen's favorite sailor was piqued – although in Spain's estimation, El Draque was nothing more than a pirate who plundered their gold along the Main.

". . . and he sailed back into Plymouth Sound with more treasure than any captain before him, receiving a knighthood and—"

The unlikely ballad of "Greensleeves" interrupted Jessica as a gaudy yellow-and-orange truck pulled up.

"I suppose you don't like ice cream anymore, shipmate." Hans winked.

"Yay!"

Examining the dated advertising stickers splattered around the vehicle's serving hatch, Hans had no idea what Feast-ivals, ZaPPers or Nize-Izes were, so he asked the vendor to suggest a local choice.

"Ninety-Nine, sir. Cornish ice cream served in a cone with a flake."

"A flake?"

"One of these." The vendor held up a catering pack containing four-inch-long chocolate logs separated into layers by corrugated paper sheets.

"We'll take two please."

Noting their accents, "Here's a song you might know!" The ice cream man chuckled and gave an impromptu blast of "Camptown Races."

As they sat on the grass to eat their 99s before the sun melted them, it occurred to Hans they were in the same spot the Beatles occupied for a picture taken when the band were in the West Country filming *Magical Mystery Tour*. Hans had seen the photograph on postcards in the souvenir stores, the Fab Four sitting in a row, gazing out to sea, wearing their attire from the movie. He asked a passing French tourist to take a snap of him and Jessica but, posing pointing to the ocean as Ringo Starr had done in 1967, a pang of grief gripped him. There were two people missing from the shot.

When they reached the lighthouse, the attendant met them at the entrance. A sprightly chap, he oozed enthusiasm for the city and looked to be supplementing his pension.

"Welcome to Smeaton's Tower, sir. I'm Jack, your captain, and we will be climbing to an altitude of forty-six feet." He grinned at his own humor, his steel-blue eyes glinting under slicked-back white hair.

"*Smeaton's* Tower?" said Hans.

"Designed by John Smeaton in 1756, sir."

"Wow, some time ago."

"Certainly is, sir. The old girl original sat on the—"

"Old girl?" Hans thought he'd missed something.

"The lighthouse, sir. Call her the old girl, see? 'Cause she's the only wife I've got!" He chuckled at another of his chestnuts and, turning to Jessica, said, "But at least this one won't be running off with the milkman!"

She smiled politely.

"Where was I?" Jack stared into nothing. "Yes, she originally sat on the Eddystone Rocks, twelve miles offshore."

"That must have been difficult – building her that far out in the 1750s."

"Revolutionary design, sir. A clever man, Mr. Smeaton." He led them back a few paces. "See how she's shaped like the trunk of an oak tree?"

"Of course." Hans lifted his sunglasses and gazed upwards.

"Her granite blocks are dovetailed to lock together for strength."

"And where was this done?"

"Millbay Docks, sir." Jack pointed to the end of the Hoe. "One thousand four hundred and ninety-three blocks in all, carved by local tin miners and ferried out to the Rocks by boat. But they had to be careful, see?"

"It was a dangerous job?"

"*Press-gangs*, sir!" The old boy fixed a knowing eye on Hans and threw in a wary nod. "If the miners were caught without their identity papers, they were liable to be kidnapped and forced to join the Royal Navy. But after standing out there protecting sailors for over a hundred years, the old girl started rocking back and forward – frightened the life out of the keeper! So they dismantled her block by block and reassembled her here for the tourists."

Hans could see the lighthouse meant a lot to Jack, but Jessica let out a second yawn, so he opened his wallet and paid the modest entrance fee. They followed Jack up a sandstone staircase winding around inside the curved walls, its steps worn into polished troughs by countless climbing feet. The first two floors were storage areas, the third housing living quarters furnished with a half-moon-shaped bench and a cast-iron stove that must have brewed many a warming cocoa on a cold, stormy night. Finally, they emerged in the glass-enclosed lantern room to find the original candelabra still suspended by its aging hemp rope.

"Phew, what a view!" Hans lifted Jessica up.

"Boats, Papa!"

Vessels of all shape and size plied the English Channel as far as the eye could see.

To their rear the city's concrete heartland nestled among neat rows of terraced housing, broken up by tree-lined parks and industry, all linked by snaking gray veins of asphalt.

"Look, Jess." Hans pointed to the marina. "Guess who I can see."

"*Future!*"

"Ha-ha! She looks like a toy from up here."

Before departing the States, Hans had doubts about the trip, particularly when well-meaning friends and relatives questioned its timing and suitability for Jessica. Now he felt excited and closer to his daughter than ever. He looked forward to setting sail and continuing the adventure.

Jack drew their attention to Plymouth's naval dockyard, which sat at the mouth of the River Tamar estuary.

"Can we take a tour?" Hans asked.

"Pleasure boat from the Mayflower Steps, sir. Best way to see the ships."

Then, laying a hand on Hans' shoulder, Jack giggled and added, "Without being arrested!"

"Or press-ganged!" Hans joked, and they both laughed.

- 10 -

Hans found it hard to believe he and Jessica were embarking on a sea voyage from the Mayflower Steps just as America's early pioneers had done in 1620. Had anyone suggested it to him a year ago, he probably would have laughed.

As they took up seats on the pleasure boat's upper deck, a horde of young people, many of whom looked to be Latino, streamed down the jetty. An eager young man wearing a North Face jacket and Timberland boots herded the excited group up the gangway and then sat down next to Hans and Jessica.

"Thank heavens I haven't lost one this time!" He chuckled, lifting his glasses to massage the bridge of his nose.

"I'm sorry?" Hans replied.

"Oh, I'm Ben." The chap smiled and shook hands. "These are my exchange students. They come here to brush up on their English. I normally lose at least one by now."

"You've certainly got your hands full. I'm Hans, and this is my daughter, Jess."

"Hello, Jess. How are you enjoying Plymouth?" Ben crouched down to meet her at eye level.

"We went up a lighthouse, and Papa bought a boat!"

"Wow! That sounds like fun. Americans? Canadi—?"

44

"Americans, from Maine," said Hans.

"Brilliant. You'll love this trip."

"You've done it before?"

"Just a *few* times. But I never get bored. Problem is, when the boat's full of foreign students the skipper skips the commentary – excuse the pun."

"Why's that?" Hans frowned, looking over to the wheelhouse to see the captain with his back to them.

"He figures they don't understand English and they're not interested anyway. But don't worry. I know the spiel off by heart."

The engine clanked into life, coughing out a cloud of sooty black smoke, the deck vibrating as the boat chugged away from the dock. In his element, Hans sucked in the salty air, the smell of rust, grease and diesel fumes reminiscent of his time in the navy. They passed a group of wetsuited teenagers taking it in turns to jump from high up on the cliff.

"Tombstoning," said Ben. "A bit of a touchy subject in Plymouth."

"Right," said Hans, picturing the health and safety cats having a field day.

Drake's Island came into view on the port side, the Hoe above them to starboard. Fifty or so ultralight dinghies skimmed across the sound, racing between two orange buoys half a mile apart, their two-person crews leaning far back over the water and working the tiny triangular sails to harness every knot from the wind. Sluggish in comparison, yachts departing the marina cut across the busy course, but despite the illusion created at sea level, there was little danger of collision.

"When Sir Francis Chichester became the first person

to sail around the world single-handed, over a million people packed the waterfront to welcome him home," said Ben.

"Another Sir Francis." Hans laughed and stroked Jessica's cheek.

"You know about Sir Francis Drake, Jess?" Ben crouched down again.

"Hmm! He had a big ship, and he sailed to the jungle, and it was bigger than *Future*."

"Future?"

"Our yacht," said Hans.

"Wow, you're a clever girl. You must know everything!"

Jessica squeezed her shoulder blades and gave her trademark toothy grin.

"Something tells me you're a military man, Hans," Ben continued.

"I did a bit of time."

"Well, right in there" – Ben pointed to a long concrete wharf lined with used tractor tires – "is Millbay Docks. You know the Normandy landings?"

"Of course."

"General Bradley and the First US Army embarked here for the assaults on Omaha and Utah Beaches."

Hans let his jaw drop in a gesture of gratitude. So many Americans would love to be here seeing this. He found himself thinking of his late grandfather, who fought in the Far East Campaign.

"Ben, I can't thank you enough."

He shook hands again.

"My pleasure, Hans. I've traveled quite a bit, and all the Americans I've met have been humble and generous

. . . *Nearly* all of them!" Ben chuckled.

"We get a bad press, huh?"

"Not with me you don't. Besides, us Brits can't say too much."

"Right." Hans nodded thoughtfully.

"Many of the survivors from the *Titanic* disaster disembarked at Millbay. And Charles Darwin left here in 1831 on the *Beagle* for his research in the Galápagos Islands."

"And Plymouth thinks *tombstoning* is touchy subject!" Hans chuckled.

"Nothing like the theory of evolution to put a biscuit in the breadbin." Ben smiled.

"You can say that again."

"James Cook – he sailed from here on HMS *Endeavour* in 1768, the first European to reach Australia. And you've heard of the Mutiny on the *Bounty*."

"Admiral Bligh?"

"That's him. Departed Plymouth to reach Tahiti, but the *Bounty*'s crew set him and eighteen of his loyal followers adrift in a rowing boat."

Hans shuddered.

"But Bligh was a nautical genius, made it thousands of miles to the Dutch East Indies in only forty-seven days. He returned to Britain" – Ben glanced at Jessica and lowered his voice – "to see the surviving mutineers hanged."

"British seafarers. I've read all about them. They're something else."

"On the subject of" – Ben broke into a whisper again – "hanging. You see the long building over there?"

"The old stone one?"

"It's the rope house in the dockyard. They still make ships' rigging there today."

"Amazing."

"But it's also where they used to string people up."

"Oh."

"The gallows still stand. You can request a visit."

"That's irony for you!"

"Yeah."

The dockyard fascinated Hans. He appreciated the way Ben explained everything to Jessica in terms she could understand.

"See that submarine there, Jess? The one that's falling apart?"

"Uh-huh." She eyed the rusting black hulk.

"It's a special one. Uses a dangerous fuel called nuclear energy."

"Does it go under the water?"

"Not anymore. It has to stay here for years and years until the fuel inside it cools down."

"Amazing when you think they used to dump them at sea," said Hans.

"I reckon some countries still do." Ben gave a suggestive shrug.

"I think you're right."

Walking back to the marina, Hans and Jessica came across a man standing on a street corner with a Jack Russell perched on his shoulders.

"Look, Papa!"

As Jessica ran over, the man bent down so she could stroke his dog.

"*Big Issue*, sir?" He looked up at Hans.

"I'm sorry?"

"Newspaper, sir. Sold by us homeless. Helps put food in Lucky's bowel. Kna what I mean? S'only two quid, sir!"

"What's a squid?" Jessica asked, getting as much attention from Lucky as she was giving him.

"It's a pound, my darlin'. Like what you guys call a dollar."

"Oh, Daddy, *pleeeease!*"

"Okay, honey. Do you wanna pay out of your allowance?"

"*Yeeeeah!*" Her smile closed the deal.

Hans swapped a ten-pound note for a copy of the *Big Issue*, signaling with a wink to keep the change.

"Aw, thanks, guv! Thank you, princess."

"Bye-bye, little doggy." Jessica gave Lucky a farewell pet.

Walking away, she turned every few seconds to wave at the man and his dog. The man waved back and grinned.

"He's a nice man, Papa."

"Yes, sweet pea. He is."

That evening, Hans, Jessica and Penny sat down to eat in a swanky Mexican restaurant on the Barbican, enjoying chicken and beef tacos topped with guacamole, salsa and jalapenos to the sound of "La Cucaracha" and other culturally themed instrumentals playing softly in the background. After the meal they walked into the city to see *The Pirates of Penzance* playing at Plymouth's modest theater.

Hans' late wife, Kerry, had introduced him to opera

back in Portland.

"Ha!" the former navy man initially scoffed. "Guys in *pantyhose*?"

"That's ballet, honey," Kerry replied, raising an eyebrow and dragging him out of the house to go and witness Carmen's demise.

During the first act he chuckled to himself, thinking, *What precocious nonsense!* In the second he started to make the connections. By the final act he sat in awe, captivated by the immense range of the performers, the imagery conjured up and the sensuous combination of libretto, score and song.

Now, watching Gilbert and Sullivan's comedy of errors, set in the adjacent county of Cornwall, Hans smiled as the girls fell spellbound to the opera's magical allure. Ever attentive, Penny made sure Jessica understood the unfolding farce.

Her discreet giggles indicated she did.

"**D**aily routine, runner bean!"

Hans geed up his daughter for their early-morning exercise, and, having downed a glass of water each, they set off for a jog around the Barbican's cobbled streets, pausing for push-ups and sit-ups on the way.

Upon their return, Penny suggested they take *Future* for a run and check out an interesting dive site. Hans and Jessica filled their air cylinders using the yacht's compressor, and following a breakfast of bacon rolls – "butties," as Penny called them – coffee and juice, they slipped moorings and cruised into Plymouth Sound.

As they passed Drake's Island and the ominous breakwater loomed in the distance, a huge white ship resplendent in blue-and-orange striping bore down astern, a plume of oily black diesel fumes spewing horizontally from its funnel before drifting upwards into a faultless blue sky.

"Brittany Ferries," Penny shouted above the thunderous noise, Hans tacking sharply to port to avoid a collision. "On its way to Roscoff in France – close to where we're heading next week."

"Well, don't they have it easy!" Hans joked. "Perhaps we're making it difficult for ourselves."

The captain of the impressive vessel gave two prolonged and deafening blasts of the horn, indicating he was passing to starboard. From the upper deck, excited passengers gave friendly waves and were delighted when the yacht's crew returned them.

Sailing around the headland, Penny kept her eye on the screen of *Future*'s sophisticated sonar, looking for signs of the shipwreck and briefing Hans and Jessica on the vessel's past as she did.

Built in the United States in 1944, the SS *James Eagan Layne* carried cargo between the UK and Europe as part of the war effort. A German U-boat torpedoed the liberty ship off the coast of Plymouth only three months into her service. Amazingly, there were no casualties, and the *Layne*'s forlorn skeleton was now one of Britain's most popular dive sites.

Hans felt a wave of excitement wash over him – and not just as a scuba diver and former naval rating. This was Anglo-American history, and to witness it firsthand was an experience he only ever dreamt about back in Portland. He felt indebted to Penny for her thoughtfulness.

Locating the *Layne* wasn't difficult. A dive boat had arrived before them, dropping buoyed shot lines on the wreck's bow and stern to act as guides for the divers. Hans furled in the mainsail, and Penny fired up the motor to prevent *Future* drifting from the spot and onto the rocky shore. As a safety precaution, Penny wouldn't drop anchor, in case the current carried Hans and Jessica away from the site during their dive or an emergency arose.

"Hello, skipper!" Hans shouted across to the dive boat. "Do you mind if we descend on your line?"

"Fill your boots, me 'andsome," the captain replied as

he handed out steaming-hot drinks to his dripping-wet divers. "Tide's slack at the minute and vis is good. So make the most of it."

True to his Scandinavian roots, Hans dived in a compressed-neoprene dry suit made by the Waterproof Company of Sweden. Designed for subzero polar temperatures and worn over a quilted undergarment, the durable black coverall would keep him warm and dry. Jessica wore her tried and tested wetsuit, not a problem even this early in the year because she never complained of the cold.

"Okay, sweet pea, remember the checklist?" Hans asked as Jessica rubbed spit on her mask to prevent the lens from fogging.

"Bangkok Women Really Are Fellas!" she replied, second nature, unaware of the joke behind the mnemonic.

Penny shot a look at Hans and suppressed a giggle.

"Go for it then," he urged.

"Buoyancy." Jessica pressed the inflation and deflation buttons on Hans' vest, waiting for a reassuring hiss of air before continuing. "Weights." She checked Hans had his belt done up with a right-handed opening in case he needed to ditch his lead in an emergency. "Releases." She patted the buckles on his equipment to indicate she knew how to undo them in a tricky situation. "Air." She made sure it flowed freely from Hans' mouthpiece and the "octopus" spare and tasted fresh and not contaminated. Then she read his pressure gauge – 250 bar, plenty enough for a standard sports dive. "Final check." She gave him a determined once-over, making sure his hoses were connected and routed properly and his mask and fins were at hand.

"Anything else, buddy?" Hans narrowed his eyes. "Like a *knnn*— "

"Knife!" she replied with a self-satisfied grin.

"Well done, honey."

Hans tapped the stainless-steel knife's plastic scabbard strapped to his chest band. Unlike the majority of divers, who attach a knife to their calf – the "Jacques Cousteaus," as one of Hans' military instructors used to mock – he knew to keep his close at hand in case he became entangled in a fishing net or kelp and was unable to reach his lower leg.

Having reciprocated the safety check, Hans conducted a dive brief. "Okay, Jess. We'll descend on the stern and it's at a depth of . . ." He looked to Penny.

"Twenty meters."

"Take it steady going down the line, control your buoyancy and remember to clear your ears. If you get a problem, give me the sign." Hans fluttered his hand palm downwards in a seesaw motion. "Then we're gonna do mask-clearing and buddy-breathing skills. Happy with that?"

"I'm happy."

"Then we'll fin along the ship to the prow – that's the front end, right?"

Jessica nodded. "How deep, Penny?"

Her father always reiterated the importance of finishing a dive in shallow water if possible to extend the no-decompression time and reduce air intake, increasing the safety margin should any last-minute issues occur.

"About twelve meters, Jessie," Penny replied.

"If you see anything interesting, give me the photo sign." Hans flexed his forefinger and patted a pocket on his buoyancy vest containing a neat underwater camera bought on vacation in Hawaii. "What marine life can we expect to see, Penny?"

"Good question. Probably a sea monster or two." Her eyes widened. "But don't worry, Jess. They only eat boys."

Jessica pursed her lips and screwed her eyelids, making the adults laugh.

"Seriously, on a good dive with vis like today you can find a lot. Check out the white anemones along the hull – they're pretty weird. You'll probably see ling and pollack, which look a bit like cod. They'll be hiding in the ship's compartments. You might come across a few crabs or a lobster, and if you're really lucky a *huge* conger!"

"What's a conger, Penny?"

"It's a very long eel, Jessie. About this big." She spread her hands right out. "But they're extremely shy and won't come near you."

"Then we put up the safety sausage." Hans waved the bright-orange marker buoy rolled up and clipped to an aluminum D-ring on his vest. When inflated using air from his regulator, the four-foot-long canvas tube would shoot to the surface on a handline and warn the surface vessels of their ascent. "Come up nice and slow, and we'll do a safety stop at five meters. Okay?"

"Okay," she replied as Penny helped her with the mask and fins.

"Any questions?"

"Dive time, Papa?"

"Let's keep it to thirty minutes. It looks pretty cold down there."

As father and daughter stepped awkwardly toward the yacht's stern, Penny grabbed Hans' arm and whispered, "Bangkok Women Really Are Fellas? What's wrong with Big White Rabbits Are Fluffy?"

"Errm . . . no answer."

Hans grinned and plunged into the sea, with Jessica close behind. After a couple of minutes on the surface to focus and do a second equipment check, Jessica gave her father the okay sign, followed by a thumbs-down for *Let's dive*.

Hans marveled at his daughter's control as she dropped to the wreck, her hand loosely clasped around the shot line for guidance. Every few seconds she pinched her nose and blew to equalize the pressure on her eardrums, putting short bursts of air into her jacket to slow the rate of descent. Hans had witnessed many far more experienced divers struggle with these basics. He floated down to kneel opposite her on the sandy bottom and made the okay sign.

Jessica was more than okay, not a hint of anxiety showing in her blue eyes.

Hans made the *Watch me* sign with his index fingers and peeled off his mask to simulate it becoming dislodged by another diver's fin. He purposely held it away from his body for several seconds to demonstrate how little an issue it was. In measured steps he stretched out the rubber headband and replaced the mask, then held the top of the lens and exhaled through his nose to expel the flooded water. Jessica followed his example with a confidence beyond her years.

Without warning Hans let the regulator drop from his mouth, chopping a hand against his throat to simulate running out of air. Jessica calmly offered him her spare, only Hans pretended it did not work either. Nonplussed, she pulled out her own regulator and handed it over. Her father took two deep breaths and passed it back. They repeated the exercise for a minute or so, until Hans patted her on the arm and replaced his mouthpiece.

Continuing the dive, Hans was impressed with the sight greeting them. The *James Egan Layne*'s barnacle-encrusted remains lay spread across the seabed like a skeleton in a boneyard, all sprouting the strange marshmallow-like anemones Penny spoke of, along with delicate coral fronds in both dull and vivid colors. Wheelhouse, winches and sheets of riveted iron bulkhead – even the porcelain in the ship's head – were still visible, coated in a thick layer of sediment and home to a variety of sea life.

Lesser-spotted dogfish lifted up out of the sand to glide snakelike through futuristic gardens of swaying green and purple kelp. Shoals of pollack holed up in the *Layne*'s murky compartments, unflinching as Hans played the beam of his flashlight on them, their algae-colored camouflage perfectly matched to this environment, their glassy black pupils bulging, as if afraid of the worst.

Hans tapped Jessica on the arm and pointed out a magnificent wrasse busy ripping barnacles off a section of bent and twisted railing with its vicious incisors. Clad in an armor of coppery scales like coins in a wishing well and swishing its spiny winglike fins, the creature gave the impression of a mystical sea dragon.

The Drift

Snapping shot after shot, Hans noticed a slight discoloration in the sand about the size of a dinner plate. Two almost imperceptible yet wonky angled eyes confirmed it was a flatfish. Evolution had allowed the species to survive through millenniums and this individual to grow to quite some age, but the American had something else on his mind – barbeque! – and the fish's contribution to the gene pool was about to end.

Hans whipped out his knife, exhaled deeply and sunk down to spear the flatfish behind its misaligned orbs. The plaice attempted to shoot away, but Hans kept the knife's point pinned to the seabed, resulting in the startled animal kicking up a storm of whirling sand with its futile butterflying motion. Hans gripped the plaice with one hand, withdrew the blade and reversed his grip, bringing the knife's hefty metal pommel down sharply to end the creature's misery, the mere recollection of frying fish and wood smoke triggering the pleasure receptors in his brain.

Hans was in the process of stowing his catch in a mesh bag when he felt a nudge on his shoulder. He looked to his side to see Jessica, who knew never to venture more than a few feet away, frantically pointing as Guz, Plymouth's much-loved sea lion, arched backwards in a graceful loop. Hans would have whooped in delight had he not had a regulator in his mouth, for this was a dive experience to beat most others. He gave Jessica the okay sign, which she returned immediately, switching the camera to video mode as he settled beside her. He had no concerns as to Guz's intentions but remained wary of the sea lion's excitement.

Fortunately, Guz just wanted to play, showing off in

58

his natural environment with more loops and turns, like a subaqua stunt pilot. Hans glanced at the rate bubbles rose from Jessica's exhalations, reassured to see she was relaxed, reading her pressure gauge to find plenty of air. True to her training, she took it as a cue to check his.

As Guz circuited the two of them, Hans had a feeling the flatfish might be the catalyst behind his display, and, not wishing to risk inviting any unwanted behavior, he pulled it from the bag. Guz's finely tuned senses saw him turn back on himself so acutely that his head traveling in one direction passed his rear flippers sculling in the other. With a gentle tug of his canine snout, Guz took the plaice from Hans' fingers and then turned to face them, bobbing his head as if to say thank you before shooting off through the deep green curtain.

Hans was about to call the dive to an end, unclipping the orange marker buoy ready for inflation, when Jessica banged him on the arm. She made a pincer sign and finned over to a ledge. Hans followed to see she had spotted a lobster caught up in fishing line.

It was an impressive specimen with a burnt-orange carapace tinged with ruby red and porcelain blue, and, over three feet in length, must have been at least sixty years old. The terrified crustacean thrashed about like a prisoner on the rack, its gigantic serrated claws powerless to extricate itself from the awful scenario.

Jessica pulled out her diving knife and began to cut the lobster free, her father helping her with the fiddly snarls while making sure the captive didn't nip them. Had the situation been different, Hans would have nabbed the lobster for dinner, but under the circumstances he was happy to see it scurry backwards under a shelf, with only the tips of its antennae still visible.

Climbing back aboard *Future*, Jessica couldn't get her words out fast enough.

"Penny! We saw Guz and we saw a lobster!"

"Wow, a lobster! Daddy said you were a good diver, but he didn't tell me you were that good! Was Guz behaving himself?"

"Ut-uh!" She shook her head. "He ate Papa's fish!"

"Oh, so we've got no lunch, hey? In that case we better find something else."

With *Future* anchored in an idyllic cove nestled amongst verdant-topped cliffs, they spent the afternoon snorkeling in the crystalline water, collecting limpets and mussels to cook over a driftwood fire on the beach. Back at the marina that evening, they rinsed the dive gear in freshwater and stowed it under the bunks, and then Hans hooked his camera up to the TV and played the video.

As Penny sipped a glass of chardonnay and praised Jessica's diving skills, her admiration for the father and daughter's unique relationship grew.

"**A**rnold Schwarzenegger," Ahmed whispered, lying on the top bunk amid the stench of stale urine, biting fleas and the muffled sob of a child.

"Jean-Claude Van Damme," Mohamed replied from the darkness below.

The young Moroccans were inseparable, blood brothers to the end, with scar tissue on their palms to prove it. Neither recalled exactly when they first met in the orphanage in Tangier. Ahmed's mother had left him on the steps as a baby. Mohamed arrived some years later when the French mission station ran out of funding. What they did remember was the bond forged between them and the promise, if called upon, to die for one another.

Now twelve and thirteen, the boys still played the Hollywood game occasionally, fantasizing that in reality their parents were movie stars, who would one day return to pluck them from obscurity with loving arms and reassurances of "We never forgot you."

"Mimi Farrar." Ahmed claimed Morocco's very own goddess of the silver screen as his birthright.

"She's *my* mother, you thief." Mohamed hissed.

"I thought you didn't know your mother." Ahmed giggled, which set Mohamed off for the umpteenth time that evening.

The door creaked open. Ahmed and Mohamed fell

silent. Lamplight bathed the crowded dormitory.

Abu Yazza, the orphanage's elderly patron, cast a drunken bloodshot eye over the sleeping children, beckoning the boy who was sobbing with a bony finger.

"Pious old pig!" said Ahmed as the door closed. "He may have the respect of the imam, but one day . . ." He leant over the side of the bunks and drew a finger across his throat.

"Abu Yazza and his baboon-faced wife are gonna show poor Omar some *hanan*." Mohamed spat the term "tenderness."

"And he will have to slave all day tomorrow, no sleep and bleeding."

In exchange for squalid accommodation and measly food, the orphans worked twelve-hour shifts in the airless basement of Abu Yazza's carpet factory.

The next morning the boys sat on their haunches in front of a traditional wooden loom strung with a half-finished rug, their nimble fingers weaving shuttles of polypropylene thread to create a striking blue, cream and red paisley motif. Mohamed coughed and rubbed his red-raw eyelids, for chemicals in the synthetic fibers often resulted in festering infections, dermatitis and asthma.

"Are you okay, brother?" Ahmed asked out the side of his mouth.

"It's painful." Mohamed blinked, trickles of sticky yellow fluid dribbling onto his cheeks.

"It's not for much longer. Remember the plan."

As youngsters, Ahmed and Mohamed had put up with the cruelty meted out to them by the heinous couple, internalizing the pain and developing coping strategies – lying, cheating, fighting and stealing – to get them through another day. Yet the pair were smart, hardening to their circumstances. Cunning replaced indifference. Plotting, the luxury of dreaming – and woe betides anyone who got in their way.

"Brother," Mohamed whispered, watching Omar scurrying around on his haunches, unable to look anyone in the eye as he swept up stray tufts with a dustpan and brush, "I remember the plan."

- 13 -

Over the next few days, while Penny spent time with Jessica fishing from the dock, rowing the tender and visiting museums, Hans made final preparations for the voyage.

Using a state-of-the-art software package, he interfaced *Future*'s electronic equipment with charts downloaded to his laptop to create a sophisticated navigation arrangement, making sure to back up the important files.

Travel visas would not be an issue, but Hans still had to make sure the yacht's paperwork was in order ready for inspection by harbormasters in the ports they intended to visit. He had the relevant tide tables and an almanac detailing the Atlantic's predicted conditions, together with a list of meteorological websites and frequencies for weather bulletins in the regions ahead. Giving a rough estimate of their arrival time, Hans emailed yacht clubs and marinas along their route to reserve moorings.

After buying scuba weights and fishing tackle in a nearby sports store, they provisioned the yacht with dried and canned victuals and enough fresh food to last them until reaching port in France. Penny helped, her knowledge of seafaring staples and British supermarkets making things a lot easier.

All Hans had to do now was take Old Glory from his suitcase and replace the English ensign flying astern.

Finally, they went to say good-bye to Old Bill, a tinkling bell above the chandlery door signaling their entrance. On bended knees, Bill stroked Jessica's cheek and pressed a good-luck gift into her hand. It was a pocketknife with a tiny silver anchor screwed to its ebony handle.

Her face lit up.

"Remember, don't cross the Biscay without a five-day window, and be sure to give her plenty of sea room when you do, mate." He winked.

"Aye aye, skippa!"

"Aye aye, me little hearty. And fair passage to 'e."

When Hans and Jessica left, Bill flipped the sign in his window to "Closed," then went into the backroom and poured himself a shot of rum. He massaged his gray-stubbled chin, knowing he would miss that nice American and his kid.

- 14 -

"**I**t is our time," Ahmed whispered, gathering his few possessions in the darkness. "There is no going back."

"Our future is bright." Mohamed retrieved his knife from under the mattress.

"Inshallah."

Using a key stolen by one of the younger children on a "visit" to the Yazza's bedside, Ahmed unlocked the dormitory. He felt nauseous, though unsure why.

Mohamed pulled a box of matches from his pocket. "Let's get the others out and torch this devil-forsaken fleapit while the filthy pigs sleep!"

Ahmed chuckled, having gotten used to his friend's impetuousness over the years.

"Not now, brother. Their time will come. Inshallah."

They hightailed into the night.

Heading in no particular direction, the boys soon found themselves walking along narrow cobbled streets deep in Tangier's Old Town. Water trickled down dank mossed walls as the faint sound of laughter emanated from underground taverns. In the glow of a streetlight, a scruffily dressed boy stood looking up and down the road. He appeared on edge, stepping from one leg to the other as the two of them approached.

"Salaam alaikum," Ahmed greeted.

"And may peace be upon you too," the boy mumbled, staring at Ahmed's palm for a moment before accepting it.

"What's your name, friend?" asked Mohamed.

"Faar," said the boy, which meant "mouse."

Mohamed wondered why Faar stood here alone in the middle of the night but didn't ask, instead letting Ahmed explain their plight.

Faar's timid brown eyes flicked alternately from Ahmed to Mohamed, until eventually "Come" he said, leading them down a winding alleyway and across a patch of wasteland. He stopped next to a pile of rubble overgrown with weeds and lifted up a sheet of rotting plywood to expose an open manhole.

"Down, down," Faar ordered, scanning the area like a soldier on patrol.

Clinging to the iron rungs of a service ladder, the boys descended into what at first was pitch-black silence, but nearing the bottom of the shaft they began to detect the flicker of firelight as the stench of human excrement and hushed conversations floated up to greet them. They stood at the base of the ladder, their vision adjusting to the dark in the cavernous space.

"This way," said Faar.

Following him along the sewer's walkway, they passed small fires and oil lamps, the flames illuminating haunted young faces and prone figures.

"*Shemkara?*" Mohamed whispered. "Glue children?"

"Yes," Faar muttered. "Here is my place."

They sat down on dirty bedding insulated from the cold stone by sheets of cardboard. Faar retrieved an empty tuna can from his shoulder bag. He levered up the lid and dripped oil from a plastic drinks bottle onto the wadding packed inside it, pulling a short length of the fabric through a hole spiked in the top of the can to serve as a wick. He lit it with a cigarette lighter and waited for the flame to take hold. Ahmed noticed Faar kept the bag strapped over his shoulder.

"Tonight you can share my blanket, but tomorrow you must find your own space. It gets cold down here."

Faar pulled a half-eaten flatbread from his bag and ripped it into three pieces.

Their eyes attuned to the darkness, the boys could make out the sewer's ancient brickwork conduit, the platform they were on set off to one side. Sewage trickled along the bottom of the pipe a few feet beneath them.

In the light of the fires, Mohamed could only see male faces. He was about to ask Faar why there were no girls when – "*Urrhk!*" – a bark shattered the subdued atmosphere, and their friend rushed to blow out the lamp.

"Shh!" Faar flattened himself against the wall. "Rat Boy!"

Sensing the fear in his voice, Ahmed and Mohamed did likewise, knowing better than to ask questions. Huddling in the shadows, they made out the silhouette of an older teenager staggering down the walkway, grunting and kicking sleeping children.

Close to Faar's bed space, two *shemkara* had fallen asleep with their lamp still burning. Mohamed lurched to extinguish it, but a terrified Faar gripped his arm.

"No!"

Taking Faar's lead, Ahmed and Mohamed buried their faces, as if in slumber, but whoever this frightening character was, it didn't fool him.

"*Urrhk!*"

He booted Faar's head, cracking it against the brickwork. The kid stifled a yelp.

In the same instant Ahmed and Mohamed went for their knives but froze at the sight that met them – a hideously disfigured head, bald with burn tissue, face melted and shriveled like a mummified corpse.

"*Sssssssss*," the creature hissed, like a snake weighing up its prey, a sole lock of hair fluttering in the subterranean breeze. Despite having no discernible features, Rat Boy appeared to give a jeering smile, pulling a knife of his own and drawing it slowly across his throat in mock slaughter.

"*Urrhk!*"

He stumbled off down the walkway and disappeared into the gloom.

15

Future carved out into the bay, responding to the slightest command like an obedient mare. For Hans it was a relief to get under way, a homecoming in every sense. Penny stood relaxed at the helm, wearing white three-quarter-length pants, Reef sandals and a blue crop top, her bronzed face glistening with sea spray. Jessica occupied herself by teaching Bear everything a stuffed toy should know about seamanship, particularly the drills her father drummed into her around safety. With sunlight dancing in the wave crests, the ocean was a delightful place to be, and at a speed of six knots Penny estimated they would reach France in twenty-two hours.

Hans settled on the cockpit cushions and opened their guidebook. He learned that Brest was the twin city of Plymouth, the siblings having a great deal in common – large universities, a strong maritime connection and a challenging vernacular. Both underwent extensive reconstruction after the Second World War, resulting in a similar conflict of architecture, although in their attempts to bomb an enemy submarine base, it was the Allies, not the Germans, who had reduced Brest's skyline to rubble.

Sailing *Future* into port in the morning, Hans mused on the likeness, as new buildings clashed with the remnants of centuries-old design. They passed the magnificent Château de Brest standing guard over the city's river mouth, the castle's crenulated walls forming a series of geometric shapes contouring the cliff side in a similar manner to the Great Wall of China. Restored to former glory, it was a formidable sight.

They rounded a point and the marina came into view, its craft nudging against lines of pontoons like components in a gigantic Airfix kit.

"Okay, me hearties." Hans interrupted a breakfast of sausage sandwiches and cereal. "Fenders in please, then hop ashore and tie us up."

"Aye aye, skipper!" Penny jumped at the task with her seemingly endless energy.

"Aye aye, skippa!" Jessica replied through a mouthful of Weetabix, unclipping her safety line and scurrying after her friend.

They each threw in a fender, and then Penny held Jessica's hand as they neared the pontoon. Hans had radioed the marina to find out their berth, and just as *Future* came abeam he blipped the engine in reverse, halting the yacht's forward momentum to allow the girls to step onto the floating dock.

"Whoooarh! That's it, shipmate."

Penny made a big deal out of pulling the boat in with Jessica and then showed her how to tie up to a cleat. With both lines secure, they climbed back on board to finish their food.

Later, as the three of them lounged in *Future*'s luxurious cockpit soaking up the morning's rays under a heavenly blue umbrella, the sound of distant rock music carried across the water.

. . . around the edge
A long way to get here
You won't see me cryin'
Just see me disappear
Without you
There is no way ahead
Without you-ooh-ooh-ooh . . .

Screening her eyes from the sun, Penny made out a yacht heading straight for them.

"Wow!" She reached for the binoculars. "She's a classic."

"What's a classic?" asked Jessica.

"It's a really old boat made from wood, honey."

"How many aboard?" asked Hans as the music grew louder.

"I'm not sure. I can only see a big fat guy.

"No! Hee-hee!"

"What?" Hans' curiosity kicked in.

"He's dancing! He's got a drink in his hand, and he's *dancing* on deck!"

"Wha—?" Hans took the binoculars.

Sure enough, a suntanned giant with a Grizzly Adams mane carved a funky groove on the cabin roof. Wearing tight yellow running shorts and Hawaiian-pattern flip-flops complete with pink plastic hibiscus blooms, he seemed blissfully unaware his overhanging gut swung in the opposite direction to the rest of his body.

As the yacht neared, they saw she truly was a thing of beauty, cherry-golden timbers gleaming lustrously beneath aqua-green sailcloth, a profile as sharp as an ax.

The only thing undermining her vintage chic was Mr. Disco and his booming rock track.

Using the same trick Hans had in Plymouth, the giant entered the marina under sail, but he dropped his canvas a touch late. Having swung his bow into the berth next to *Future*, he rushed forward, clutching his cocktail, to grab the mooring line.

"Hallo!" was all he managed, in a Dutch accent, before the yacht thumped into the pontoon, sending him reeling forwards, somersaulting across the walkway and into the sea on the other side. He surfaced still holding his glass.

"Hallo!" The giant grinned, shaking water from his hair and beard. "Is it okay to park my boat here?"

Jessica and Penny fell about laughing, Hans jumping up to help the guy ashore.

After securing his yacht and changing into dry shorts, the Dutchman came and introduced himself, bringing along a gallon can full of his favored concoction, along with the pungent whiff of marijuana.

"Hallo again!" he slurred, clambering into the cockpit. "My name is Marshell. And who's this liddle princess?"

"I'm Jessica."

"Ahhh . . . *Jesshica*! I heard all about you, the most beautiful princess in the whole world!"

She giggled.

Marcel – his name when sober – got down on one knee and kissed her hand. "Will you marry me . . . *pleash*!"

"You talk funny!"

"Funny-money-bunny-honey! Wanna drink some mojito?" He held out the gas can.

"Uh-huh!" Her eyes lit up.

"So, Father, can the princess have a liddle drink?"

"She can if she wants." Hans winked at Penny. "But she better not have too much, unless she wants to be sick as a pig."

"Okay, with some lemonade then."

Penny fetched a can of soda from the fridge.

"So, princess, if you gotta boat, I suppose you got boyfriends all around the world!" He tickled her ears.

"No! I *haven't* got a boyfriend!" She gave a determined headshake, unsure what to make of this strange man.

"Okay, then let's have a drink!"

In the ensuing conversation they learnt that Marcel had made a fortune in fine art. When his wife died, he'd retired to spend his days aboard her namesake, *Sietske*.

"So how is it crossing the Atlantic?" Hans asked.

"Oh . . ." Marcel's face flushed, his eyes flitting around the cockpit, looking anywhere but at Hans. "Er . . . yeah, it's okay. You gotta pick up the trade winds, you know?"

"Right," Hans replied.

16

For the next three years, Ahmed and Mohamed lived in the maze of crumbling sewers below Tangier's hectic streets, adapting to the ways of the *shemkara*, so-called for their inhaling of adhesive to banish a sense of rejection and indelible memories of abuse.

The boys spent their days hustling for dirhams by any means possible – collecting empty bottles and cans, begging for change, expropriating any item of value not under lock and key, and always as a pair, always watching each other's backs, forever planning, forever scheming for the Big Out.

Life belowground was harder still – securing a sleeping area, keeping hold of their belongings and maintaining face among the other urchins. Rat Boy was gang leader. Mutilated as a child when a begging syndicate poured acid over his face to increase his marketability, he had escaped his captors, but his grotesque appearance prevented him renting his body out to the perverts cruising the city's sordid backstreets. Out of necessity he had mastered the art of rat catching, gutting them with his teeth and eating their carcasses raw. With no hope of transcending the sewer's malodorous depths, Rat Boy maintained control through intimidation and violence, not hesitating to unleash it by way of a rusty blade carried in the waistband of his ragged pants.

The gang's female members cropped their hair, dressed as boys and adopted male names – anything to put off the vile predators who viewed them as subhuman prey. Every so often a child disappeared, kidnapped by one of the many trafficking syndicates and sold into sweatshops, drug operations and prostitution, the girls often destined for the Gulf States to begin lives as slaves.

One night Rat Boy returned to the hive drunk on a bottle whiskey taxed from little Faar, who stole it from a bag of duty-free purchases while portering at the ferry terminal. Rat Boy exuded venom at the best of times, but under the influence of alcohol his mood became unpredictable and usually spiraled out of control. Spying Mohamed asleep, he whipped out his knife and pounced, pinning him to the sewer's walkway with his legs.

Mohamed awoke in a daze, his mind fogged from inhaling lighter fluid, to find the blade shoved against his windpipe.

"*Urrhk-urrhk!*"

Rat Boy's guttural commands made no sense, an indication he was wasted and out of control.

Struggling for breath, Mohamed fought to control his fear, staring into menacing eyes sunk deep in the sockets of a disfigured head. With alcohol fumes enveloping them, masking the stench of human excrement, he considered his options – moreover, the swiftest way to inflict pain on his attacker. He would willingly risk having his throat slashed so long as he exacted revenge before the life drained from his body.

Mohamed reached for his own knife, a three count coming from within. He was about to plunge the blade into Rat Boy's kidney when he spied a movement in the gloomy corridor.

"Pssst!"

Rat Boy turned to see Ahmed holding out a bunch of bills, all the money the boys made that week.

"Here, take it."

Despite blood dripping down his neck, Mohamed attempted to object, but Ahmed placated him with a slow nod.

Rat Boy stood up and grabbed the dirhams.

"*Urrhk!*"

He staggered off down the tunnel toward his flea-infested mattress.

"Why did you do that?" Mohamed scowled. "I could have beaten him!"

"You will beat him." Ahmed raised a finger to his lips. "But the best answer comes to the man who isn't blinded by anger."

"Of course." The remaining enamel on Mohamed's blackened teeth flashed in the darkness.

"Keep your brother by your side, for without one you're like a man rushing into battle without a weapon."

"One hand cannot clap," Mohamed agreed, knowing Ahmed proffered the wisdom of someone five times his age.

"When we hit, we make it painful. The consequences are the same."

Ahmed tugged the sleeve of Mohamed's grubby T-shirt and they sunk into the shadows.

An hour passed then Ahmed nudged Mohamed and pointed a forefinger into the blackness. Careful not to wake the other scamps, they sneaked along the walkway toward Rat Boy's sleeping space.

"*Sahkaran*," Mohamed whispered, spying their leader facedown "drunk" on his bedding.

"Wait!" Ahmed put his arm out. "We make a plan."

In hushed tones, they agreed roles. Ahmed would dive on Rat Boy and restrain him while Mohamed stomped on his head. If things got out of hand, they would pull their knives and stick the leader without mercy.

As they crept forwards, a child started coughing. The boys froze, hearts pounding, waiting for the pitiful rasp to cease before continuing.

Reaching Rat Boy's comatose figure, they paused just long enough to acknowledge the look in each other's eyes.

Ahmed leapt through the air and landed heavily with his knees on the enemy, knocking the wind out of him as Mohamed stabbed a foot down hard.

"*Urrhk!*"

Rat Boy shot upright, years of self-preservation wiping aside the fog of liquor. He grabbed Ahmed by the throat and slammed his head against the sewer wall, knocking him unconscious.

Mohamed's heel smashed into the concrete.

"*Ahhhh!*"

He grimaced, pain rocketing up his leg.

Rat Boy pulled his knife and in a fluid motion slashed at Mohamed, nicking him just below the eye.

Mohamed drew his blade, and as Rat Boy reversed his swing he shoved it through the gang leader's wrist.

Rat Boy's weapon dropped from his grip, the metallic clatter echoing in the hollow confines of the lair. He stared at the object spearing his forearm, disbelief in his tortoise-like eyes as he realized his opponent had the upper hand.

Mohamed yanked the blade free and struck again, bringing his arm around in a wide arc. Rat Boy ducked, fumbling in the gloom for his own knife but finding the empty whiskey bottle. He smashed it against the brickwork to form a shank.

Overbalancing, Mohamed flailed his arms to stop himself reeling backwards off the platform. Rat Boy reveled in the horror on Mohamed's face, sneering behind his ugly mask. He raised the jagged bottle neck above his head and brought it down hard—

Ahmed thudded into Rat Boy using the mattress for protection.

"Oooph!"

Rat Boy flew through the air, a sickening thud as his head smacked against the far wall. His limp body rolled down into the river of human waste.

The boys fell silent.

Woken by the commotion, the street children gathered around them, peering down at Rat Boy's motionless form in disbelief.

"Inshallah," Mohamed whispered.

Ahmed hopped of the walkway into the flow of sewage.

"Inshallah." He held up the fold of money retrieved from Rat Boy's pocket.

When morning came, their former leader had fled.

- 17 -

Future's crew visited a hypermarket on the outskirts of Brest, to find the enormous store, the size of several football fields, packed with aisle upon aisle of discount food and drink.

"Chocolate, Papa!"

Jessica zeroed in on a shelf stacked with supersized bars.

"In the cart then, greedy pants."

Hans smiled as she heaved a two-foot-long slab onto the growing pile of beer, wine, coffee, canned meats and other treats. He picked up a bulk pack of mini-firecrackers, figuring he would have a bit of fun with them at some point.

"Say, is anyone else hungry?"

"I thought you'd never ask," Penny replied, her appetite boosted by the surrounding delicacies.

"I thought you'd never ask." Jessica stood mesmerized by a gigantic stack of Toblerones.

They took up seats in what had to be the smartest restaurant Hans had ever seen. Furnished in rich mahogany, with cream satin tablecloths, mirrored alcoves and pastel-painted murals depicting folk scenes from all around the world on every wall, it truly was a gem, the view of the Château de Brest a bonus. Hans marveled at Penny's competency in French as she ordered from the menu, delighted to find out they shared an appetite for the exotic when frog legs and escargot arrived for their starter.

"Escargot, Jess?" Gripping the mollusk's shell with a set of tongs, Hans eased the slimy morsel from its home with a cocktail fork.

"What is it?"

"It's a snail, like we have in the yard at home."

"*Urrrh!*"

No, this one's real nice, cooked with garlic butter and parsley."

"Hmm?" She frowned, not convinced and looking alternately at her father and Penny.

Hans popped the snail in his mouth, and Penny followed suit, both making a pretense at enjoying the dish – although in truth escargot didn't taste too great. Never one to be left out, Jessica nodded her approval, but as she chewed on the rubbery offering her grimace said otherwise.

After two days in port they got the five-day weather window, as Old Bill had insisted. Hans and Penny were well aware that the Bay of Biscay between Brest and La Coruña in northern Spain was not a body of water to mess with. Storms out in the Atlantic sent waves barreling in to meet shallows created by the continental shelf, forming mountainous breakers. Along with cargo ships and cruise liners, the Biscay had claimed many a yacht with its cantankerous bent. Keeping well out to sea, they agreed, would be the key to a successful passage.

On *Future*'s last night in the marina, Marcel invited

them aboard *Sietske* for a barbecue. By now this kindhearted Dutchman had made quite an impression on them, so they happily accepted.

Having grown up on her parents' wooden yacht, Penny was thrilled to spend an evening aboard *Sietske*, but as they stepped over her coaming, the scene greeting them was something of a shock. Empty beer cans, cup noodle pots and potato chip wrappers littered the cockpit floor, along with valuable items of equipment.

"I guess each to their own," she whispered to Hans.

Sensing their unease, Marcel made his excuses. "Ah! You know us Dutch. Anything for a pardy!"

He shoveled a load of litter into a pile with his foot, picked it up and disappeared into the cabin, reemerging with his mammoth grin and a tray of Tequila Sunrises.

"So, princess, when you marry me, we can tidy this place up together, you know?"

"Uh-huh." She nodded, her little eyes sold on the idea.

As the sun dropped below the horizon and an amber blaze spread out through burnt-red wisps tinged with pinks and blues, the evening turned into one to remember, Marcel supplying them with copious drinks and burgers and hilarious anecdotes from his experiences sailing the coast of Europe and North Africa.

"So, I'm in the Casbah, right? And I got a liddle drunk and I bought a monkey."

"What's a Cashbar?" Jessica asked.

"A Casbah . . . It's like a marketplace, you know? In Morocco they sell everything there – pots, pans, jewelry, carpets – and liddle monkeys like you!"

"I'm *not* a monkey!"

"Monkey-funky-hunky-bunky-honey!" Marcel wetted a forefinger and shoved it in her ear.

"Urrrh . . . yuck!" She punched his enormous stomach.

"Anyhow, where was I? Oh yeah. So I got this monkey back to the boat, and he ran away. So the next day I'm in the Casbah again and I see the same guy selling the same monkey. And I say, 'Hey! Why you selling my monkey?' And the guy says, 'Sir, iz not yurr monkey. Iz *twin* brother'!"

Chuckling as Marcel cracked them up for the umpteenth time, Hans wondered why this larger-than-life character never talked about anything closer to home. Picking his moment, "What about *The Card Players*?" he asked.

"Cards?" Marcel replied. "You wanna play some cards? Oh, I don't got any cards." He frowned and shook his head, looking upset he couldn't oblige.

"Never mind," said Hans.

Jessica let rip a monster yawn.

It was getting late, so Penny seized on the opportunity for them to say goodnight. Throwing a mock-seductive look at Hans, "*Voulez-vous venir avec moi?*" she asked, fluttering her eyelashes.

"Huh?"

"It's French. It means, 'Would you like to come home with me?'"

"Oh! Er . . . *oui*, madam."

"Madam!" She feigned outrage. "*Mademoiselle*, if you please!"

They thanked Marcel for his hospitality and, following hugs all round, climbed back aboard *Future*.

"I hope you find your monkey, Marshell!" Jessica shouted.

"Hey! Monkey-funky-hunky-bunky-honey!"

After sending Jessica to sleep with a tale of mermaids and dolphins, Penny joined Hans in the galley as he boiled water for a nightcap.

"You don't trust him, do you?" She ran a hand down his back.

"Don't trust him? What gives you that idea?"

"The card players thing. You weren't suggesting we play Texas Hold'em, were you?"

"No, I wasn't. It's a series of paintings by Cézanne. One of them went at auction last year for two hundred and fifty million. I saw a Discovery on it. Anyone with an idea of art would have known what I meant."

"So you don't believe his story."

"Listen" – Hans put his arm around her – "the guy's real nice. Look at the way he treats Jess. She adores him."

"She's a liddle princess!"

"Ha! It's just that he ain't no retired art dealer. Look at the garbage can he lives in – *stinks* of pot! That's not someone who knows how to make a million bucks."

"You can say that again."

"I just have a feeling there's more to this guy than he's letting on."

"I think you're right."

- 18 -

With their newfound status as gang leaders, life became slightly more prosperous for Ahmed and Mohamed, who imposed a modicum of tax in return for protecting the other members. It was far from enough to live off, though, and their hustling continued, always scheming and every day dreaming of the Big Out.

Sniffing around the medina one afternoon, they came across a battered orange pickup parked in the courtyard behind Old Man Ali's carpet shop.

"You go," said Ahmed, spying a tarpaulin covering goods in the back of the truck. "I'll keep watch."

Mohamed dashed forward, intent on taking a quick peek and retreating to make a plan. But the goods were heavy, the tarpaulin folded tightly around them.

Seeing his friend struggle, Ahmed ran over, and together they managed to loosen the canvas enough to expose its contents.

"Wow!" He shot a look at Mohamed, who stood mouth agape in a trance. "No way!"

Spilling onto the truck's rusting bed were bars of the finest hashish, likely a hundred or more, all carrying a stamp in the form of a monkey.

"We're rich!" hissed Ahmed.

"We're rich!" Mohamed replied.

"You're dead!" A sinewy arm locked around Mohamed's neck.

Ahmed was off on his toes, but turning to see Mohamed held captive, he slowed to a halt.

"If you run, I will kill him," the man said, and both boys knew he meant it. The cruel scar running from eye to chin spoke for him.

Instinctively, Ahmed sized the man up. Dressed traditionally in a dark-brown ankle-length djellaba and maroon skullcap, he was by no means an imposing figure, but there was something in the way he held himself – perhaps the cold, confident eyes – that said he was not a person to mess with.

"If you pull that, I'll snap his neck," the stranger warned, reading Ahmed's mind.

Reluctantly, Ahmed reached around, removed the knife from his waistband and threw it onto the pickup, a curt look signaling Mohamed to do likewise.

"*Shemkara*?" the man asked, releasing his hold on the boy.

"*Sayyid*." Ahmed nodded, staring at the dusty, grit-strewn ground.

"Then I have a better offer for you." He flicked his head toward the door of the truck.

The boys obliged, climbing in the passenger side.

The man drove out of the city for an hour and up a steep and winding mountain pass, Ahmed and Mohamed spellbound by the open countryside yet terrified of the dirt road's sheer drop, which had doubtless claimed the occupants of many a carelessly driven vehicle. On the approach to the village of Azila, the man stopped the truck on a particularly vicious bend. He killed the engine and lit a cigarette.

Ahmed looked to his right to see the scrubland falling

away hundreds of feet below. A small stone plaque sat concreted to a rock in the hillside.

> *My beloved Safiya, Amir and Hassan. Though you fly with the angels, your memory forever sings in my heart. Saleem.*

"I will make it simple for you," the man began, looking dead ahead. "I am Naseem, son of Saeed." He paused to let his words register, the boys instantly recognizing the birth name of the one known throughout the land as Al Mohzerer, "the Grower."

"The product is the best, and you will work hard to keep it the best. There will be no drugs, no pilfering and no shirking. In return you will not have to live as excrement in the city's asshole. You will have a roof over your heads, food in your bellies, and no one will touch you."

Ahmed and Mohamed shifted uncomfortably on the truck's bench seat.

"But do not cross me . . . if you value the air in your lungs and wish to see tomorrow's sunrise."

- 19 -

In the morning, as Hans and Penny readied *Future* for departure, Marcel emerged from *Sietske*'s cabin clutching a scuba mask and a pint of black coffee laced with cognac. With his still-in-bed hair and dumpling eyes, he looked on the delicate side of fragile.

"So you guys leaving now?" he asked, his voice as rough as sandpaper.

"Yeah, see you in La Coruña!" Penny blew a kiss and threw off the mooring line.

"*Ja*! I see you guys there."

"See you there, Marshell!" Jessica waved Bear in the air.

"I'm following you, princess!"

They chugged out of the marina in conditions the bulletins had promised, but as Penny cut the engine and Hans made good the mainsail, something of a commotion broke out on the dock.

"*Attendez! Attendez, s'il vous plaît!*"

Running along the pontoon toward *Sietske* were two of the marina's officials, looking as though they wanted a word with her skipper. But as Marcel swung the yacht around in a frantic reverse arc, the scuba mask resting on his head and water dripping from his shaggy mane, he didn't appear keen to oblige, leaving his pursuers lurching over the dockside waving their fists like extras in a Bond movie.

"What was all that about?" asked Penny. "And what was with the diving mask?"

"If I had to guess, I'd say it might be the little matter of mooring fees." Hans chuckled. "The mask, I have no idea."

At one point it looked as if Sietske would catch up with *Future*, but eventually her serene pace proved no match for the modern yacht's racing line. With clear sky and fair northerlies as predicted, the first part of the crossing went smoothly. Hans and Penny made a great team. When it came to seamanship, both instinctively knew each other's strengths, Hans trusting Penny's superior knowledge and she his scrupulousness and pragmatism. Penny's bond with Jessica made the whole deal tighter.

"Crew briefing of the century!" Hans announced.

"Crew briefing of the century!" Penny echoed.

"Crew briefing of the century, Bear!" Jessica grabbed her furry companion and joined them on deck.

Hans addressed the issue of abandoning ship, explaining how the life raft worked and why it was important to don survival suits in an emergency. He showed Jessica how to set the handheld VHF radio to the correct frequency and broadcast a Mayday, and how to deploy the EPIRB should they have to leave the yacht.

"What's the emergency channel, First Mate?"

"Sixteen, Pap— er, skippa."

"Well done."

For a bit of fun they each had a go at operating the hand-cranked desalinator. Working on the principle of reverse osmosis, the pump turned salt water into fresh, but as Jessica found out, it took significant effort to produce even the slightest trickle.

The next day's weather bulletin dampened their spirits with a report of the Azores High moving off toward the Eastern Seaboard, leaving choppy conditions and variable wind in its place. Over a late lunch they discussed their options, Penny serving up chunky slices of whole-wheat baguette laden with French pâté and potent-smelling cheese.

"Papa!" Jessica shrieked as she gazed over the coaming.

"Dolphins, sweat pea."

"Porpoises," Penny corrected him.

Six gray friends zipped through the water at *Future*'s bow, flashing white bellies as they turned on their side every so often to fix a beady eye on the spectators.

"That one's looking at you, Jess!" Hans put an arm around his daughter.

"Heeee!"

So enchanting were their companions, *Future*'s crew watched mesmerized for over an hour, until a rumble of distant thunder sent the porpoises shooting off. Penny looked up to see a bank of dark cloud moving in from the west.

"Too late to turn back," she whispered.

Hans nodded as a gentle swell erased the cat's paw-print effect on the sea's previously polished surface.

By late afternoon a force six headwind slowed *Future*'s progress. The barometer plummeting, Penny furled a third reef in the mainsail.

"It's going to be a long night." She smiled. "Will Jessie need a seasickness tablet?"

"Please, Penny. If you can keep her occupied below, I don't mind taking the first couple of watches, and we better close the companionway."

"Aye aye, captain," Penny replied, deploying the "last-chance" line abaft before disappearing inside.

True to its name, the hundred-yard-long rope knotted at three-foot intervals offered a last chance to stay with the boat should one of them fall overboard while alone on deck. Grabbing it would trip the self-steering mechanism, slewing the yacht into the wind and bringing her to a standstill.

While *The Lion King* played on DVD, Penny fetched an ornate wooden box from her kitbag, opening it up to reveal a veritable Aladdin's cave of colored beads, gemstones, leather thongs and silver chain. Great fun, her jewelry making generated a significant second income as she traveled the marinas of the world, hawking her avant-garde trinkets to rich and often bored yachting wives. She stripped wire from a spool and, using a pair of needle-nosed pliers, twisted the end around the eye of a small metal clasp. Having measured the bracelet for size around Jessica's wrist, she snipped the wire to length and let the little girl choose which beads she wanted on it.

Delighted with her gift, Jessica snuggled up against Penny to watch the movie.

"JJ loved *Lion King*."

"Did he?"

"Hmm. Mommy called him Simba."

"Really?"

"Hmm . . . but they got dead."

"Oh, honey. Daddy told me." Penny welled up,

putting her arms around the little girl, wishing she could do more.

"A bad man hurt them. But Papa says it's okay because they will always be with us when we look at the flowers and the trees and the sea."

Jessica looked up at Penny, tears pouring down her cheeks as she sought affirmation.

"Oh, sweetheart." Penny pulled Jessica close as her tiny shoulders shrugged up and down. "Papa's right. They'll always be here. You know those porpoises that visited us today?"

"Uh-huh, uh-uh."

"They came to tell us that Mommy and JJ are happy and smiling, and everything is going to be all right."

"I just want Mommy and JJ to be here, Penny . . . uh-uh."

"I know, sweetie. I wish that too."

- 20 -

"The kif in the Rif is the Rif in the kif!" shrieked
Ahmed, whacking the garbage bag of dried marijuana
with two sticks like a drummer in a rock band.

"The Rif and the kif are one and the same!" Mohamed
replied, completing their youthful mantra.

High up in Morocco's Rif Mountains, the view
stretched to the shimmering waters of the
Mediterranean Sea, yet in the murk of the hut the boys
concentrated on beating the kif plants, stripping them of
their valuable buds for processing into the finest
hashish.

"This is boring. I wish we were picking." Mohamed
sighed, his thoughts flicking to harvesting the pungent-
smelling blooms out on the miles of man-made terraces.

The Berbers had inhabited this region of North Africa
since prehistoric times and, over the last century,
cleared vast tracts of pine forest, wild flowers and rocky
outcrops for cultivation.

"You blinkered baboon!" Ahmed pretend-whipped
his friend. "Remember the plan!"

"Am-ster-*daaaam*!" Mohamed's face lit up

"Girls, girls, girls!" Ahmed grinned, exposing a row of
blackened teeth that "girls" would surely die for.

A year had passed since Al Mohzerer first brought
them to the hut, situated on a mountain farm his family
had owned for generations. Compared to sleeping in a

93

sewer wondering where their next meal came from, it was a great improvement and far better than the depravity of the orphanage and the unhealthy grind in the carpet factory.

They awoke every day at dawn upon hearing the *adhan* piped from the village mosque's ancient minaret. However, the boys never paid homage to Allah. Even if they had wanted to pray five times a day – which they did not – Al Mohzerer forbade such a practice, for time was money, the competition fierce in this industry. After a breakfast of bread and sweet black coffee, the boys went to work, relentlessly thrashing the cannabis stems or harvesting the plants out on the slopes.

Every so often a Dutch buyer or a group of backpackers arrived at the farm to witness production, a highpoint for Ahmed and Mohamed, the visitors showering them with gifts and dirhams and teaching them phrases in English. Some of the girls wore shorts and skimpy tops, a source of amusement and intrigue for the cheeky pair, who worked their puckish charm for all it was worth to receive hugs and pecks on the cheek.

"Mon-ni-ca!" Mohamed often teased, reminding Ahmed of the French girl he'd taken a shine to last year. "Kissy, kissy, kissy!"

He would clasp his hands to his chest and jiggle them up and down.

"Idiot!" Ahmed always flushed.

Naturally, many of the guests jumped at the chance to purchase hashish. The boys would slip them quarter ounces of the "squidgy black" they made by spitting on palmfuls of hash powder and kneading the mix into malleable lumps with their fingers, giving strict instructions not to disclose the transaction to the other workers, especially Al Mohzerer, who'd chopped people's hands off for less.

Every dirham earned went into a can hidden beneath the hut's floorboards, ready for the day they would leave this place and head for the bright lights of Amsterdam, where people bought cannabis on the street, smoked it in cafés, and girls sat half-naked in the glow of red bulbs wantonly awaiting young bucks such as them. When the time came, the two of them would steal as many blocks of Al Mohzerer's hashish as they could carry and a boat from the harbor in Tangier, then sail across the Strait of Gibraltar to Spain and hitchhike to the land of milk and honey.

One Sunday a month Al Mohzerer allowed the boys to travel to the city with him. While he attended to the business of delivering Golden Monkey, they would watch a movie, sneaking below the ticket booth window to save their hard-earned cash for the Big Out. As for entertainments snacks, Ahmed distracted the storekeepers while Mohamed shoved them into his pockets. The rest of the sojourn they spent at the ferry port or backpacker hostels, touting their squidgy black lumps to dope-loving tourists.

"Jiggy, jiggy, jiggy!" Mohamed pouted his lips, jiving with his hands as if flying a kite. "Am-ster-*daaaam!*"

"Vroom, vroom!" Ahmed beamed, steering an imaginary sports car around an imaginary bend. "BMW!"

"Ferrari!"

"Rolls . . . *Royce!*"

Whipping the dried plants, the boys fell silent under

the allure of their long-planned adventure, minutes passing as the highly prized follicles of marihuana accumulated in the bottom of the garbage sack.

"Footyball!" Mohamed piped up, his thoughts flicking to the homemade soccer ball they had made by wrapping hundreds of carrier bags around each other. Amongst the endless rows of weed, it was easy to have a discreet kickabout.

"Beckham!"

"Ronaldo!"

Their boyish banter continued – anything to relieve the monotony of a twelve-hour shift in the hut.

Without warning the door flew open, kicking up a cloud of yellow dust as sunlight poured into the room. The teenagers fell silent, neither daring to look up.

In walked Al Mohzerer.

As a glittering golden haze swirled about them, Ahmed and Mohamed went at the task with renewed vigor. Al Mohzerer stared at them for a few seconds, then picked up a plastic barrel brimming with potent plant matter, loaded it onto his battered truck and drove off.

"Ketama!" Ahmed chirped with a grin, mimicking the visiting Dutch dealers.

"Sputnik!" Mohamed replied – another brand name the region's hashish went by in the coffee shops of Amsterdam.

"Zero Zero!"

"King Hassan!"

"Rifman!"

And so it went on.

- 21 -

Conditions worsened, the wind growing stronger and increasingly unpredictable, the mainsail flogging around like a bucking stallion. Hans focussed on keeping *Future*'s nose pointed into the oncoming swell, a formidable task as waves smashed into the yacht from all angles. The rain turned from lazy slugs into a barrage of biting pellets, torrents of spray drenching him further, and as the once-distant cloud bank blocked out the remaining daylight, a bolt of lightning zigzagged down to stab the sea in the distance. It arced brighter twice, as if Mother Nature had fired a Taser and then double-zapped her victim, leaving an image of a snaking white bungee burned into Hans' retinas. Thunder rumbled seconds after, a sign the worst was yet to come.

Future rode up endless rollers that built still higher, but just as the yacht looked to founder, she crashed down their steep faces into the black troughs below, a deluge of white water cascading over the bow and threatening to pitch her end over end. Like a whale coming up for air, she shrugged off the liquid avalanche and charged into the next berg with her indomitable spirit.

Used to such conditions, Penny prepared for the worst, stowing all the gear in the cabin and strapping Jessica and Bear down in their bunk, no easy task as

Future careened into the maelstrom.

"Don't worry, darling. Neptune's just playing with us."

"Who's Neptune, Penny?"

"Well, once upon a time . . ."

The constantly changing wind threatened to knock *Future* down, so high-pitched it reminded Hans of Indy 500 cars changing gear. He checked the wind indicator to see it pegging seventy knots, confirming that these were by far the worst conditions in which he had skippered. Furling in the remaining canvas, he unclipped his safety line ready to go forward and set the storm jib, but an almighty gust slammed the mainsail down into the seething ocean, plunging the starboard beam deep underwater.

As Jessica screamed, Penny flew across the cabin, smashing her head against the opposite bunk, her body collapsing onto the sole as the yacht rolled upright.

"Papa!"

Hans had problems of his own. Tons of seawater poured out of the cockpit, sucking him overboard into the path of a breaking giant. He drew a sharp breath and attempted a duck-dive, but it was too late. The wave crashed down, knocking air from his lungs and tumbling him around until there was nothing but cold, black silence.

Desperate to breathe, Hans kicked for the surface, but foul-weather gear and sea boots retarded his progress, the deep layer of froth offering little resistance for his determined strokes.

Stay calm! His military training came into play, but,

breaking through the surf, he saw *Future* had sailed on. She was thirty yards away and moving further every second.

"Penny!" Hans screamed to no avail, realizing his only chance of survival was the man-overboard line. He ducked under, pulled off his footwear and, leaving his life jacket deflated so as not to impede his movement, struck out in a direction perpendicular to the *Future*'s wake.

By now she was sixty yards distant. Hans put this out of his mind and plowed on through the breakers, desperate to feel an arm chop down on the rope but knowing the massive swell would considerably shorten its hundred-yard length.

Crossing *Future*'s wake by a good ten yards, Hans still couldn't find the line and, treading water, wondered if he had swum over the top of it. He was about to resign himself to fate when a fluorescent float came skimming across the foam toward him.

"*Arrrhh!*"

He lunged, grabbing the last foot of nylon as the yacht began dragging him through the wave crests like an oversized fishing lure.

Using his palm as a hydrofoil, Hans popped his life jacket, and although creating drag, it kept his head above water, its pull-down hood fending off spray and enabling him to breathe.

Why doesn't the tension on the rope trip the self-steering? he wondered as *Future* forged ahead, making their reunion a formidable task.

His strength waning, Hans inched along the rope, relieved to grasp the half hitches tied every three feet.

Ninety yards . . . sixty . . . thirty . . . So close but so far.
"*Noooooo!*"

Forced to give up, Hans did not have the energy to heave anymore or to tie the line around him.

Good-bye, my beautiful baby.

He prepared himself for the inevitable, ready to let go and surrender to nature's wet embrace.

I'm sorry, my sweet pea. I'm so sorry.

Light flooded the cockpit.

"Papa!"

"Jessie!"

Above the noise of the howling wind and crashing ocean, Hans screamed, "Honey, swing the wheel around! *All* the way, like Daddy showed you!"

He could see his daughter struggling to carry out his instructions, the storm tumbling her insignificant figure around the cockpit.

Finally the line went slack.

Oh, my girl!

With a second wind, Hans swam the last few yards, spitting violently to expel the water invading his mouth and attempting to drown him. He clung to the stern ladder, regaining the strength to climb back aboard.

"Penny, Papa! Penny's *not* moving!"

Hans swept her up and, seeing she had put her life jacket and harness on correctly and secured a safety line, burst into tears. Penny lay still in the cabin, Jessica having placed her in the recovery position. Hans checked her airway and breathing and her body for injuries. He found a nasty lump on the back of her head. His fingers came away wet with blood.

"Jessie, I'm gonna strap Penny in her bunk. I need

you to get in yours too while I go and set the storm sail."

He pulled the cover over Penny and saw her eyes flicker.

"Hans . . . is that you?"

"I'm here, honey."

"Hmm." She smiled, clasping his hand before drifting into sleep.

Leaving to go on deck, Hans heard "Papa!" He turned to see Jessica holding Bear out.

"Huh?"

"For Penny," she whispered.

Al Mohzerer pulled up outside an ancient stone building on his farm. He flicked a half-smoked cigarette aside and hauled the plastic barrel off the pickup, eyeing the rusting tailgate with contempt. It was a bitter reminder that although his gang played a key role in the hashish trade, the majority of the profit filled the pockets of European drug lords.

"Salaam alaikum." Saleem, his aging foreman, appeared in the doorway, patting plant dust from his djellaba in a gesture of subservience.

"And may peace be upon you," Al Mohzerer replied in Arabic, before switching to French. "*Le produit est prêt?*"

"Of course, *sayyid*. Allah has been good to us. Come, come." He beckoned with his palm facing down.

Behind the outhouse's ramshackle façade lay a hive of activity as workers, eyes red from the cloud of cannabis dust, set about the final stages of preparation. Unlike Ahmed and Mohamed, these men had long since served out their indenture, earning the approval, if not the respect, of Al Mohzerer.

Two of the gang beat the base foliage a second time and, using a sheet of muslin, sieved out the minute epidermal cells containing the highest level of tetrahydrocannabinol (THC) the plant's psychotropic chemical, resulting in buckets of pure hash powder.

Another team poured the valued commodity into cellophane bags and taped them up to form packets. They spiked the packets with tiny holes to prevent escaping air bursting them in the press. The machine itself consisted of a hydraulic truck jack set into a custom-built metal frame, which crushed the powder to create a block of hashish so solid you could hammer a nail in with it. The mold left an imprint of a Barbary macaque on the block to identify the product as Golden Monkey in the marketplace, a source of pride for Al Mohzerer. The final part of the process involved sealing the goods in wax and dusting them with fragrant powder to foil sniffer dogs before wrapping them in layers of brown parcel tape for export.

The Grower sat cross-legged on a floor cushion as Saleem lifted a pot of mint tea from a wood-burning stove, filled two thimble-sized cups and dropped a sugar lump in each, the accepted protocol prior to discussing business.

"Once again you have done me proud, old brother." Al Mohzerer rarely bestowed such terms of endearment. "May Allah rain peace upon you."

"You are too kind, *sayyid*. I am but a simple man who does his best for his master."

Talking the talk handed down through the ages, Saleem crumbled ash from the fire into the bowel of a sipsi pipe and sprinkled on a layer of hash powder. Igniting the mix, he knew better than to offer it to the Grower, who would stick to his Maxims, a cheap imitation of the mighty Marlboro, knowing that for his boss the resultant paranoia from smoking the herb had long since outweighed its beneficial effects.

"We go back a long way." Al Mohzerer paused to empty his teacup. "A journey not without hardship."

Saleem stroked his beard and nodded thoughtfully, picturing the evil mountain bend and the faces of his wife and two boys. He shook himself. "And for our fathers before us, master."

"Indeed. Your father begged mine to break from the war and tend to the farm."

He spoke of the war of independence fought against the Spanish in the early part of the twentieth century.

"But yours was a man of great honor who put the interests of the clan first and led its warriors into battle until the bitter end." Saleem eased himself up, wincing as he refilled their drinks.

"They both came home broken men," Al Mohzerer muttered.

"The only two who did return." Saleem shook his head slowly.

"But to what?" the Grower spat. "To fields gone to waste. My father leading a clan of women and dead men."

"Inshallah, *sayyid*. We cannot change the past. You did your best to recover the farm."

"For a while it was good."

"It was glorious." Saleem gazed at the embers smoldering in the pipe's bowel and smiled. "Supplying the greedy infidels with the magic herb made you a rich man."

"Then the cursed fungus destroyed the plants and made me poor once more. I sold off much of my family's land to survive yet still had to pay the workers and the never-ending bribes." The Grower swirled the dregs of tea around in the cup and then flicked them on the dusty floor.

"It will come again, *sayyid*. There are moves far and wide to legalize the herb, and then there's the medical market in Europe and America."

"You speak kind words, old friend, but the infidels grow their own product now. They no longer need our fertile earth and the blessed weather from Allah. It can all be bought on this thing they call the Internet and grown in their pox-ridden homes under artificial light that shines brighter than the midday sun."

Sensing Al Mohzerer's growing antipathy, Saleem changed the subject.

"And what of the two boys, *sayyid*? They show promise, no?"

"Ha! *Shemkara*. Rats from the gutter with filthy poisoned lungs and treacherous minds."

"Please do not be hard on them, *sayyid*. They have only known suffering in their short years and could be your biggest asset in times to come. They carry the fire in their hearts . . . like we once did."

Future rode out the storm under bare poles, a parachute sea anchor streamed from the bow to keep her into the wind and prevent further drama. When resetting the last-chance line, Hans found out why it had been difficult to locate and not tripped the steering mechanism – it had hooked around the rudder when *Future* keeled over. After checking on the girls, he changed into dry clothes and filled a thermos with soup for the long night ahead, spent sitting upright in his sleeping bag catnapping in the cockpit.

"Hello, handsome." Penny handed him a mug of coffee.

"Uh . . ."

"Guess we had quite a night last night."

"You could say that. How's the head?"

"It's nothing."

"I superglued the cut while you were out of it."

"Really?" Penny fingered the painful bump. "You're quite the GI Joe, aren't you?"

"I've seen worse, but you should get it checked out when we reach La Coruña. How's Jess?"

"Zonked." Penny smiled briefly before catching the emotion in Hans' eyes. "What happened, honey?"

With the sun burning a hole in the miserable gray ceiling and *Future* making light work of the remaining swell, Hans retold events.

Penny listened aghast. When he had finished, their mutual silence conveyed the debt of gratitude owed to this marvelous kid.

After a time Penny chirped up, "Hey! You know what they say?"

"No. What do *they* say?"

"Worse things happen at sea."

Her quip lightened the mood and, together with the morning rays now ricocheting off the water, reminded Hans this trip was supposed to be fun.

"Hot chocolate?" he tempted. "With a li-ttle shot of rum?"

"Hmm!" Penny beamed. "Be rude not to."

Snuggling together, the spirit working its magic, both experienced sheer bliss in the calm after the storm.

"Après ski," Penny murmured.

"Après ski?"

"This feeling – like downing a large brandy after a day on the slopes."

"Right, erm, hot bath after a jog in the rain?"

"Mmm . . . Fire on the beach after a dip in the sea."

"Sauna after rolling naked in the snow . . ."

"Hey?"

"Oh, must be a military thing."

Whatever the feeling, neither of them wanted to be anywhere else at any other time in history.

"Sandwiches!"

Standing in the companionway, mouth smeared in blackcurrant jam, the first mate looked pleased with her effort.

"Oh, sweet pea! Did you make them for us?" Penny

took the plate stacked with irregularly chopped offerings.

Upon closer inspection, "sandwiches" proved to be a generous description in view of the distinct lack of filling splattered between slices of bread like Rorschach's inkblots, but Hans and Penny wolfed them down nonetheless.

"So who was a big, brave girl last night?" Penny cleaned Jessica's face with a wet wipe. "Did you tell Daddy I banged my head?"

"Hmm! Daddy got *all* wet."

"So I heard."

"Will Marshell be okay? Did *Siska* fall down too?"

"Oh . . ." Penny glanced at Hans. "I'm sure he'll be fine. He's been in much worse weather than this."

Sweeee-sweeee! A tiny bird alighted on the spreader, fluffing its orange and turquoise plumage to dry off the spray.

"Land ahoy!" Hans spotted the Spanish coastline on the horizon. "La Coruña for lunch!"

An hour later a rocky headland covered in sparse grass like a worn-out toupee loomed over them.

"Check that out." Standing at the helm, Penny pointed at the cliff top.

Hans and Jessica looked up to see a bunch of weird Easter Island–like statues and someone's idea of a futuristic take on Stonehenge.

"Modern art?" asked Hans.

"I guess so." Penny grinned. "But that tall building there—"

Hans eyed the striking obelisk.

"Tower of Hercules. World's first-known lighthouse.

Dates back to Roman times."

"Wow, that's four hundred years earlier than our oldest Native American monument."

For Hans the trip was already the experience of a lifetime, despite last night's challenges. In the military, while on NATO training exercises in the Norwegian Arctic, he had taken a week's leave to explore his roots in neighboring Sweden. Indulging in enormous smorgasbords washed down with *brännvin* and *öl* while immersed in the history and culture of his Scandinavian ancestors had been a revelation, and visiting a Viking museum in picturesque Stockholm a welcome break from skiing for days in full equipment and living in snow caves. But something about Europe was unique, as if it offered a lens through which to view the United States into context.

- 24 -

"**H**e has the heart of a rock." Mohamed attacked the plate of olives, goat cheese and flatbread.

"And the bitterness of a thousand lemons." Ahmed spat a stone into the long grass.

"Do not be so quick to judge another before you have carried the weight of their burden and understand what it is that makes them heavy of chest," Saleem interjected, though in truth he empathized with the boys.

Ahmed and Mohamed swapped glances, knowing exactly where their loyalties lay.

They looked forward to lunch with Saleem, Al Mohzerer's trusted foreman. A kindly old man, he lived in a cottage on the farm, his history with the Grower spanning generations. Eating with him in the soft grass in front of the farmhouse provided a welcome break from the boredom of the hut and the endless harvesting of plants out on the terraces. As with countless waifs over the years, Saleem had taken the youngsters under his wing, showing them the love he once felt for his own two boys.

"Look about you." Saleem cast an arm over the land. "One hundred years ago this farm thrived, yielding rich crops of barley and wheat, while herds of sheep and goat grazed as far as the eye could see."

Only knowing the farm to grow marijuana, Ahmed and Mohamed were fascinated, as always falling under the spell of Saleem's fatherly talk. Not a single cloud interrupted the pristine sky, just the fluffy white plumage of Atlas flycatchers as they climbed and dipped in search of juicy delights to feed gluttonous clutches.

"What do you know of the Berbers?"

The boys looked at each other, faces a blank.

"The clans have lived in the Rif since time began. Fierce men, loyal women, no one would ever take this land from them, and certainly not the Spanish invaders."

As the old man spoke, a butterfly alighted on his knee and began to pad around in a clumsy circle on the white cotton of his djellaba. A collage of zebra stripes, sunburst reds and yellows and oranges, and mock eyes emblazoned the finely ribbed sections of the insect's wings, and despite failing eyesight, Saleem could make out tiny black arrowheads marking the wings' serrated edges.

Prior to their arrival at the farm, the boys had never seen such beautiful creatures, but out of habit Mohamed raised his palm and took a swipe.

"Stop!" Ahmed blocked his friend's arm and gave him a look of thunder.

"The ancients believed that when a butterfly lands you can give it a message to take to loved ones in heaven," said Saleem.

As the insect lifted into the air, he appeared to lose his train of thought before continuing the story. "Al Mohzerer's father was the great Saeed, leader of the Zayenesh clan, shrewd but compassionate and greatly respected by his people. In the summer of 1921, he sat in this exact spot" – Saleem stroked the long green stems – "applying a splint to the leg of an injured lamb. He heard the sound of beating hooves and looked up to see a figure approaching on horseback. A boy your age" – Saleem's eyes glinted as they had at this part of the tale many times before – "dismounted and delivered a message that would change the family's fortune forever."

The boys followed his gaze to see the stone trough the messenger's horse drank from all those years ago.

"Spanish troops had breached the Rif's eastern border and set up a military outpost in the foothills of the Abarran Mountains. The great Saeed had heard enough. 'We ride!' he replied, and within an hour the men of the Zayenesh mounted and rode east to join the coalition, their horses kicking up a plume of dust visible for miles around.

"The Berber tribesmen had a long tradition of fighting and a high standard of fieldcraft, but lacked weapons. Saeed advised Abd el-Krim, their charismatic leader, to send men into battle with a rifle between two, so should a Berber fall his brother could continue the fight."

"Men went into battle without a gun?" Ahmed looked at Saleem in disbelief.

"The men went into battle with the loyalty of the clan and the hearts of lions. A force of five hundred descended on the Spanish, rifles blazing and scimitars drawn, massacring two hundred of the infidels. Word spread, and the Riffian ranks swelled. They attacked a hundred more encampments, employing guerilla tactics, captured weapons and killed thousands more enemy, laughing as the Spanish fled north to the coast."

"Al Saeed was a hero!" Mohamed stared into Saleem's cloudy eyes.

"Saeed was a simple farmer who had to decide

whether to return to his land and tend to the crops and livestock or stay by the side of Abd el-Krim. He chose to remain."

"Did they slay the remaining infidels like dogs?" Ahmed's pupils widened as he spoiled for the fight.

"The Spanish troops were no match for us Berbers, who have only ever known hardship and suffering. Our numbers grew to eighty thousand, and we drove the remaining scum back to Melilla in the east."

"Yaaaah!" Mohamed swung a mock scimitar, imagining a lopped enemy head spurting blood as it flew through the air.

"But Abd el-Krim made a foolish error. Rather than close in on Melilla and cut the infidels down like grass" – Saleem ripped up a handful of stalks and let the breeze flutter them from his palm – "he began to wage war on the occupying French in the west."

"Why let the snake grow another head?" Mohamed felt betrayed.

Saleem pulled a sipsi pipe and a small ivory box from the sleeve of his djellaba. "You are wise for one so young." He took a pinch of hash powder from the ornate holder and thumbed it into the pipe's bowel. "Abd el-Krim feared reprisals from other European nations who had interests in Melilla." He lit a match and circled it around his preparation while drawing on the pipe's stem, blowing a plume of yellowy-brown smoke into the fresh mountain air.

With a look of bliss settling over his leathery face and softening the appearance of a beaked nose, the old man resumed his history lesson. "But by taking on the French he made a big mistake. The garlic eaters could not risk rebellion spreading through their African colonies and sent a massive army, with planes and artillery support. The Foreign Legionaries" – Saleem took a long pull on the pipe, holding in the magic fumes as they transported him backwards in time – "they were ruthless in battle, executing prisoners and" – he drew a finger across his throat – "decapitating the fallen."

"But Abd el-Krim and Al Saeed, they must have killed them all!" Mohamed spoke with the same passion as the young Berbers drawn to the slaughter.

"Ho Chi Minh, Mao Zedong, Che Guevara – they all learned from Saeed's legendary leadership, but the humble farmer could do nothing to stop the infidels unleashing vile chemicals on the villages. Babies, children, adults and elders writhing on the ground, suffocated by the foul gas, lungs on fire and drowning in their own blood as the foreigners counted their greedy profits.

"Abd el-Krim was forced to surrender and banished from the land. Saeed returned to his farm a broken man, a leg crippled by shrapnel, his lungs starched by the devil's mustard breath, his workforce dead."

"Did he die too?" Mohamed spoke through a mouthful of bread and olives, his rotten teeth making ugly work of masticating the bolus.

"How could he die, you idiot?" Ahmed pretended to slap his friend but instead forced Mohamed's gaping maw shut. "He is the father of Al Mohzerer."

"Allah blessed Saeed with twenty more years, but alas he joined the Holy Prophet – may peace be upon Him – two days before Naseem entered the world to inherit a farm gone to rack and ruin." Saleem looked out over the fields as if to acknowledge his own stake in the land, his family working the farm for generations, his father fighting by Saeed's side.

"His mother, the beautiful Aisha, told the young Naseem tales of his father's military prowess, his agricultural genius and the praise he received as head of the Zayenesh. But times had changed, and following the Berber's defeat, the remaining clan developed infighting and factions, denying Naseem the chance to prove himself as successor."

"But he is *Al Mohzerer*, known *throughout* the land."

Mohamed struggled to accept the scenario, which did not fit with the image of the legendary Naseem.

"He was not always the Grower." Saleem began reloading his pipe. At eighty-four years old, his wife and boys long since claimed by the cruel mountain pass, he felt good sitting there with the sun on his face, the scent of the land in his nostrils, imparting treasured memories to fresh ears. "Back then he was just a child filled with anger and resentment. He gained a reputation for fighting and clawing his way through life and had none of his father's compassion. He would do all it took to reinstate what he saw as rightfully his. You see the knife scar on his cheek?" Saleem ran a finger down his own face.

The boys nodded.

"A mere scratch compared to the pain he has inflicted upon others."

"But how did he become Al Mohzerer?"

Ahmed's respect for their employer's deviousness grew, but it would not stop him double-crossing the stinking jackal at the earliest opportunity.

"In the sixties, infidels appeared in the region once more, ghoulish trash with lank, greasy locks hanging against gaunt spectacled faces." Saleem coughed up a chunk of brown phlegm and spat it into the grass. "Filthy clothes patched like paupers, guitars dangling on rainbow-colored straps from their drug-addled frames."

Ahmed and Mohamed pictured some of the Europeans who arrived at the farm to buy hashish, the privileged young dopeheads wearing fat, flea-ridden dreadlocks with a pride bordering on arrogance.

"And all desperate to buy marijuana," Saleem continued. "Smoking their way along the Hippy Trail – what us impoverished mortals call 'life.' But Naseem was not stupid. He seized the opportunity, sowing the seeds that would see him become Al Mohzerer, his plants flourishing in the Rif's blessed soil."

- 25 -

Brightly painted fishing craft and modern yachts packed a large basin surrounded by lofty white buildings, their spindly framed frontages stretching up five stories to give the appearance of gigantic birdcages on stilts, the warm inshore air and clear sky pure sensory pleasure following their ordeal on the ocean. With *Future* moored in one of Club Nautico's inexpensive berths, Hans, Jessica and Penny showered in the clubhouse and went in search of lunch. They walked through Maria Píta Square, home to La Coruña's magnificent town hall, its three copper domes shining like rosy-red apples in the midday sun.

A bronze statue portrayed Maria, Spain's sixteenth-century hero, glaring down, spear in hand, from an ornate stone plinth. Her army captain husband lay at her feet, killed while defending La Coruña from the English. History has it an enraged Maria then rallied the townsfolk and fought off the invaders.

"Hey, Jessie. Do you remember Sir Francis Drake, the Queen of England's favorite sailor?"

"The man who liked to go bowling?"

"That's him. You know he fought the Spanish and their ships?"

"In a bigger boat than *Future*, with a hundred men."

"That's right. Well, one time he sailed here from

England, like we did, and he and his sailors attacked the local people and tried to steal all their money. And you'll *never* guess—"

Jessica wasn't listening. She stood fixated on the depiction of Maria's spouse lying awkwardly on his back, wearing the unmistakable mask of death.

"Who's that man?"

Hans looked at Penny and then crouched beside his daughter. "That's Maria's husband. He was a Spanish soldier."

"Why did he die?"

"He got killed in battle fighting to protect his family and friends."

"Did Maria sprinkle him?"

"Yeah, I'm sure she did."

"Is he in the flowers now?"

"Of course. He's in the flowers and the birds and the trees."

Jessica broke into a grin and skipped over to hold Penny's hand.

"Who's hungry?" Penny beamed. "Shall we go find some food?"

A cobbled backstreet led to a crazy-paved courtyard surrounded by open-fronted restaurants, a sea of red tablecloths flowing out from solid marble-slab counters. Unsure which establishment or dish to favor, Hans stooped to read an A-frame blackboard.

"We can have pulbo . . . á . . . feir—"

"Hey! Hunky-funky-bunky-monkey!" boomed a voice they all recognized.

The Dutchman sat grinning behind a massive plate of paella and empty Estrella bottles.

"Marshell!" Jessica ran over and scrambled onto his lap.

"Where you been, princess? The pardy's started, you know?"

"Marcel, we were worried about you." Penny gave him a heartfelt hug.

"Worried! About *me*?"

"Yeah, the storm!"

"Storm?"

"In the Biscay. You must have run into it?"

"Oh . . . I'm not sure. Probably had a few beers, you know?"

Over seafood and sangria, they filled Marcel in on their experience, the big man making an extra special fuss of "the best girl in the Biscay," as he referred to her.

Hans suggested they accompany Penny to the local hospital to have the gash checked out, but she shook her head.

"You guys stay here and have some more drinks. Jessie, do you want to come with me?"

"Uh-huh."

She sprung from her chair.

"Okay, we'll grab a cab there and see you two back at the marina later."

"So, Hans, dat's two wonderful women you have there," said Marcel as they watched the girls disappear.

"Thanks. But only one of them is mine."

"Ah, come on, man! Penny thinks the world of you. Anyone can see that. Er, you're divorced, right?"

"My wife was killed last year, and our son Jacob."

"Oh . . . friend. I'm sorry. I-I-I had—"

"No, it's okay. I'm dealing with it . . . for Jess, you

know?"

"*Ja*, sure. She's a great kid."

"Thanks."

Hans hailed the waiter and ordered beer and another jug of sangria. "So what's your story?"

"Oh . . ." The gentle giant picked up his fork and began pushing a sliver of chicken around his plate. "I made a few bucks in the art world and—"

"Marcel! You can stop the pretense."

"Pretense?"

"Does 1891 to 1895 mean anything to you?"

"Should it?"

"To a retired art dealer, it should. According to our guidebook, it's the years Picasso lived in La Coruña."

"Ah." Marcel picked at the label on his beer bottle. "Busted, huh?"

"You were busted from day one, but my daughter thinks the world of you, so you've had the benefit of the doubt."

A look of gratitude replaced embarrassment.

"So, no million-dollar art business?"

"Postman."

They burst out laughing.

The tale Marcel told Hans was fascinating yet sorrowful, and though the Dutchman was no choirboy, the American felt a great deal of empathy.

Bullied at school for being chubby, he had been a shy and introverted kid, worsening when his mother abandoned the family when he was nine. His father, who actually was a big name in the art world, died from alcohol-related illness ten years later.

At sixteen, Marcel became a postal worker, a role

suited to his solitary nature. Only he had a problem. From a young age he'd learned that the red wine he took sneaky sips of while his father lay comatose made him feel better about himself. Reaching adulthood, Marcel was drinking ten beers a day and chain-smoking cannabis – and this was before his delivery round. A liter of vodka every evening only added to his hangover. Attempting to regulate the liquor's side effects, he began using harder drugs – cocaine and speed – or prescription medication swindled from his doctor.

Eventually, he lost his job and his few friends, and his health began to suffer. On his twenty-first birthday, Marcel received his inheritance and decided to break free from the chains of addiction. Following a spell in rehab, he sold his parents' house, put on a backpack and spent the next three years traveling the world, ending up in Ibiza, where he invested in a restaurant venture.

"And there she was . . ." Marcel gazed at the tablecloth. "'I'm Sietske. I'm here for the waitressing job.' And dat was it."

"Love at first sight?"

"*Ja*! And the crazy thing was she came from the village next to mine back home."

"You hit it off immediately?"

"No, we spent more and more time together, and then one day *bam!* I realized the girl loved me for who I am – or who I was."

"Meaning?"

"Meaning anyone can be a nice when they're sober and living in paradise with a successful business. We got married and had a good few years. Would've had kids but . . ."

"You started drinking again?"

"And the rest, Hans. Ibiza's a hedonist's playground. Thought I could handle it. Best of both worlds. Mr. Cool Guy."

"What happened?"

"She got to see the real me." A tear rolled into Marcel's beard. "A drugged-up bum who drank, snorted and gambled his restaurant and savings away."

"She didn't hang around?"

"No, she didn't. I was devastated. Couldn't stay on the island any longer. Bet what I had left in a poker game – came away with five thousand euros, a French watch and a nice boat."

"*Sietske*?"

"How did you guess?"

Hans eyed the Cartier, its patent leather strap and striking gold case looking dinky on the Dutchman's fat wrist. Everything made sense – the yacht, the charade, the drinking – but it didn't explain how the Dutchman managed to fund five years at sea. Over more beer Hans divulged a little of his own checkered youth and then decided to ask.

Marcel's eyes took on a piratical glint. "Shall I explain over a joint?"

"Ha! I haven't smoked that stuff in years, but I suppose it would be rude not to." Hans chuckled.

"Let's go back to my boat."

26

"**A**l Saeed was a *hero*!" Ahmed mocked that evening.

"Ah, shut your face, you drunken baboon!" Mohamed hated it when Ahmed made fun of his naivety.

"But he is *Al Mohzerer*, known *throughout* the land." Lying on his makeshift mattress, Ahmed sniggered into his hands.

"His father was a warrior, a brave man," Mohamed stated with conviction.

"Yes, but Al Mohzerer is nothing but a sly old fox who thinks we are for the taking, like his scraggy hens."

In the flicker of the oil lamp, Ahmed's eyes smoldered, reminding Mohamed they had a plan to see through no matter what.

Despite the ribbing, Mohamed knew he would be lost without the older boy's guidance. Ahmed possessed a maturity way beyond his years, a product of his harsh upbringing. Hard as a diamond, he refused to take second place to anyone yet was loyal to his friends without bounds.

"So if he is a fox, what must we be?" Ahmed continued.

"We must be wolves!"

Right on cue a blood-curdling wail broke the silence on the mountainside.

"It's a sign!" Mohamed hissed.

"No, it's just a mangy wolf rallying his pack to hunt

down one of Farmer Hamsa's fat cows." Ahmed leant over and placed a brotherly arm on Mohamed's shoulder. "And what did I tell you about signs?"

"All signs are good signs."

"And who is the wolf afraid of?"

"He is afraid of nothing and no one."

"And what must the wolf do to survive?"

"He must improvise, adapt and overcome."

"Well done!" Ahmed was pleased his nurturing had started to show promise. Improvise they certainly could do. The oil lamp fashioned from a soda can, and their mattresses – hessian sacks sewn together and stuffed with dried weed – evidenced that. Adapting to life on the farm came easily too, especially with every second invested in the plan to reach Europe.

They produced increasing amounts of their own hashish, one working doubly hard in the hut while the other spat on palmfuls of the rich powder and massaged it into squidgy lumps. On the monthly visit to the city, they had refined their operation. Mohamed would sneak into the cinema and watch a movie – preferably one in English to improve his skill in the language – briefing Ahmed on the plot later to provide a cover story should the Grower ask them what they had seen. Meanwhile Ahmed would dash around their most profitable marketplaces, zeroing in on any tourist sporting dreadlocks or carrying a rucksack, launching into sales pitches laden with heartstring-tugging charm.

Following their individual missions, they would meet up at the city's harbor. Decrepit in comparison to the Mediterranean's more upmarket ports of call, the anchorage's laissez-faire attitude toward paperwork and mooring fees made it a popular option for yacht crews on a budget.

Ahmed and Mohamed had perfected their approach. Having pinpointed a shoestring skipper, they would amble along the wharf and bid a cheery "Hello! How are you?" and if the response was amicable strike up an "endearing" conversation through which to glean all they could about sailing, using a mix of French, broken English and gesticulation.

"What *gasolina* this one?"

"How to start?"

"How put up this one?"

"Wind come this way, how make this way?"

Figuring they were getting the authentic travel experience, skippers and crews would go to great lengths to make sure the boys understood, often inviting them aboard to run up a mainsail or go through the ignition sequence for the engine.

"Ouch!"

Ahmed slapped his neck, swatting the offending mosquito. He inspected the squished mess, wondering if the inordinate amount of blood smudged across his palm was his own. Fortunately, at this altitude the Rif remained free from the annoying insects most of the year, but in the summer months the animal troughs and latrines created the perfect environment for hatchlings to morph into adulthood.

"Pussy!" Mohamed giggled in the lamplight. "Ouch!"

"You were saying?" Ahmed held back a grin.

After a time Mohamed piped up. "Hey, brother."

"What's up?"

"I've been thinking . . . This sailing business seems quite hard. Why don't we steal a boat with a motor?"

"I've been thinking that too. We'll check it out."

27

Sitting amongst the clutter in *Sietske*'s cockpit, Marcel spliced two cigarette papers using glue leeched from a third.

"Us Dutch, we like a smoke, huh?"

He heated a cigarette with a lighter flame and blew through it, expelling the redundant nicotine, tar and moisture in noxious wafts.

"Gotta toast the tobacco."

"I never saw that before." Hans watched, fascinated. "Folks smoke it pure back home."

"That's okay for grass, man, but for flat press you need some tobacco."

"Flat press?"

"*Ja.*" Marcel tossed him a light-brown block the size of a matchbox. "Moroccan hashish. Crushed pollen, high THC content, almost the best you can get."

"And the best?"

"Number One – from Pakistan. Looks like an after-dinner mint. You don't see much of it in Europe."

"How come you know so much?"

"You really wanna know?" Marcel sparked the reefer, took a couple of puffs and passed it to Hans. "I'll show you."

He went into the cabin, emerging seconds later with an underwater flashlight, diving mask and fins. Flopping over the side, he looked like a fat frog on a mission.

Seconds ticked by before he surfaced.

"Here, take this." He held up a sausage-shaped rubber fender, surprisingly heavy, and then hauled himself aboard. "Have a look in the side."

Hans turned the fender in his lap until he spotted a long slit. Pulling it apart, he uncovered a nylon capsule the size of a spaghetti jar and a scuba weight to anchor the contraption on the seafloor.

"Well, I *wonder* what we have here."

"Just a few pardy prescriptions." Marcel wiped it with his towel. "I make this trip every year. Spend a month in the Netherlands seeing some old hippy friends and finish up in the Dam."

"The Dam?"

"Amsterdam." Marcel unscrewed the lid. "I pardy for a few days, stock up on some good ecstasy" – he waved a ziplock bag full of pink pills with Mickey Mouse's face stamped on them – "then I head south for Morocco, pick up a load of top-grade hash real cheap and sail to the Canary Islands to sell it to the dealers. The tourists can't get enough."

He emptied out three fat rolls of banknotes bound in elastic bands.

"You don't worry about getting caught?"

"When I pull into harbor, this thing sits under the boat. Nothing to do with me, right?"

"Right."

"At sea, if the coastguard ever pulled me I'd throw it overboard. But it's never happened."

"The cash too?"

"It's drug money. How could I explain it? Besides, I

can always make more."

"And other narcotics . . . Coke?"

"Nah!" Marcel shook his head. "Dat's a fool's game, man. I'm not greedy – just make enough to stay at sea. I don't mind to sell cannabis. It's less harmful than alcohol."

"I guess you don't see too many potheads crashing cars or smashing people over the head with pool cues."

"That's right, and the pills are for personal use."

"And this pays for you to stay at sea."

"Pays for me to stay away from reality – mortgages, cell phones, nine-to-five. Who wants the hassle?"

Understandable. Hans always spotted the plank in his own eye before pointing out the splinter in others'.

"But enough about me." Marcel relit the joint. "Penny said you're some kind of detective."

"Private investigator."

"Hell, now *dat's* a job! Were you a policeman before?"

"Military. Navy SEALs."

"I *knew* it! I *knew* there was something about you!"

Hans smiled.

"Those guys, they're real tough, huh?"

"Well . . ."

"Ah, come on." Marcel took a long pull on the spliff and held the smoke deep in his lungs before exhaling a silvery brown plume. "*Huhph-huhph!*" he coughed. "You're being modest – *huhph!* Everyone knows you guys are born killers."

"To be honest, Marcel, most of the guys I knew were pretty down to earth. Just normal kids who wanted a bit more excitement than the regular military offered."

"But you must have been superfit. You don't just fall

into dat kinda job, huh?"

"Funnily enough, I did. Like I said, I spent most of my youth bunking off school in my boat or reading adventure books. Didn't pass any exams. Joining the navy was pretty much on the cards. But manning a radar screen twelve hours a day became boring, so I applied for special forces."

"You must have some stories to tell. You parachuted?"

"Yeah, an amazing experience."

"So how was it – to jump out of an aircraft?"

"Insane. We did our basic training at the Army Airborne School in Fort Benning."

"I'm listening." Marcel began skinning up another joint.

"You're throwing yourself out of mock-up planes and off this massive tower on a zip wire, rolling about the place, and all the time the instructors are stressing the importance of pulling your reserve if you have a malfunction."

"Malfunction?"

"Yeah. Like they keep hollering, 'What do you do if your chute don't open?'"

"Pull your reserve!"

"What do you do if your lines are twisted and you can't kick 'em out?"

"Pull your reserve!"

"What do you do if your chute rips apart?"

"Pull your reserve!"

"*Ja*, safety first, man."

Marcel crumbled a generous amount of flat press onto a bed of toasted tobacco.

"So we got this one guy – funny dude, Zebrowski, from New York – never stopped talking! We're in the bar one night and he starts telling us about this Action Man he had as a kid. You know Action Man, right?"

"*Ja*, we have dat in Holland, Hans."

"So he's got this Action Man, and he loves his Action Man. Takes him everywhere, puts him through all kinda crazy stuff. Then one day they bring out Action Man Sky Diver – but Zebrowski can't afford one. Besides, he loves the one he's got. So he makes a parachute for him out of a plastic bag – you know, with strings taped to it an' all?"

Marcel chuckled and passed Hans another beer.

"Well, Zebrowski lives on the twelfth floor of an apartment block in Queens. He launches Action Man outta the window, then takes the elevator down to see if his experiment worked."

"Did it?"

"Hell no! Action Man's laying there, his parachute's come apart, his head's missing, and he's flat as a pancake 'cause he's gotten run over by a car. So us rough, tough SEALs are all listening like schoolboys, and Monroe, this real gentle guy from Muskogee, leans forward and asks, 'What happened?' Zebrowski just shrugs and says, 'Forgot to pull his reserve'!"

"Haaaa-ha-ha-haaah!"

"But there's more." Hans took a toke of the doobie. "We're doing our first jump – from a C-130."

"The Hercules?"

"Right. And I'm the guy in the door, and I'm all hooked up, parachute on, kinda revved up but nervous. The ground's whizzing by a thousand feet below, and all the roads and fields and houses looks so damn small.

The engine's deafening, and all you can smell is hot avgas, and I'm putting a brave face on it – my first jump an' all. But just as the green light comes on I feel this tap on my shoulder, and Zebrowski shouts, 'Remember my Action Man!'"

- 28 -

The crow of Kekee the Rooster woke Ahmed. He stretched and nudged Mohamed and then went to the well to splash water on his face and fill up a pan for their morning coffee. Rather than return to the hut immediately, he hopped up onto the well's brickwork surround and sat awhile, taking in the fresh air and watching the sun sparkle life into the landscape.

Upon his return to the hut, the pong of burning marijuana met him at the door. Scowling, he stormed inside to find Mohamed sitting in a cloud of smoke, puffing away on a soda can pipe.

"What the hell are you doing!" He smacked the contraption out of his friend's hand, a shower of burning embers flying through the air as it clattered across the floor.

"Just a little awakener," Mohamed replied indignantly.

"Awakener?" Ahmed grasped the little fella's shoulders. "Your eyes are bloodshot, you fool, and the *smell!*"

The consequences of Mohamed's actions did not bear thinking about. Al Mohzerer had strangled workers to death for smoking the product.

Ahmed opened the shutters. "I'm going to the village to get bread. This stink better be gone when I get back."

Mohamed sat staring at his feet, unable to meet

Ahmed's fiery gaze, bottom lip thrust out like a petulant child. When the door slammed, he leant forward and picked up the Coca-Cola can, knowing he should hide it in the trash pile but feeling reluctant to do so. They worked with the damn stuff every day, so what was the harm in sampling the goods? Still in his underpants, he mulled over Ahmed's rebuke and was in the process of formulating a comeback when the door flew open.

"Look, Ahmed,' he snapped, turning to face his brother. 'You—"

Al Mohzerer stood there, silhouetted in the morning sunshine. Mohamed shoved the pipe behind his back, as if hiding the paraphernalia would discredit the telltale cloud.

"I need you to . . ." the Grower began as the scene registered.

Mohamed's eyes bulged like those of a rabbit caught in car headlights. His legs went weak. In what seemed slow motion, Naseem took a pace across the room, nostrils flared and face darker than hell. He grabbed Mohamed by the hair and dragged him off the mattress, then threw him facedown on the floor and began stomping on his head and torso. Mohamed was too frightened to take in what was happening, though vaguely aware of a warm, wet sensation in his groin.

Instead of calming, Naseem's rage grew worse with each kick and blow rained down of the terrified boy.

Please let it stop, was all Mohamed could think, tasting of blood and dust as he lost consciousness.

Ahmed entered the hut clutching two flatbreads and a bag of oily black olives.

"Here you go, fool—"

His blood ran cold. Mohamed sat on the floor, ankles crossed and knees locked together, rocking back and forward, his hideously smashed-up face buried in his arms. Too confused to speak, he prayed Ahmed would make everything right, as he always did.

"Oh, brother. What has he done to you?" Ahmed burst into tears.

"I'm sorry." The emotion in his friend's voice set Mohamed off, a mixture of shock and humiliation leaving him sobbing like a baby.

"No, nothing to be sorry about," Ahmed whispered, kissing Mohamed's blood-and-dirt-matted hair.

They hugged for several minutes, Ahmed fighting intense rage to put Mohamed's needs first. He stripped off his T-shirt, dipped a corner into the pan of water and began wiping the congealing maroon mess off Mohamed's distorted features.

"How is it?" Mohamed croaked.

"Acht, nothing too bad, soldier," he lied, horrified by deep cuts and swelling worse than a wannabe prizefighter's after ten rounds with Ali. He kept quiet about Mohamed's broken nose and missing teeth. "How's the ribs?"

"Hurting, but not broken, I think."

"Okay, I'll get you some freshwater and then I will kill Al Mohzerer."

"No!" Mohamed clutched Ahmed's arm. "I can't leave the mountain like this. We must wait – and then take the swine for everything he has."

A fat moon shone down through the warm night air, stars exploding across the sky to put life into perspective. Penny cuddled with Hans in *Future*'s cockpit, Jessica tucked in her bunk by a woman that could do no wrong.

"I'm glad they didn't shave my hair."

"The hospital?"

"Yeah. They were impressed with your improvised surgery."

"Not really improvised. It's what superglue was invented for – in Vietnam."

Hans was about to add something but instead stared into his mug of coffee.

Penny let the silence hang awhile, sipping her drink as unanswered questions ricocheted around her mind.

"Hans, can you tell me about Jessie's mum?"

"Her *mom*?"

"It's just that she's so confused by what happened. I feel I ought to know more."

"Sure, sure. Of course. Do you want it long or short?"

"We've got all night." She stroked his cheek.

"I met Kerry back in 2000. My SEAL team had been unofficially attached to your Royal Marines' Special Boat Service – you know, the SBS?"

"The Cockleshell Heroes – who doesn't?"

"We'd been tasked with a mission in Sierra Leone – the civil war there?"

"Something about rebels wearing women's wigs . . . and always drunk."

"Yeah, the West Side Boys – the group we were after. Real head cases, always high on drugs and the local hooch. Modeled themselves on Tupac Shakur, the gangster rapper. Most of them were former child soldiers, or still were. Our intel was they'd taken a group of American and European medical workers hostage in an old hospital on the coast and were using the building as their headquarters. We were on standby on an aircraft carrier out in the Atlantic, and our orders came through to drop into the sea from choppers and swim ashore under the cover of darkness. The marines would then go forward and carry out reconnaissance, find out where the nurses were, then scout an LZ for an SAS strike force to land in the morning. My team's instructions were to go to ground in the jungle to give covering fire should the marines get compromised."

"Scary stuff."

"It would have been a big result, especially if the leader of the West Side Boys, Fodim Kassay, and his lieutenants were present. But it didn't go to plan. The birds were delayed getting us off the carrier, waiting for clearance from the Pentagon for us Yanks. By the time we'd gotten a green light, the sea conditions had changed. What should have been an easy swim turned into a battle for survival. The tide was on the move, a swell kicked up, the one mile we had to cover became the equivalent of three. Waves were smashing down on us like apartment blocks. Thirty-two went into the water

. . . only six got out."

"No!"

"Thirteen of my closest buddies gone, and most of the marines. You don't wanna know what they did to the bodies that washed ashore. Those of us left regrouped and continued the mission."

"You must have been exhausted. I . . . can't imagine."

"Exhausted, in shock real bad, running on autopilot. But to stop and think about it would have ruined us. At first light we heard the choppers and crawled into position to give support."

"What happened?"

"It was unbelievable. I thought the SEALs were a force to be reckoned with, but these SAS guys" – Hans shook his head – "they were something else."

"In what way?"

"Like totally calm. I mean, *real* calm, as if they were arriving at a ball game. And so professional – yet complete nutjobs! Forget all this military discipline you see in movies. Half of them went into battle wearing jeans, T-shirts and sneakers. Later, when I asked why, they started laughing, and one of them said his mom shrunk his uniform in the wash. That's British humor, right?"

Penny smiled.

"Us Yanks took everything so damn serious, like a high school football team. The Brits got the job done *and* managed to laugh their way through it. One team roped onto the hospital roof – near blew the damn thing off – pouring so many rounds down it was like they were hosing the lawn on a Sunday morning. The second team surrounded the building and threw in stun grenades.

Hell, half the guys followed them in before they'd even exploded!

"The West Side Boys were sleeping off hangovers, and most didn't stand a chance, but a handful came out fighting, high on some drug and wearing these magic amulets they believed made 'em invincible. They made a break for the jungle and . . ." Hans stared into his coffee again, then got up to fetch a bottle of rum from the galley.

"Are you okay?" Penny held out her mug and accepted a slug.

"I only ever signed up because I loved the sea and wanted a challenge, yet here I was laying down fire and chucking grenades at kids."

"Whoa!"

Hans bit his lip and nodded.

"And the medical workers?"

"Huddling in a room, terrified."

"And one of them was Kerry?"

"Yeah, one of 'em was a nurse called Kerry. We flew them out to the carrier and sailed for Dakar. Got pretty close during those days at sea."

"Enough to get married?"

"No. We saw each other off and on for a few years, but I left the military after a couple of Middle East deployments and – well, my life fell apart."

"How come?"

"I was angry – at losing friends, at the navy, the enemy. Hell, I was angry at everyone. I'd get menial jobs working for peanuts, ordered about by some little Hitler who'd never been out of the States in his life. I couldn't believe what the workers put up with, just accepted, like it was all there was to live for."

"And what happened?"

"What happened was I started drinking, fighting and getting depressed."

"Do you think it was PTSD?"

"That's what the docs said, but I couldn't see it at the time. Thought I was normal, that everyone else had issues."

"And Kerry?"

"I woke up in a hospital in Cleveland. Like an idiot I'd gotten in my car drunk to go and see her and totaled it on the freeway. Luckily, no one else was hurt, but I was pretty busted up – in a coma for twelve days. When I woke, she was there holding my hand."

"Really?"

"Yeah! Working in the same hospital. They say there's no such thing as coincidence. I kinda started believing it that day. She nursed me back to health. Said God sent her an angel down there in Africa and she wasn't about to let him have me back."

- 30 -

On the next trip to Tangier, Mohamed pulled his cinema trick while Ahmed went on the hashish round, striking it lucky with two Australian backpackers, who paid top whack for all the squidgy lumps in his pocket and would have bought every other drug known to man had they been available. Ahmed briefly considered rekindling some old acquaintances but thought better of it, knowing the cheating scumbags would only rip him off. Besides, he had to meet Mohamed to go clothes shopping for Europe.

"What do you reckon?"

Mohamed held up an imitation number 10 shirt in the national team's colors.

"Very nice – but you need an Amsterdam one. To blend in, you know?"

"Don't you mean a Dutch one?"

"Yes, a Dutch-Amsterdam one."

For the first time in their lives, the two of them had money to buy clothes rather than having to rely on cast-off goods donated to the missions. Shoplifting them had always been out of the question, for wearing new attire as a street kid only invited trouble. They decided against stealing outfits for Europe, as the last thing they wanted was a shop owner catching them in the act and thwarting their plan at this late stage.

Rather surprisingly, the stall in the bazaar was a little

short on Dutch soccer shirts, so after trying on a whole range of clothes and footwear – most of them ridiculous, the boys having no idea of Western fashion – they settled on the ones they liked the most and went to pay.

"Wait!"

Mohamed dashed back though the racks, returning with two Day-Glo orange parkas complete with toggles and fake-fur-trimmed hoods.

"It's cold in Europe."

"Yes, you are probably right."

The final item on the list was a travel guide. Almost all the tourists visiting the farm carried a *Lonely Planet*, and Ahmed deemed it imperative to have something similar. There was a secondhand bookstore in the bazaar, so they went in to have a look around.

"Here!" said Mohamed after browsing a couple of minutes, holding up the *Encyclopedia of the European Monetary Union* with a triumphant grin.

"En-cy-clo-peee-dia!" Ahmed beamed, delighted to show off his growing proficiency in English yet oblivious to the tome's intended audience.

"Look! Cheechee and Chongee!"

Mohamed recognized the world-famous stoners from his trips to the cinema. Having giggled all the way through *Still Smokin*, he figured *Cheech & Chong: The Unauthorized Autobiography* would help them corner the hash market in Amsterdam.

They stowed their books and new wardrobe in a locker at the ferry port and walked to the harbor. After chatting to a friendly Swedish couple, who invited them aboard *Lille Maria* for a meal of meatballs and mashed potato served with a delicious red-berry sauce, the boys went in search of local fishermen, intent on investigating the possibility of crossing the Strait of Gibraltar in a motorboat.

An elderly man sat cross-legged on the dock next to a rusting trawler, weaving a shuttle of green twine through a damaged net at lightning speed. The boys' minds flashed back to their work in Abu Yazza's carpet factory. Despite the afternoon heat, the man wore a black woolen hat and a set of yellow rubber dungarees that has seen better days, along with a good few tons of sardines.

"*Pas de problème*," he replied with a nonchalant shrug.

"And how many hours does it take to reach Spain in a boat like this?" asked Ahmed in French.

"*Trois.*" He held up three callused fingers. "*Avec suffisamment diesel.*"

"Oh." Ahmed frowned. "And what would happen if we don't have enough diesel?"

"*Bonjour, Atlantique – phhhsssk*!" The old man flicked a hand through the air, dramatizing the worst-case scenario – dragged out into the North Atlantic by the unforgiving current.

Mulling over the old man's words, the boys headed toward the medina for their rendezvous with Naseem, eventually dismissing the idea of stealing a motorized vessel. They couldn't simply pull up at the fuel pump in the harbor in a stolen boat, and if they ran out of diesel midpassage and drifted out into the ocean with a load of hashish on board it would be game over.

Mohamed was unusually quiet, hands in pockets and staring down as they walked.

"What's up, sister?" Ahmed ruffled his hair.

"This crossing . . ." He sighed. "Are you sure we can make it? Why don't we just run away now and live like we used to?"

"All our money is in the hut."

"You know what I mean."

"Listen!" Ahmed grabbed Mohamed's arm and pulled him to a halt. "Anywhere we go in this place, the Grower will find us. And you know what that means."

"How about Algeria?" Mohamed looked up inquiringly.

"Ha! Swap a pig for a hog?" Ahmed spat in the dirt.

Mohamed knew it to be true.

Ahmed softened his tone. "Look, little brother, the hut is our honeypot, our ticket out of here. I promise you it will be worth it when we step ashore in Spain as free men."

He cocked his head at the sea to remind his friend how close their destination was.

"Am-ster-dam-am!" Mohamed broke into a grin.

"Jiggy, jiggy, jiggy!" Ahmed threw a high five, and to cheer Mohamed up further, added, "Hey, you can read English?"

"Of course."

"Look what I got!"

He reached under his manky T-shirt, pulled a hardback book from the waistband of his pants and waved *Den Kompletta Guiden till Segling* in front of Mohamed's face as if hitting the jackpot.

"That's a *Swedish* sailing book, you idiot!"

"Oh . . ." Ahmed was crestfallen for a moment before beaming again. "Hey, we can look at the pictures!"

Approaching the medina, Ahmed remembered

Mohamed hadn't briefed him on the movie. It was important to get their story straight before meeting Naseem.

"It was about a man with a *brave* heart in Scotland Land. They call him Wall-yam Willis, the *Brave* Heart Man." Mohamed fell silent, looking somewhat nonplussed.

"What is it?"

"It's . . ."

"Come on, tell me!"

"Ahmed?"

"What?"

"Is Amsterdam like Scotland Land?"

"No, I don't think so. Why?"

"In Scotland Land the men have blue faces and they wear short skirts, like the infidel women. And they are savages – *really* savages. Fight like the Berber!"

"**N**ext stop Portugal!"

Hans was in good spirits as *Future* sliced through a moderate sea in close proximity to land. Marcel had agreed to meet them in the Canary Islands, but was heading *Sietske* for the Moroccan port of Tangier first "to see some 'guys,' you know?"

"Bop rabbit!" Penny paused to adjust her blindfold before tapping the rubber fender down gently.

"Missed me!" Jessica squealed, kneeling opposite on deck. She loved playing Bop Rabbit, trying to guess where your opponent is and "bop" them accordingly.

With the sun on his face, Hans enjoyed the moment. It had been a while since he felt so relaxed. The endless phone calls, emails, lab reports, court appearances and surveillance operations crammed into a week at the Larsson Investigation Agency were far from his mind, as was the awkward ritual of receiving condolences and well wishes.

Unbeknown to Penny, Hans filled a bucket with seawater. *Shh!* he signaled to Jessica, climbing up beside her.

As their shipmate raised the bunny whacker and announced "Bop rabbit!" a second time, Hans delivered an impromptu shower.

"Ahh! You *swine!*" She lifted the blindfold to find the

Larsson family in stitches. "I'll get you back, you know!"

"I wouldn't have it any other way." Hans grinned and tipped the remaining water over her.

The two days to Lisbon made for dream sailing. Although low in the water from ample provisioning, *Future* lay well over and ran before the breeze like an excited stag, her brilliant-white sails a perfect match for the cottony wisps drifting across a sapphire sky. As far as the eye could see, glistening wave crests gave the impression of herds of buffalo roaming the plane.

Humans are born on land, so what is it about the sea? Hans reflected, imagining centuries of clippers and whalers plying this same route.

By now they had settled into an easy routine, Penny and Hans alternating turns at the helm to keep Jessica occupied with games, seamanship and schoolwork. Hans appreciated the interest Penny took in his daughter and the extra mile she always went without hesitation.

"She's so clever," Penny remarked as Jessica sat on deck twisting her Rubik's Cube.

"She is. Took me twenty years to solve that thing."

"She can *solve* it?"

"In under three minutes." Hans chuckled. "You'd be too young to remember the craze."

"There was one?"

"Yeah, pretty much every kid in school had a Rubik's Cube, but only the brainboxes could do them. Made it look easy. The rest of us struggled to get a side the same color or resorted to taking them apart and putting them back together again. She gets it from her mom – the intelligence, I mean."

"Of course. I didn't think she got it from you."

"Hah! She gets her looks from me."

"That's obvious." Penny prodded him in the ribs. "So her mum was pretty smart?"

"Her IQ was off the scale."

"Really?"

"State Scrabble champion five years in a row. Could make words you didn't know existed."

"So that's where Jessie gets it."

"Look at her scuba diving. You're an instructor, right?"

"I am."

"How many kids do you know that are as competent as she is?"

"I've never met any kids her age who can dive."

"Exactly. Makes me laugh when I see parents posting videos on YouTube of their eight-year-old, claiming they're the youngest open-water diver ever. Jess dived off Maine at five."

"It's remarkable."

"She's always been advanced for her age – crawling, talking, reading. Problem was she got way ahead in class and started to lose interest. We had her moved up a year, and Kerry spent time in the evenings homeschooling her."

"How did that go?"

"Really well. Kerry was good at that kinda thing – math, English, music. Hell, she could speak Spanish and German fluently."

"Sounds like a tough act to fol– " The words tumbled out before Penny could stop them.

"No!" Hans kicked himself. "Don't think that. Kerry

was Kerry and . . . well, that's it."

They fell silent a moment, listening to the waves splashing against *Future*'s hull.

"And was JJ the same?"

"No, JJ was a plodder like his father, but uncannily pragmatic."

"That figures."

"They were good together. Balanced one another. But it's been hard to . . ."

"To explain to Jessie what happened?"

Hans nodded, his jaw clenched. "She would understand death better than most adults. It's just . . . I don't want to put my grief onto her. Don't wanna steal her innocence. She's smart, but she's still a child. Does that make sense?"

"Perfect sense. It's why she carries a teddy."

Hans smiled. "I've done my best to explain it to her. You know, without resorting to angels in heaven or a full-on science lecture."

"You've done a great job, Hans. You always do. I see the way you take time to teach her things, like the history in Plymouth. Most parents just drag their kids around, overlooking the fact they're a receptacle for knowledge."

"Ha! You've had the rundown on Sir Francis Drake?"

"Queen's favorite sailor. Big ship called a galleon. Sailed to faraway places like the jungle – and don't get me started on nuclear submarines."

"She's a cracking kid."

"She certainly is. And bereavement isn't something you can deal with through logic, no matter how smart you are."

"You're right." Hans put his arm around Penny and kissed her hair. "Say, you hungry?"

"I'm always hungry, Hans. You should know that by now."

"Then it's Scooby snack time! Jessie, wanna eat something?"

"I'm okay, Papa." She concentrated on putting the colored squares in place for a fifth time.

"Got plenty of escargot, if you want some."

"Urrrh!"

Hans went into the galley and began pulling items from the fridge, timing his forays with the roll of the yacht like a sketch in a Laurel and Hardy movie. He emerged with two baton rolls loaded with enough ingredients to stock a deli.

"Hot sauce?" He waggled the bottle in front of Penny as she set the self-steering mechanism.

"Erm?" She eyed the label "Louisiana Mega Death" and its skull-and-crossbones logo with suspicion. "I think I'll pass."

They sat in the cockpit working their way along the torpedo-sized sandwiches.

"You said you liked smorgasbord, Hans, but this is ridiculous!" Penny tried not to let the thick slices of chorizo, wild boar salami, chunks of goat cheese and salad sneak out of the perimeter. Having polished off the sub, she wiped her mouth with a tissue and stared out to sea.

"What's up?"

"Nothing." She gazed dead ahead.

"Must be something?"

"It's that . . . I've never asked you what happened."

She turned to face him. "Not that I want to pry, but if you need to talk . . ."

Hans rubbed his neck and stared down at the cockpit's wooden decking.

Penny regretted her comment, fearing she had overstepped the mark, though she need not have.

"Penny, I've always found it strange, almost despised the way people deal with death. I don't know if it's a military thing or just the result of my upbringing. My parents divorced, and a whole load of chaos came with it. But I always refused to feel sorry for myself, you know? Even homeless and wandering the streets at one point, I told myself this is life, and just get on and deal with it. When I got older and people started dying – relatives or friends I grew up with – I applied the same thinking. I guess when you understand from an early age that life ain't fair you learn to take things in your stride. Hell, when my parents died I hardly shed a tear, even though I missed them as much as anyone."

Penny tried to understand, but she had been raised at sea, which meant relatives were always at a distance and their deaths had little impact on her life.

"People tread on tiptoes and use expressions like 'passed away' and insist on wearing black to funerals and getting all pious and stuff. Everyone wants to tell you this is gonna take time and that grieving works in mysterious ways. And I just think, 'They haven't "passed away" – they're *dead*.' And it's only gonna take time if you choose it to. I down a bottle of Jack and get on with it."

"Isn't that what shrinks call 'detachment'?"

"Shrinks can call it what they like. I figure it's best to

see life the way it is and move on."

"But this time it's different, isn't it?"

Hans slipped a hand over Penny's. "You have a way of seeing things."

"When you've crewed on as many boats as I have, you get used to weighing people up – kind of a survival mechanism. You meet some challenging people in this line of work."

"So you see me and Jess as a challenge or just work?" Hans lightened the mood.

"I see Jess as utterly adorable, and you . . ." She paused, looking into his eyes and choosing her words carefully. "Put it this way. In all my years of sailing you were the first person I ever saw enter a marina under canvas."

"Real Tarzan, huh?"

"To this Jane, yeah. But we're not talking about me."

"Oh."

"Hans" – Penny stroked his knee – "it's okay to grieve."

"I know. But now when I should be grieving, when I *want* to grieve, I can't."

"Why?" Penny spoke softly.

Hans stared at the cockpit floor once more, contemplating his response. "Because I have unfinished business."

Penny saw a look come over Hans' face she had not seen before, dark, brooding and violent. "And is this to do with your work?"

Still looking down, Hans bit his lip and nodded.

"You feel guilty, don't you?"

"More than you'd ever believe."

They both fell silent. Even if Penny knew what to say, this was not the time to say it.

"I've done it six times!" Jessica held the completed cube aloft.

"Wow!" Penny climbed up on the cabin roof. "And what about Bear? How many times did he do it?"

"He didn't even do it once." Jessica shrugged, looking doleful. "He can't really do anything."

"Oh, sweetie." Penny pecked her on the cheek.

"Well, how about taking Bear below and showing him how to fill out yesterday's log?" Hans suggested, knowing being trusted with this task meant a lot to Jessica. "And afterwards I think we should break open that big bar of chocolate."

"Aye aye, skippa!"

An excited Jessica ran aft, forgetting to unclip her safety line. Yanked off her feet, she crashed unceremoniously onto the deck.

"Ahh!" She pushed up onto her knees and eyed the offending restraint with disdain. "You *swine!*"

Penny glanced at Hans and ducked inside the cabin.

- 32 -

That evening, as Mohamed rattled on about the Brave Heart Man and the curious nature of Scottish culture, Ahmed leafed through the Swedish couple's *Complete Guide to Sailing*, studying the pictures and diagrams with interest. Everything started to make sense, fitting with knowledge gained from their impromptu lessons at the harbor.

"Wee!" Mohamed grinned, appearing pleased with himself.

"What?" Ahmed looked up from the page.

"The Scot-*tish*, they say 'wee' instead of 'small.'"

"I thought you were supposed to be improving your English."

"But this was a Scot-*tish* movie."

"Oh . . . well, next time watch an English one."

"Okay."

Ahmed leant over and blew out the oil lamp. "Sleep," he ordered, lying back on the weed mattress, visions of Swedish women and enormous meatballs running through his mind.

Mohamed dreamt he was chasing Al Mohzerer through the endless rows of marijuana. Every now and then the Grower would turn to face him, brandishing a scimitar . . . *the size of a pocketknife?* Mohamed wielded a two-handed claymore like his hero the Brave Heart Man. Only, as opposed to the five feet of savage steel in the movie, his was the length of a scaffolding pole. Blue faced, longhaired and skirted, he cut Naseem in half repeatedly and then ran through the fields, whooping and slicing down tennis-court-sized swaths of their evil boss's beloved crop.

All too soon the fantasy ended. Ahmed, with the self-discipline of a monk, sat up, stretched and lit the lamp. He retrieved a couple of candy bars and poked one at the little snorer.

"It's time."

" Ah! Just a few more minutes."

"No, it's past midnight. We go now."

Ahmed got up off his mattress.

Every night for the past week they had crept over to the outbuilding where Naseem's older hands pressed the hash powder into blocks of Golden Monkey, using their knives to scrape away the dirt at the base of a row of boards blocking an old animal entrance in the stonework. The boys had replaced the rubble to conceal their efforts, ready for the day they absconded with as much of Naseem's prize product as could be carried between them.

The plan was not yet watertight. They still needed to figure a way to get down off the mountain and cover the thirty miles to the port in Tangier. Mohamed was all for drugging Naseem and then stealing the keys to his truck. They could use the small black berries from the Belladonna, which grew in abundance on the slopes. In ancient times Moroccan women would drip the poison juice into their eyes, its dilative effect deemed to enhance beauty, hence the plant's name. Nowadays, along with cheap pharmaceuticals, the growers used the berries to fortify a low-grade form of hashish known as Soap Bar in the United Kingdom – its biggest importer – for its shape and taste, the latter a byproduct of the garbage bags and other waste plastic used as a bulking agent. Ahmed was not so sure. Getting the right dose and figuring a way to deliver it would be hit and miss, and despite their hatred of the Grower, they did not want to kill him and have the police on their tail.

Outside there was a light covering of cloud, just the sound of the odd clucking hen and the breeze rustling through the rows of marijuana. Mohamed lay in the long grass surrounding the hut, keeping a lookout as Ahmed crept across the courtyard and secreted himself in a slight depression at the side of the outbuilding. The farmhouse was directly across from him, at this time in darkness as the Grower slept soundly in his bed. Ahmed pulled out his knife and began raking the loosened dirt back out of the hole at the base of the boards.

Mohamed stifled a yawn and allowed his chin to rest on the back of his hands.

Up on the hillside *Canis lupus* lifted his nose and sniffed the air, detecting the scent of chickens in Naseem's henhouse, along with the unusual odor given off by the two-legged beings. Years of evolution saw *Canis lupus*, the "wolf dog," freeze and slowly lower to his haunches, straining his powerful neck and pricking his ears.

Instinctively, the younger wolves fell into a flanking formation around the alpha male and adopted the same posture. As the wolf dog began to creep forward, his mottled-gray fur camouflaged against the grass, the pack moved as one, the way their ancestors had done for millenniums.

"*Pbuck-pbaaark!*"

Damn bird! Ahmed finished excavating the last of the rubble and turned his attention to the rusting nails holding the wood in place.

Canis lupus went to ground just feet from the courtyard, his pack acting as one in an arc around him. With superior night vision, he viewed the strange creature lying in the grass with cold indifference, sensing gentle snores, as loud to him as if broadcast to humans from the loudspeakers atop the village minaret. He was wary. He did not know why. He did not need to. The prone figure's scent and regular breathing told the born killer that this specimen was healthy and might put up a fight. But the wolves were hungry, the females weak and their body fat dangerously depleted from suckling cubs back in the den. All were desperate for a kill to ensure the survival of the pack.

Canis lupus rose, the tendons in his legs as taut as bowstrings.

"*Pbuck-pbaaark! Pbuck-pbaaark!*"

The rest of the wolves followed suit. Spread out like the horns of a bull, they would come at Mohamed from all angles to prevent any chance of escape, clamping down on his limbs with bone-crunching strength and ragging him about to expose his jugular and suffocate the life from body.

"*Pbuck-pbaaark! Pbuck-pbaaark! Pbuck-pbaaark!*"

By now the chickens were making such a racket that Ahmed, managing to loosen two of the three boards required to squeeze inside the outbuilding, decided to call it a night. He eased the wood back into place and reinserted the nails, using the hilt of his knife to press them home, replacing the dirt and patting it down to hide his efforts. Just as he was about to scamper back to the hut, the farmhouse door creaked open, and lamplight doused the courtyard.

Ahmed dropped onto his stomach, the light just catching his backside as he flattened in the gulley. He turned his head slightly to see the silhouette of Al Mohzerer projected onto the building's wall, along with the unmistakable outline of a shotgun. He watched in horror, metallic spit in his mouth, the shadow growing smaller and the sound of the boss's footsteps louder as he crossed the courtyard.

This must surely be it!

Ahmed tried in vain to calm his breathing and a heart pounding in his chest.

Years of cunning told *Canis lupus* to quit now and to skulk off into the dark, but his hunger and sense of duty to the cubs took over. Like a coiled spring, he leapt from the grass, growling and baring his teeth, ready to bite down on Mohamed's neck.

The silhouette of the shotgun swung around.

Ahmed stifled a scream.

Bang!

His body jolted as the pellets hit home, *Canis lupus* yelping in pain and fleeing back up the mountain with the pack.

- 33 -

Hans, Jessica and Penny entered a large flagstoned plaza in the center of Lisbon. Surrounded by open-air bars and eateries, it was a popular venue for locals and tourists, the verdancy of the Portuguese oaks dotted about melding with the pleasant night air to create an atmosphere of tranquillity. All of the restaurants offered a similar cuisine, so they opted for Bar Mar, sitting down at a picnic-style bench to order food.

"So, shipmate." Hans began debriefing the first officer. "What did you write in the log?"

"That" – Jessica's brow furrowed – "the winds are *light* and *aerial*."

"Don't you mean light and variable?" Hans squeezed Penny's leg.

"Yes!" Jessica gave a resolute nod and shake of her head.

They heard a commotion in the distance, looking up to see a large group of young men and women walking toward them. In high spirits, they were having a whale of a time and had drunk more than their fair share of alcohol.

"*Os inglêses*," muttered the waitress taking their orders, hostility radiating from her gypsy brown eyes.

"*São marinheiros?*" Penny queried.

"*São*." The woman nodded.

"British Royal Navy," said Penny.

"I kinda figured," said Hans. "Guess they're not too popular around here."

"The Portuguese are hospitable people, but there's a line you shouldn't cross."

As Penny spoke, a noticeable tenseness replaced the easygoing comportment of the bar staff.

More groups of service personnel arrived, congregating at the watering holes lining the far side of the plaza, all tanked on happy juice and looking to imbibe more. Hans, Jessica and Penny continued their conversation, but the noise grew louder, the scene more animated, as sailors peeled away from the counters balancing trays loaded with drink.

"Mind if we sit here, mate?" inquired a piggy-faced matelot wearing Yoko Ono wraparounds.

"Be my guest," Hans replied, clocking the irony of the slogan "Life's Too Short to Dance with Fat Chicks!" emblazoned on the young man's T-shirt.

"Wanna get away from the riffraff! Know what I'm saying?" He chuckled.

"What's a riffraff?" Jessica asked.

"That lot over there, sweetheart." He gave a clumsy wink and cocked his head at his shipmates. "Bleedin' lunatics the lot of 'em! I'm Bonny, short for Bonington. You know, like the mountain climber."

"Bonny's a girl's name!" Jessica put him in his place.

"Oh . . ." It dawned on Bonny that his well-rehearsed military patter wasn't having the desired effect on this seven-year-old American. "Yeah, but I'm part of the woodwork on HMS *Invincible*," he attempted to recover.

"Really?" Hans looked at him askew. "I thought they

built them out of steel nowadays."

Bonny was baffled for a moment, unused to such interrogation, then broke into a smile. "That's a joke, right? 'Cause ships ain't made of wood anymore!"

"Who's your friend?" Penny asked.

"This is Gibbo." He slapped his buddy on the back. "But he don't say much, do you, shippers?"

Gibbo, a hatchet-faced lad with eyes like a cartoon frog, stared at the label on his beer bottle.

"You've done a bit of time yourself, right?" Bonny gave Hans a mock-boisterous punch on the arm. "Come on, what were ya? Army, Marines . . . National bloomin' Guard!"

"Navy," Hans replied. "Like yourself."

"Ahh!" Bonny viewed Hans with suspicion. "You strike me as the special forces type – you know, dagger in the teeth, take no prisoners, that sort of thing."

"Radar operator," said Hans, humoring the young lad. "USS *Nimitz*."

"Aircraft carrier – like us! Bet you seen a bit of the world – least more than bleedin' Portugal."

"I've seen some. So has Penny. She's a—"

Gibbo stood up, mumbled something about finding a toilet and wandered toward the bar.

"Is he okay?" Penny asked. "He looks a little . . . distracted."

"Gibbo's all right." Bonny checked his friend was out of sight before continuing. "He's a devil worshipper, you know."

"Someone has to be," said Hans.

"I'm serious." Bonny lowered his voice, as if fearing reprisal from the Dark Side. "He don't say much about it, but one of the lads on our ship lives in the same town as him – Penzance, down the arse end of Cornwall."

"Pirates!" Jessica piped up.

"Yeah." Bonny looked surprised. "How do you know that?"

"Because we saw some," she replied firmly. "They sail on the sea, and if they catch a ship with orphans on board, then they let it go."

As Hans and Penny smiled at Jessica's recollection of the opera they had watched in Plymouth, Bonny continued to look bemused.

The waitress arrived with their drinks. Super Bock, a strong pale lager brewed locally, and a Coca-Cola for Jessica. Penny accepted a glass, but Hans always sipped from the bottle.

"Any chance of another beer, me darlin'?" Bonny attempted to lay on the charm.

"*Momento.*" Her lack of eye contact signaled he'd failed.

Oblivious to the put-down, Bonny gulped his dregs and continued. "Yeah, so this Cornish lad tells us how Gibbo got in a fight in the pub – local heroes trying to act tough and picking on a little sailor. Gibbo was having none of it. Comes out with all this kung fu stuff and puts four of 'em in hospital."

"Really?" said Penny. "He's smaller than I am."

"Yeah, he don't look much."

"You don't need to when the devil's on your side." Hans grinned.

"But get this!" Bonny leant forward, building the suspense. "The coppers turn up and arrest Gibbo and chuck him in the back of a police van. So Gibbo sums up this . . . esotelic power—"

"Esoteric?" Penny fought back a smile as she unfolded her napkin.

"Yeah, that's it. Breaks the handcuffs apart, kicks the door open and dives right out."

"Of a police car?" Jessica stared at Bonny, eyebrows raised.

"At full speed! The *Penzance Gazette* reported he ran off into the night howling like a werewolf."

"Are you serious . . . about the handcuffs?" asked Hans.

"Dead serious. When the coppers caught up with him the next day, he was still wearin' 'em – except they weren't handcuffs anymore. More like bangles."

As they all laughed aloud, Hans wondered if Bonny meant to be hilarious or whether it was a byproduct of his naivety.

Gibbo returned, and their merriment ceased. He looked agitated.

"You all right, Able Seaman Gibson?" Bonny threw a drunken arm around his mate.

"Just a hole in the ground," Gibbo muttered, staring into space, shaking his head.

One of life's characters, Hans mused, noting Gibbo wore well-pressed chinos, schoolteacher shoes and a yellow check shirt like grandpa has in his closet. Folks who go through life oblivious or unconcerned at others' pretentiousness always humbled Hans. He suddenly felt uncomfortable in his Ralph Lauren shirt and Armani jeans.

The waitress arrived with their food. "*Açorda de marisco.*" She placed steaming bowls in front of them, along with a basket of chunky brown bread.

"Beer?" Bonny flashed a moronic smile, holding up his empty bottle and pointing a finger at it in case she didn't understand what "beer" meant.

She scowled and brushed him off once more.

"Don't know how you can eat that foreign muck." Bonny eyed their food with disdain.

"Shellfish and coriander stew," said Penny. "Classic dish. You should try some."

"Nah, I'll stick with Macky D's, babe." He attempted to wink at Penny, who had a good ten years on him, but couldn't shut one eye at a time and looked as though he had an affliction.

"Go! Go! Go! Go!"

The ship's company chanted as a chap with high-and-tight hair inched his way up a flagpole in the center of the square.

"That's gotta be a Royal Marine." Hans chuckled, noting desert boots on the guy's feet and a bulldog tattoo on his bicep.

"That's Pin Head – mad dude!" A look of pride washed over Bonny's chubby features. "Them marines, they're *all* bloomin' mad!"

Pin Head neared the top of the forty-foot mast, his shipmates egging him on with wolf whistles and screams of encouragement. Clinging to the pole's truck with one hand, he plucked a bottle of beer from his waistband and began sipping nonchalantly while surveying the scene all around.

As the crowd clapped and cheered, one of the ship's stokers, "Knocker" White – too intoxicated to calculate his money in sterling, let alone euros – accused a bartender in Castelo de Cartas of shortchanging him, something easily resolved had he not grabbed the Portuguese's apron with his banana fingers. With Latino pride at stake and in a well-rehearsed routine, the barmen pulled batons, chains and knuckledusters out of nowhere, leaping over the counter and raining them down on the dumb Yorkshireman without mercy. His messmates came to his aid, only to receive the same serving of pent-up frustration.

Within seconds violence erupted at the far side of the square. Chairs crashed into optics and glasses and punches flew, the barmen rallying and fighting back as sailors and marines attempted to pummel them to the ground. Chaos ruled the moment and gave no indication of stopping.

The distant sound of sirens grew louder, and before long a stream of police vehicles and ambulances entered the plaza, deafening the drinkers and diners and bathing the area in flashing blue light. The cops also adopted a no-nonsense approach to dealing with disorderly foreigners, particularly the Royal Navy, who didn't do themselves any favors in these parts.

Like a Mexican wave, calm rippled through the seething mass, the sailors realizing the stakes had upped and liberty and careers were on the line. This did nothing to curb the enthusiasm of the law. Chests thrust out and chins high, they leapt into action, dragging anyone with a pasty complexion from the fold and throwing them into the back of a police van.

"No!"

Bonny sat openmouthed, as if personally involved with each person arrested.

"That's Brown . . . and Smudge . . . Bailey and Marchy . . . and . . . oh, that's the *padre!*"

Every time the officers slammed the van's doors, the faces of his shipmates pressed against the meshed rear window.

"Padre?" asked Hans.

"Father Michael," Bonny replied, fixated on the scene. "Ship's padre. This is the second time."

"Second time?"

"Yeah, he got arrested in GUZ last week trying to split up a fight on Union Street. The rozzers threw him in the Paddy wagon, and he turns round to 'em and says, 'But I'm a Roman Catholic priest!' and the sergeant says, 'I'm the bleedin' pope, so pull the other one.'"

Gibbo, who had a pathological hatred of police and everything they stood for, got up and began walking toward the commotion, the same blank look on his face that was his default.

"Oh, oh, oh! 'Ere he goes, watch!"

Bonny seemed as excited as a Steven Seagal fan when their hero's about to kick ass in Chinatown.

In hubris and ignorance of British Forces' mentality, the cops had left the keys in the wagon's ignition and the engine running. Gibbo hopped into the driver's seat, shoved the gear stick forward and, wheels spinning like *The Dukes of Hazzard*, sped out of the square, taking his incarcerated shipmates with him.

The police stopped beating people up, in freeze-frame as they attempted to make sense of what just happened. The ship's company roared like Spartans on the battlefield, seizing the opportunity to get one over on the locals. Chaos reignited, and glasses and fists flew. More vans arrived on the scene, and black-clad riot squad officers began pumping gas pellets into the crowd.

"Time to leave."

Hans grabbed Jessica around the waist, bid Bonny a hasty good-bye and ducked off down a side street with Penny. Just as Penny breathed a sigh of relief, a patrol car screeched to a halt in their path and two officers sprung from the vehicle, truncheons raised and adrenaline-fueled confusion in their eyes.

"*Filho da puta!*" the first one proffered, so hyped up he failed to register they were tourists with a child in tow.

Hans set Jessica down. The police officer swung his baton. Hans blocked it with his forearm and chopped a hand into the man's throat. The cop reeled over backwards, landing in a gagging heap on the sidewalk. A kick to the second officer's groin hit the mark, followed by a crunching head butt and a fist to the solar plexus.

"Amateurs," Hans muttered, and went to grab his girls.

Jessica broke away and ran over to the police officer who lay on his back clutching a broken nose and kicked him in the shin.

Back aboard *Future*, Penny still trembled, her face pale.

"Hans, those policemen, they would have beaten us up."

"Beaten on us, thrown us in jail and placed Jessie in the care of social services until a court date came around – finally came around, that is."

"But we'd done nothing."

"Doesn't matter. Give young men weapons and put

them in a position of authority, and the power goes to their heads. Wearing a uniform doesn't make you the smartest cookie in the jar. Think how it is in war."

"I'd rather not."

"Listen" – he put his arms around the two of them – "I'm never gonna let anything happen to you. Okay?"

"Bear too?" Jessica waggled her furry friend.

"Bear too, honey."

As Jessica tucked Bear into the bunk beside her that evening, she repeated the sentiment.

- 34 -

Al Mohzerer's pickup rolled down the rocky track out of Azila. Stacked under a tarpaulin were two hundred blocks of prime merchandise destined for small-business owners in Tangier, who jumped at the chance to supplement meager incomes by peddling Golden Monkey to tourists and other customers.

Dark clouds gathered around the mountain peaks as long-awaited rain looked set to bless the fertile plains once more. Local urchins ceased playing games in the road and scurried off to the side, for young and old knew better than to get in the way of the Grower.

One of the village's flea-ridden mutts was not so lucky. Too fixated as it gnawed on the remnants of a road-killed macaque, the puppy looked up just as the truck bore down on him. Al Mohzerer had no intention of swerving. Displays of kindness to humans were rare; an animal had no chance. Under the darkening sky his ugly scar could easily pass for a grin as the little dog yelped and a rainbow of intestines spewed across the dirt.

Naseem encountered numerous checkpoints on the mountain pass, but the police waved him through, for they would never question the Grower. Besides, cigarettes, alcohol and other contraband coming in the opposite direction from Europe formed the focus of their searches, not an innocent weed boosting the local economy. Still, it didn't hurt to tip a token amount of baksheesh to some of the more senior officers, many of whom Al Mohzerer had known since childhood.

As the pickup neared Tangier, the weather cleared and minarets and sparkling white roof terraces came into view. The familiar stench of rotting food and sewage spiked with frying meat and vehicle fumes permeated the afternoon heat. Al Mohzerer threaded his truck through the city's maze of backstreets, past peeling pastel-painted premises – butcher's shops, hardware stores and other family-run businesses – and under crumbling archways, narrowly missing the multitude of street vendors crowding the route.

Upon reaching the old town, he pulled into a walled courtyard and stepped out to the more inviting fragrance of exotic spices blended with caramel, almonds, perfume and incense. His customer, Old Man Ali, had owned a carpet shop in the medina as far back as Al Mohzerer could remember.

Old Man Ali's shrewd character and keen business acumen, combined with a genuine interest in people, put Al Mohzerer on edge, despite their lengthy relationship and a family connection spanning generations. Altruism was not a concept the Grower understood. For him, you were only nice to others if you stood to gain something, the carpet seller's near blindness doing nothing to diminish his mistrust.

The old man's partisan approach had seen him through ninety-plus years, good times and bad, conflict and upheaval, his milky eyes not a barrier to selling the carpets for which he cared passionately. A simple smell and touch told him all he needed to know – weave, dye color, manufacturer and whether the product was handmade or machined.

Al Mohzerer parted the beaded fly screen to find the proprietor drinking tea with a large European man wearing garish yellow shorts, a vest and flip-flops and sat sweating profusely atop a pile of intricately woven prayer mats. The Grower's antennae pricked up. He took an immediate dislike to the infidel, yet years of cunning saw him hide his suspicion, leaving only a hint of contempt in his reptilian gaze.

Following introductions, Al Mohzerer took a backseat, feigning disinterest in the English banter yet taking in every word, noting the fat man was drunk and that the flashy timepiece on his podgy wrist was worth ten times the Berber's own salary. The carpet seller took a long pull on a hookah pipe, the apple tobacco smoke bubbling up through water trapped in its cherry-red glass bowl.

"So how is the boat?" he asked gently.

"*Sietske*'s fine," the fat man replied. "My savings, plus the money I make when I off-load this in the Canaries" – he patted the plastic bag at his feet – "should pay for some repairs, you know?"

It was an unusually large purchase for the Dutchman, but he had a plan.

"Six kilos of Golden Monkey will bring you a fine price, my friend – far greater than in our poor land. And when do you sail?"

"In the morning. With any luck I will be in Las Palmas for Wednesday."

"May Allah bring you fair winds and blue skies."

As the European walked back to his boat that evening, having sunk several beers in his favorite bar, he did not notice a man with a cruel facial scar following him.

- 35 -

Marcel tied *Sietske* up in the marina in Las Palmas, not bothered who occupied the berth or – more to the point – who had paid for it. He didn't intend to stay long nor report his arrival to the harbormaster. His sole concern was handing over the consignment of pot to his trusted source and setting sail for the nearby island of Tenerife to catch up with Hans, Jessica and Penny. The mere thought of seeing them again filled him with the warmth of acceptance.

Rather than walk out of the marina's main gate and risk a confrontation with officials, he unstrapped *Sietske*'s tender, dropped it over the side and transferred the all-important contents of the rubber fender into a white plastic bag. With a set of oars retrieved from the cabin and clutching his shipment, he lowered himself into the tiny dinghy, which immediately threatened to sink under his weight.

Singing to himself as he rounded the harbor's protective wall – "*Marshell rowed the boat ashore, ha-ley*-luuuuu-*yah!*" – he'd never felt so on top of life, yet to anyone witnessing the spectacle of a twenty-stone man in a yellow vest and shorts crammed into a yellow inflatable with toy-sized paddles, he looked like a rubber duck with issues – issues observed through binoculars ever since *Sietske* arrived in port.

Marcel dragged the tender above the high-tide mark on the shore and set out to find a pay phone.

"*Quieres comer comida del norte de África?*" he asked. "*Voy a traer seis amigos.*"

The invitation to eat "North African" food with "six companions" was all that needed to be said.

Bar Macondo was half-full at this time in the morning, a mix of Canary islanders and tourists enjoying seafood platters to the sound of Spanish romantic pop serenading in the background. Yellow-and-blue umbrellas pinned round tables to a large wooden deck surrounded by date palms, the view across the promenade taking in golden sand and the inviting blue water beyond.

After ordering a beer from a bartender in siesta mode, Marcel sat opposite a local man so engrossed in his Wi-Fi connection he didn't bother looking up. Coincidently, he too had a white plastic carrier at his feet.

The big man sunk his Dorada Especial in three gulps, swapped bags and left the bar's congenial atmosphere, the alcohol dulling the possibility their transaction might not have been hush-hush. He rowed back to the yacht and stowed the best part of twenty thousand euros, along with the rest of his savings and party drugs, in the keep-safe rubber fender, which he left lying innocuously on deck.

Filled with bravado, Marcel went to pay the mooring fee and present his paperwork to the harbormaster, knowing he needed to fill up from the marina's diesel pump and take a cab from the main entrance to go food shopping.

"Did you radio ahead, señor?" The official's eyes narrowed.

"*Ja*! Sure did, man. I spoke to . . . *Miguel*?"

"Miguel doesn't work here anymore."

"Oh! *Miguel* . . . *Manuel* . . . Er, I had a few beers, you know?"

The harbormaster was further unimpressed to learn that *Sietske* occupied *Growing Old Disgracefully*'s berth – but fortunately for the Dutchman, retirees John and Margie Grenson had decided to spend the week anchored off Lanzarote.

Enjoying fair winds, *Sietske* made good progress northeast to Tenerife the next morning, but an afternoon lull saw her sails flapping back and forth with indifference. Never one for passing up the chance to relax in the sun, Marcel went below to roll a couple of doobies and mix a jug of his preferred potion, whacking up the volume on Led Zeppelin's "Heartbreaker" as he did.

As Marcel prepared his vices, pausing regularly to slug Havana Club, he heard the sound of an outboard engine grow louder. He assumed it was local fishermen, who bravely – or foolishly – thought nothing of motoring ten miles offshore in their aging skiffs to secure a catch. With the booze taking hold, cradling him in a sentimental caress, Marcel fell into a daydream. He pondered where to head after his stop-off in Tenerife. Ordinarily, he would return to the Dam and spend chill time with friends before sailing *Sietske* south to commence the hash run once more. But there was something about the Larsson family and the delightful Penny he had not experienced in a long time. *They make me feel good about myself. Hell, Hans even invited me to visit them in the States.*

Marcel sparked one of the blunts, took a long pull and was halfway through exhaling when his musing hit home and he came up with an idea.

"Huhph!" he coughed. "*Sietske*, my dear, we are going to Maine!"

It made perfect sense. Hadn't Penny said she would love to visit too? Perhaps he could buy her an air ticket, or better still, she would meet him in South America after skippering for the Parisian couple and they could sail north together.

Yes!

He started putting a plan together, shaking and sweating more than usual. *How about spending time in the Caribbean en route?* They could stop off at his hero Bob Marley's birthplace – wasn't it Jamaica where the weed was so strong it rendered you incapacitated?

Marcel rifled through his CD collection, interrupting "Bring It On Home" to play "Buffalo Soldier" at full volume.

And Cuba – *Cuba libre*! – Che Guevara sailing from Mexico in 1956 on the leaking cabin cruiser *Granma* with only eighty-two men to overthrow the puppet Batista and his corrupt regime. The place where Hemingway wrote *The Old Man and the Sea*, the lonely fisherman finding inner peace battling his demons, along with a mighty marlin, on a mightier ocean. *Now there was a guy who could write! Could drink his weight in rum and still knock out a literary classic!*

Marcel had dreamed of visiting El Floridita, the bar in Havana where Hemingway knocked back glass after glass of mojito while discussing the Great American Novel with friends. From there they would travel to the Florida Keys and up the Treasure Coast, taking care *Sietske* did not join the numerous Spanish galleons that had foundered on the perilous reefs, their holds weighed down with doubloons still searched for by fortune seekers today.

And how about pulling in to Sebastian in Florida to meet his old mailman chum who now owned a skydiving center there? Plummeting through the air from fifteen thousand feet was on his bucket list – actually, the only item on the list, but that was about to change.

It has to be done! Marcel screwed the cap back on the bottle of rum.

Above the sound of "Redemption Song," the noise of the once-distant outboard engine became too loud to ignore. Marcel felt a bump against *Sietske*'s hull. He grabbed the schooner of cocktail and went up through the companionway to investigate.

A dark-skinned man, barefoot and dressed in ragged denim shorts and a filthy New York Yankees vest, stood in the cockpit pointing an AK-47 at him.

"I don't suppose I can offer you a mojito?" were the Dutchman's last words.

37

The tourist haven of Tenerife proved to be every sailor's dream destination. Hans, Jessica and Penny enjoyed long sunny days, walks on palm-fringed beaches, local tours and delicious food, all the time looking forward to Marcel's arrival.

"How do you fancy diving on a reef, shipmate?"

"Hmm!" Jessica gave Penny her excited *I'll do anything you do* look.

"Do you know much about reefs? Have you dived on one before?"

"I haven't dived on one before, but I've seen pictures in my books. It's rocks and flowers and red and yellow fish and blue sea."

"Good girl! And do you know what those flowers are called?"

Jessica shook her head.

"They're corals, made by lots of little animals, known as polyps, that eat seaweed and other little animals. They spit out the bits they don't like, which build up over the years to create the pretty rocks."

While Penny and Jessica pulled the dive gear from under the bunks and kitted up, Hans sailed *Future* a few miles up the coast to a reef known locally as Rainbow Mountain, giving a clue as to the myriad of colors awaiting the girls. One of the dive centers in Santa Cruz recommended the site in view of its shallow depth and good visibility.

A number of buoys bobbed in the turquoise water, the island's conservation society urging boats to make use of them rather than drop anchor and damage the fragile coral below. Penny conducted a dive brief, and she and Jessica went through their checks. Hans would remain on board as surface cover.

"Out of air signal, honey?"

Although a qualified scuba instructor, Penny understood the importance of agreeing buddy-to-buddy communications, which varied between dive-training organizations, as well as countries and individuals.

Jessica chopped a hand against her throat.

"Air pressure?"

She tapped two fingers against her forearm.

"Watch me."

The little girl pointed index fingers at her eyes.

When Penny was satisfied, she said, "Watch this!" and did a spectacular forward roll off the yacht's stern.

Hans chuckled.

Jessica clamped her mask and regulator in place with one hand and her weight belt's quick release buckle and instrument console with the other and leapt after Penny. They regrouped for a final check and then sunk below the surface of the warm water.

Immediately apparent was the reason why locals called the reef Rainbow Mountain. As opposed to the coarse black volcanic sand the island was noted for, the sand here was fine, almost white, making the vivid pigment of the coral stand out all the more. Fan, staghorn, table, star, lettuce and other similes used to describe the calcium carbonate built up over millenniums were instantly ascribable. It was easy to see why biologists refer to coral reefs as the rainforests of the sea, each organism playing a unique role in perpetuating the delicate ecosystem and balancing the planet's biosphere.

Elkhorn coral lined the outer edges of the reef, protecting it from the Atlantic's crashing waves. Brain corals acted as cleaning stations for gobies and other small fish. Coralline algae strengthened the reef's structure with limestone deposits, and so Mother Nature ran her course.

Not surprisingly, the reef spawned an abundance of marine life. Brightly colored fish – porgies, damsels, jacks – hovered in schools in the current. Puffers, wrasse and basslets zipped between crags. Moray eels, crabs and octopi hid in dark crevices. A stingray glided toward them. Bigger than Jessica, the attention-seeking fish allowed the girls to tickle its soft white underbelly.

Finning along with the little girl, Penny felt utterly contented. The previous year she had skippered for a group of Scandinavian scientists on an expedition to Antarctica, sailing from Ushuaia in Tierra del Fuego – the Land of Fire, on the southernmost tip of Argentina – for a seven-day crossing of the treacherous Drake Passage. They encountered icebergs the size of small countries and waded through vast colonies of adelie penguins in the South Shetland Islands before venturing into the Antarctic Circle to dive in the continent's pristine waters, snorkeling with leopard seals and watching orcas hunting in pods. Exploring the rugged white wilderness had been the experience of a lifetime, something Penny never dreamed to surpass, but being here now floating hand in hand with her friend through the coral idyll easily beat it.

A large shadow on the sand interrupted Penny's thoughts. She looked up expecting to see another stingray, her delight turning to horror as a seven-foot-long bull shark cruised just feet above them. Ordinarily, Penny would not have been overly concerned, despite the shark's reputation for attacking humans, but with its pectoral fins pointing downwards as it cut an abrupt zigzag pattern through the water, she could tell the animal was in hunting mode.

Ascending was out of the question. Their silhouette might prove too tempting for the predator. Instead, Penny placed an open hand on her head in the shark signal, followed by thumbs-down for "descend." She didn't want to alarm Jessica, but it was important her buddy knew what was happening to prevent panic.

Penny made a finning sign with her index fingers and pointed to the entrance of a small cave at the base of the reef. Amazed at how calmly Jessica carried out her instruction, she followed behind, relieved to find it large enough for both of them.

After checking Jessica was okay, Penny turned to face the danger, pulling her knife from its sheath. She knew not even the sharpest blade would penetrate the skin of this prehistoric killing machine, though a well-placed jab might serve as a deterrent. She prayed the bull shark would lose interest, but instead the angry fish swam in ever-tighter circles, getting closer each time before veering off at the last moment. It would not be long before the beast took a test bite of her with its fearsome jaws or their air ran out. Penny would not risk either scenario.

As the bull shark commenced another circuit, Penny put a plan into action, signaling for Jessica to take her emergency regulator. Jessica complied without hesitation, swapping to the yellow octopus spare, as she had done with her father hundreds of times before.

Penny unbuckled Jessica's buoyancy vest and cylinder and laid them on the seabed, then inflated the bright-orange marker with a blast of air from her mouthpiece. It shot to the surface, pulling line from the hand reel. Hans would spot the sausage-shaped buoy and close in to pick them up, and by clipping the reel to Jessica's equipment Penny could retrieve it later.

The bull shark became increasingly agitated, bashing its ugly snout into the cave entrance and smashing off chunks of coral. Rotting fish flesh streamed from rows of savage teeth like morbid souvenirs. Penny eyed the gruesome pennants and shuddered.

For the briefest of moments Penny's mind fixated on the enormous danger they were in. Her adrenaline waned, weakening her resolve. *People don't survive shark attacks – not without serious injury!*

Her breathing was out of control, wasting precious air, and she suddenly felt nauseous.

Remember Jessica! What would Hans do in this situation?

As if Neptune had prodded her with his trident, Penny snapped back into action, closing the valve on Jessica's cylinder and purging the system of air so she could unscrew the hoses. Then balancing the tank on her knee, she waited for the shark to return.

Seconds ticked by . . .

With a rapid tail-finning motion, the shark attacked, its mouth opened wide, exposing soft pink throat tissue. Penny cranked the valve and sent a jet of high-pressure air shooting into the beast's cold black eyes. The shark jolted and peeled away.

It was now or never . . .

Hearing *Future*'s motor overhead, Penny placed the equipment on the sand with the cylinder's valve fully open. She grabbed Jessica around the waist and pushed off with her feet, using the frenetic screen of bubbles as both cover and deterrent. She held a finger down on her buoyancy vest's air-inlet button until the overfill valves vibrated.

They rocketed upwards.

Catching sight of the marker and the constant stream of bubbles, Hans knew something was wrong. He positioned *Future* a few feet away, donned a mask and fins and was about to dive overboard when the girls burst to the surface. He wrenched his daughter from the sea with one hand, dragging Penny unceremoniously up the ladder with the other. They collapsed in a heap in the cockpit.

"No safety stop then?" Hans raised an eyebrow.

"Thought we'd give it a miss, honey. We had company," Penny panted.

"A big shark, Papa! He tried to eat Penny!"

"Well, it's a good thing he didn't. She's cooking supper."

38

Following their close encounter with the barrel of Naseem's shotgun, the boys hadn't ventured out of the hut at night except to visit the latrine. Ahmed figured they had loosened the outhouse's boards enough, that a sharp tug would see them swiftly inside and securing at least thirty kilos of hashish between them. They spent the dark hours improving their English and poring over the diagrams in the Swedish sailing guide.

The next trip to Tangier began as usual, Al Mohzerer ordering Ahmed and Mohamed to load the pickup with blocks of Golden Monkey, ready for delivery to his customers in the city. The boys stacked the regular amount in a neat pile in the corner of the flatbed and were in the process of pulling over the tarpaulin when the Grower interrupted them. "No. *More!*

"How much more, *sayyid*?" Ahmed asked.

"All of it."

The boys' spirits sunk.

There must have been a thousand half-kilo blocks in the outbuilding – four months' worth of production – delaying the boys' escape indefinitely. Hiding their shock, they continued the task in silence, but at the first opportunity Ahmed hissed, "We're ruined!"

"No, we still have our savings."

Stashed under the floorboards in the hut was over a thousand dollars in euros, converted from dirhams in preparation for the trip.

"It's not enough!" Hard as he was, Ahmed looked on the verge of tears.

"Hey!" Mohamed took Ahmed's hand and squeezed it. "What would the wolf do?"

"He would improvise," Ahmed replied reluctantly.

"And?"

"He would adapt . . . and overcome."

"See? I have taught you well, friend!" Mohamed grinned.

Ahmed couldn't help but smile.

Footsteps approached, catching them off guard. Their hands dropped.

"What do you talk about?" Al Mohzerer demanded, his scar turning the question into a sneer.

"We say we must work extra hard to replace the product, *sayyid*."

He grunted and nodded to the door of the truck.

- 39 -

On the fifth day in port, Hans was lounging in the cockpit inventing pictures for Jessica to draw with her Etch a Sketch when Penny returned from the marina's clubhouse visibly shaken, tears pouring down her face.

"Jessie, could you take Bear inside and play awhile?"

"Okay, Papa."

Hans stepped ashore and ran toward their companion. Penny stumbled along the pontoon as if drunk, until her legs gave way. Hans crouched beside her as she sobbed uncontrollably.

"Baby, what's up?"

"It's all over the Internet, Hans."

"What is, honey? Come on, you can tell me."

"*Sietske*. The crew of the *Jenny H* found her drifting ten miles off Las Palmas and pulled alongside to see if Marcel needed help."

"Did he?"

"He wasn't there, Hans. Just some rough-looking locals crashed out drunk. And they had guns . . . *uh-huht-huh*."

Over the next few days, Hans and Penny attempted to make sense of what happened, the yachting community alive with gossip and all-round disbelief. Hans learned from the harbormaster, whose thirty years on the job saw him a man in the know, that the Canadian couple found *Sietske* with her sails flapping and dark-red blood splattering the cockpit. He believed pirates had murdered Marcel and thrown his body overboard.

Piracy was a constant topic in the media due to a spate of container ship hijackings off the coast of Somalia. Prior to the trip, while researching on the web, Hans learned these attacks had been going on for years and yachts were easy targets. The harbormaster's grave nod confirmed this.

Penny recovered from her initial shock but remained noticeably nervous – obviously worried they might experience a similar fate. Hans did his best to assure her he would not let that happen. While in the UK he'd considered buying a firearm on the secondhand market to stow aboard *Future* for such an occurrence. But knowing the trouble it would create if a customs search uncovered the weapon upon their arrival in a foreign port – namely, him being arrested and Jessica placed in the care of social services – he'd decided on a less overt arrangement.

That evening, as Jessica slept in her bunk, Hans and Penny mixed up mojitos and lit candles next to a postcard-sized picture drawn in pastel chalks. It was of the three of them together with Marcel, sitting in *Sietske*'s cockpit in Brest, arms around each other, all smiling and raising cocktails and set against a beautiful sunset. Hans had found it taped to the helm when they departed Spain. In the corner of the drawing, high in the sky, was a little stick man with what looked to be a spliff stuck between his lips and a speech bubble that read, "Ahhhhhhhh!" On the back of the card, scrawled in spidery handwriting, were the words "Don't forget to pull your reserve! Big love, Marcel. X."

Downloaded to Hans' laptop, "How Fast Can You Live?" by the Stoner Brothers played quietly the background.

> *... around the edge*
> *A long way to get here*
> *You won't see me cryin'*
> *Just see me disappear*
> *Without you*
> *There is no way ahead*
> *Without you-ooh-ooh-ooh ...*

Setting a solitary flower adrift on the water, they cried some more.

The Grower looked on edge as he navigated the perilous bends carving down the mountain. The boys knew better than to say anything, both staring ahead as a million questions buzzed in their minds.

Once in town Al Mohzerer dropped them off outside the cinema with strict instructions to meet him at Old Man Ali's carpet shop in the medina at three o'clock.

"What shall we do?" Mohamed looked to his friend for guidance.

Ahmed stared upwards for a second. "We continue as normal until we can work out what's going on. Besides, I need time to think."

Ahmed went up to the ticket booth and asked the attendant for directions to a nearby restaurant. When the man walked outside with him and began pointing up the street, Mohamed slipped into the cinema. Ahmed thanked the attendant and bolted off to peddle more squidgy black hashish.

The boys reunited at the harbor in the afternoon and began chatting with a crew of young English guys, who were more intent on discussing soccer than the art of seamanship. With their endeavor now thrown into jeopardy, the boys were happy to talk about something other than sailing.

Walking toward their rendezvous with Naseem, Mohamed stopped in his tracks, looking outraged.

"Beckham! Why he don't play for an English club?"
"He's gone overseas, where the money is, fool!"
Ahmed grabbed his friend's ears. "Like we must do!"

As far as sailing was concerned, the hop from the Canary Islands to Cape Verde proved to be the most enjoyable part of the trip, though thrust to the back of Hans and Penny's minds was the loss of a friend and parting company on arrival.

Not since meeting Jessica's mother had Hans experienced such a strong connection with a member of the opposite sex, not to mention the base desire whipped up by their union. He could tell Penny had feelings for him too, figuring they were both hesitant to act on them for fear of creating additional confusion for Jessica.

Awaking at dawn to take over on watch, Hans emerged from the cabin to find the cockpit deserted. A bikini top and denim shorts lay on the cushions.

No!

Hans' mind attempted to make sense of the situation. A chill crept through him. Had she taken advantage of a lull in the wind to go for a dip, only to see *Future* sail on without her? Or perhaps suffered some kind of breakdown? Either way he felt sick as he pictured explaining this to Jessica.

"*Penny!*"

The sound of water sloshing on deck stopped his panic in its tracks.

"I'm right here!"

Hans turned to see a naked Penny grinning as she took a bucket shower. "Oh! I was worried you'd fallen overboard. Er, I'll give you a minute."

"Don't be so silly! I was hoping someone would soap my back!"

Hans let out a nervous chuckle. Every so often on the trip, glimpses of unadulterated femininity escaped Penny's tomboyish exterior, drawing him in with an allure he neither could nor wanted to resist. He was deeply in love, and every cell in his body knew it.

Hopping onto the cabin roof, he felt a range of emotions and adrenaline pulsing through him, resulting in a pleasant state of anxiety. Streaked blond by the sun, Penny's damp tresses cascaded down her back, white bikini lines interrupting her deep tan to add further lasciviousness to her natural beauty. Hans trembled like a teenager on a first date.

Penny passed the bar of soap over her shoulder in a fake attempt at modesty. Hans took it in one hand, slipping the other under her breasts to pull her close.

She turned her head . . .

The soap fell . . .

Their lips met—

"Fishing time!"

A fiberglass pole emerged from the cabin, flopping around as the seven-year-old on the other end attempted to control it.

"Well, well, well!" Hans winked at Penny. "We could just do with some fish for breakfast. In fact, seeing as though the wind doesn't want to play, I think today should be a fun day."

"Yay!"

Making good progress in these warmer climes, they were able to take plenty of time out, furling in the mainsail to fire up the barbeque, grab the fishing and snorkeling gear and make the most of their ocean playground.

"Birds in the water!" Hans echoed a line from *The Perfect Storm* as Jessica lowered a set of spangled lures over the side, controlling the spool with her thumb to prevent it paying out too fast and tangling. "So what are we going for, First Mate?"

"Fish, Papa!"

"And what kinda fi—?"

Jessica's pole slammed against the guardrail. "Penny!" she screamed as line ripped from the spool.

"Let it run, sweetie." Penny leant over and loosened the clutch on the reel. "You've hooked a beauty!"

Up until now the only thing they had caught were horse mackerel and baitfish, but this time pulses raced all round. After a minute or so the fish ended its run, and Penny urged Jessica to reel in, but the animal shot into the depths and tore off more line. The pattern continued for a good twenty minutes, until Hans, even with his hands-on approach to parenting, felt obliged to assist.

"Nah!" She gave a firm shake of the head, focus unwavering as her exhausted arms trembled.

Eventually, the catch weakened, flashing silver as Jessica brought it to the surface, yet a final bid for freedom saw the line tighten and stay that way.

"Agh! It's hooked around the propeller," said Penny, craning over the side shaking her head.

"You swine!" Jessica shook hers.

"Come on, sweet pea, time to go swimming." Hans vaulted into the cockpit, dashing through the companionway to grab snorkeling gear and a knife. "Are you ready?" he asked as they stood on deck kitted up.

Jessica nodded – the same nod she would give if her papa announced they were going to fight bears.

"Right, let's go fishing."

With a big grin, he picked her up and flopped over the side.

Breaking the surface, Jessica blew seawater from her snorkel and scanned below. Indeed, the line had snagged around the propeller, the exhausted tuna giving the odd flick of its tail in a vain effort to escape.

Hans duck-dove and swam down through the warm blue water. He cut the nylon free and drew the fish toward him. As he was about to kick upwards, Jessica appeared, finning like crazy, by his side, reminding him of the wind-up scuba toy she and JJ used to play with in the tub. He wrapped the line around her hand and gave the thumb sign for *Let's surface*. She returned it, and they floated upwards.

"Well done, honey. You got us a yellowfin! Don't let go now."

"Onk-onk!" Through her snorkel, Jessica sounded like a goose.

"You clever girl!"

Penny helped her up the steps and then gaffed the tuna through its gill – for, weighing a good ten pounds, it could easily rip itself off the hook if hauled by the line.

Using the gaff's hefty handle, Penny dispatched the fish, and Hans showed Jessica how to prepare it. Soon there were ten ruby-red steaks sizzling on the barbeque, all splashed with Worcestershire sauce, a tangy British condiment chosen by Penny. Hans threw the fish's head onto the coals, ready for a dare with Jessica.

One time while serving in the SEALs, Hans had been sitting outside a restaurant in West Africa finishing off a fried snapper. A group of ragamuffins assembled and began ogling what to him was an empty plate. Hans gestured there was nothing left except bones, but a couple of kids rushed over and plucked out the fish's eyeballs, wolfing them down and indicating with belly rubs they were an important part of the dish. It was a memorable moment, bringing home to Hans how privileged he was to be born into a culture that could afford to throw perfectly good food away. Ever since, he had customarily followed their example while reveling in nostalgia.

Jessica eyed the translucent globule with suspicion, the staring black pupil adding creepiness to the off-putting "delicacy."

"*Yuck!*" Her face screwed up.

"I will if you will." Penny snatched the other eye and popped it in her mouth. "Hmm . . . not bad." she fibbed as blood and goo ran down her chin.

"Hmm . . . not bad." Jessica was never one to be left out.

- 42 -

Mitch didn't know anything about sailing. There was not much call for it in Fort Worth, Dallas. He spent his time watching DVDs, *Discovery* and playing *Gulf War II* on his Xbox when not working a twelve-hour shift in the call center – or the Shed of Broken Dreams as he thought of it.

A girlfriend seemed a long way off. He had not been in a relationship since splitting with Darlene, and that was seven years ago and counting. And he certainly wasn't the sporty type, despite running a half marathon a couple of years back following a drunken wager with a colleague – near killed him, and two hours forty wasn't exactly something to be proud of.

Now, browsing shopping sites on the Internet, Mitch considered splashing the $1,400 in his savings account on one of these widescreen televisions that had suddenly become so popular. Watching a recent documentary, he learned that the factories in Japan could not churn out the sets fast enough. Packed into huge containers, they would then be loaded onto cargo ships for delivery worldwide. Apparently, thousands of these containers fell over the side in rough seas every year, floating around for months and creating a significant hazard for yachts.

The money was supposed to be for Vegas. He and the Budmeister planned to hire Harleys and ride there next summer. Only Bud had gotten all sensible, tied the knot with Jeanie and moved to the East Coast, so that trip was doomed.

Come on, Mitchell, think! He rubbed his eyes. *You work your ass off all week. You don't exactly socialize much, and you ain't got any hobbies other than spending time in front of the TV. And that little set you've had since college is on its last legs.*

Yes, he reasoned, he would treat himself. After all, the Hitachi 42-ES-1080 came with HD, surround sound and VGA connector – a gamer's paradise!

With a feeling bordering on surreal, he clicked the "Buy" button on Digital Direct's website and then typed in his address and credit card details.

- 43 -

Hans and Penny cozied up in the cockpit as *Future* made three to four knots under a canopy of stars.

"Hans, how did you get into detective work?"

"Oh, good question. You know I said I loved reading as a kid?"

"Hmm."

"There used to be a book series, the Hardy Boys, about two brothers who solved crimes and stuff. Did you have this in England?"

"Of course. And don't forget Nancy Drew."

"What about the Three Investigators?"

"Hah! Jupiter . . . ?"

"Jones and his buddies Pete Crenshaw and Bob Andrews, the supersleuths, always jealous of Skinny Norris because he was old enough to drive a car."

"I read them all."

"Me too. I even went through a spell with my friend Adrian when we made ourselves detective kits. You know, like in hopes we'd solve a mystery of our own."

"Detective kits?"

"These little backpacks. Put all kinds of stuff in them, like magnifying glasses and talcum powder to dust for fingerprints. Used to collect spare keys in case we might be able to open a door with them. Stole our moms' hair grips to try and pick locks."

"Any luck?"

"Not a lot, but we figured out how to escape from a locked room."

"Tell me."

"You push a sheet of newspaper under the door and poke a knife blade through the keyhole. The key drops onto the paper, you pull it back under the gap and – hey presto! – you let yourself out."

"Neat trick."

"It was at that age. We even made blowpipes from the bamboo plants in Adrian's backyard and little darts out of sewing needles and bird feathers. Kinda thought we were James Bond."

"Did you ever solve any crimes?"

"No, we never came across any, just liked the excitement of living like our heroes. One time I even wore a disguise – like those guys were always putting on disguises, right?"

"Uh-huh."

"I had on my mother's fur coat and these long boots, and I pulled a big flowery hat down over my face."

"You're joking!"

"No, I'm serious. I wanted to experience being undercover – to see if I'd get away with it. Took my little brother's pram and pushed it around the block. Walked right past a load of kids I knew and none of them said a word."

"No one recognized you?"

"Nah. When I told them later, they said they thought it was some weird old lady passing by. I wish I never told them, though . . ."

"How come?"

"You try explaining why you're wearing women's clothes when you're an eleven-year-old boy."

"I see."

"Some of them still remind me of it today." Hans chuckled.

"So you always wanted to be a detective?"

"Kinda, but mostly a pipe dream. Like a lotta things in my life, I ended up falling into it."

"As you do." Penny looked up and smiled.

"A lot of my SEAL buddies left the navy around the same time I did, during the Iraq conflict. Jobs came up in the Middle East doing private security work, and guys could get paid three times as much on contracts out there than they did working for Uncle Sam."

"And you did that?"

"It was tempting. Every man and his dog was doing a year and paying off their mortgages, even national guardsmen with no experience of combat. I couldn't get to grips with the ethics of it all. I'd seen enough senseless killing – certainly enough of the desert – and Kerry was pregnant with Jess."

"What did you do?"

"I wanted to join the police department as a rookie and work my way up. The DUI on my record put paid to that."

"Drunk driving?"

"Yeah, said I could get a job in admin – answering the phone in traffic or typing up witness statements. Like I was gonna do that."

"So you started an investigation agency?"

"Not quite. Kerry was always real positive, you know? Kinda like you."

"Aw." Penny snuggled tighter.

"No, I mean it. Always the glass half-full. She said, when you need an answer, open your eyes and it will find you. So I'm sitting in a bar one night, doing what I did best back then – drowning my sorry ass – and I get talking to the guy on the next stool. Harry Ross was his name – 'Rosco.' Turns out he's a private eye – real old-school type like Mike Hammer, with the same drink problem."

Penny didn't know who Mike Hammer was but nodded anyway.

"So after a time listening to him talk about his work, I asked straight out if he could give me a job."

"Did he?"

"No, he laughed. Said there's a lot more to detective work than you see on TV."

"In what way?"

"Well, for a start folks only hire PIs when they're desperate."

"Meaning?"

"Meaning if the police and all their resources can't get the answer they're looking for, they turn to you. You're one guy trying to solve a mystery a hundred or more professionals just gave up on . . . which to be honest ain't always a bad thing."

"It's not?"

"Cops always look for the quick result, and they can be pretty useless at the best of times. Then there's the boredom factor. Starting out, you're likely to be sat in your car for hours drinking coffee and trying to stay awake, just to expose a spouse's infidelity or a fraudulent disability benefit claim."

"Hardly exciting."

"Not exactly busting the big stuff. Anyway, Rosco says to come by his office and he'll give me details of a case he's been working on. A real tough one, where he reckoned the cops hadn't done their job."

"I'm listening." Penny went to check on Jessica and returned with a couple of beers. "So if you got to the bottom of it he'd take you on."

"That's how I understood it, but we were pretty drunk. He didn't expect me to show up."

"But you did."

"My diary was kinda empty, and it's not like I had anything to lose. Neither did he." Hans pulled the tab on his beer. "Turns out a retired businessman had offered to pay two hundred thousand bucks to find his daughter. Said 'Keira' went missing on a scuba dive down in the Keys while vacationing with her husband."

"A scuba dive? How did he expect you to find her body? I mean, they must have carried out searches and stuff."

"Ha, that's a story for another day."

"So you solved the case and got a job as a private eye?"

"I got more than that. Rosco was looking to retire. He gave me a half share of the reward money and eventually let me buy him out of the business."

"The Larsson Investigation Agency."

"That's what it became."

The two of them cuddled in silence for a while. Penny desperately wanted to ask Hans about Kerry and JJ's deaths, but she knew he would tell her when the time was right. She put it to the back of her mind and instead mused on how fortunate she was to have met him. She hadn't felt this way for quite some time.

After a while, "Penny, you ever gonna tell me your story?" Hans asked.

"Mine?"

"You pretty much know ours."

Penny was about to remind Hans that a crucial chunk of the Larsson history was missing, but, not wanting to ruin the moment, she kept shtum.

"How did you end up on a yacht in the North Atlantic?"

"It's what I've always done, Hans – nearly always. I graduated from uni as a veterinary nurse. Because I grew up on yachts, my parents wanted me to experience a 'normal' career."

"Not for you then?"

"I enjoyed it, don't get me wrong – practiced for three years in London after graduation. But the pull of the sea . . . It's hard to resist."

"So what happened?"

"I got a job on a luxury yacht owned by the sultan of Oman, traveled the world working my way up from deckhand to get my skipper's ticket. Been crewing ever since."

"And you never felt like settling down – getting married, having kids?"

"Of course I thought about it. But relationships at sea tend to be pretty short-lived."

"Passing ships?"

"Exactly."

"So there's never been anyone special?"

"There was one guy, from Miami, hired me to sail his yacht around the Caribbean. He was young, handsome and wealthy, and I was . . . well, young and naïve. We had what you might call a passionate romance. I really thought it was meant to be."

"What happened?"

"On the way back to the States he disclosed a wife and two kids."

"Oh."

"You can say that again! I guess the Cher keep fit and Disney DVDs were a bit of a giveaway."

They laughed and snuggled tighter.

"Penny, can I ask you something?"

"Sure."

"It's just that Jessie, she thinks the world of you – and I do too."

"Aw." Penny buried her head in Hans' chest.

"Would you come visit us in the US? I mean, I'd pay your flight and everything, and you wouldn't need to spend a dime—"

"Honey!" She cupped his face in her hands. "I make a great deal of money ferrying rich businessmen around the globe and teaching their pampered brats to scuba dive, and it's not as if there's a lot a girl needs to spend her money on in the middle of the ocean. Of course I'll come, *and* pay my own way. It's about time I tested my land legs."

"Are you sure?"

"Yes! I'm assuming there are sailing schools in Portland?"

"*Sh*yeah!"

"Well, in that case I might just stay awhile."

Their lips met – and this time no one interrupted them to go fishing.

- 44 -

As Kuro stood on a production line in Japan, wearing primrose overalls, a protective hairnet and antistatic boots, sailing was far from his mind. In fact, he had never been on a yacht in his life.

The working day started as normal. Rise at 5:00 a.m., shower, fresh shirt and the same sickly yellow tie, eat a breakfast of steamed rice, miso soup and rolled omelet with his parents, and then take the high-speed rail link from their home in Hasuda to the factory in Oyama.

A shift at Hitachi always began with a motivational speech delivered by Minakuchi-san, the plant manager. Somewhat lacking as an orator, Minakuchi-san simply regurgitated white-collar rhetoric, which proved a constant source of amusement for the younger employees, who would drop such jargon as "product focused" and "target driven" into their lunchtime conversations, along with furtive giggles. Then came the morning warm-up routine, exercises deemed to create *wa*, "harmony," in the working environment.

Graceful, confident and in time with the clonking piano waltz piped over the public address system, the beautiful Aiko had yet to realize Kuro stood near her whenever a space was available. The thoughts and feelings the young man experienced were confusing and somewhat shameful, certainly not ones to air over family dinner when asked how his day went.

Kuro would happily have spent the entire shift bending and twisting to the manager's stilted instruction if it resulted in further peeks at Aiko's pert figure and proximity to her magical aura, but the music ended abruptly, and the employees turned in file and scurried to their workstations.

Kuro's role in the manufacturing process was plugging diodes, capacitors and microchips into circuit boards, ready for soldering and fitting into the company's latest widescreen television, the Hitachi 42-ES-1080. Complete with HD, surround sound and VGA connector, the set was taking the market by storm, particularly in the US, where shipments couldn't reach the distributors fast enough. If he proved his worth on this section of the conveyor belt, in the next two to three years he could see promotion to quality control – test-inspecting the motherboards' complex architecture to prevent imperfections entering the build phase.

Who knew: the year after he could be looking at a supervisor's position. And boy, with the big bucks rolling in he could save up the deposit for an apartment and make his move on Aiko.

45

When Hans relieved Penny for the 4:00 a.m. watch, he could see she was exhausted, the events of the previous week having caught up with her. Penny's mind had been working overtime, and sleeping was a problem, so Hans fetched a double-strength Valium from the first aid kit.

Sitting in the darkness, Cape Verde sixty miles ahead, he reflected on the trip so far and what an education it had been for Jessica. He also thought about their dear friend's untimely demise, something he decided to keep from his daughter.

The low but distinct rumbling of a diesel engine interrupted his muse. Instinctively, he scanned around, expecting to see another boat passing in close proximity, a regular occurrence when sailing near to land. All he saw were far-distant cargo carriers and tankers spread out across the horizon like a string of fairy lights.

This ship was much closer, and the fact it was under way with no running lights put Hans instantly on guard. He switched off *Future*'s navigation beacons and listened. Sure enough, the dull throbbing grew louder as the unknown vessel approached.

Changing course to run with the breeze, Hans hoped it was a maverick fishing trawler whose captain held scant regard for sea safety. Yet after forty-five minutes it became obvious the mystery craft was tracking *Future* on radar.

In the emerging half-light, Hans made out an ugly black hulk less than a quarter of a mile to starboard. Through the binoculars he could see activity on deck as the crew lowered a skiff onto the water. He felt certain he knew what was on the cards and considered waking Penny but then dismissed the idea, figuring in her sedated state she could serve no purpose. He also thought about radioing for help, but this far offshore it was not as if the Cape Verde coastguard would miraculously appear on the scene. Besides, if the other vessel was listening in it would warn them, and the uninvited guests might arrive with guns blazing.

Instead, Hans lowered his shoulders and took a few deep breaths, visualizing the tension flowing from his body. Then he went into the cabin and fetched a bucket from the cleaning store, the emergency flare gun and a two-gallon can of gas. As an afterthought, he grabbed the bulk pack of firecrackers bought in the hypermarket in France. Back in the cockpit, he filled the bucket with fuel, fitted a cartridge to the gun and shoved the opened packet of bangers in the waistband of his shorts. Then he did what Navy SEALs do best – he watched and waited.

The skiff approached at speed.

Hans continued his reconnaissance, observing three ragtag Africans on board, one of them operating the powerful outboard motor. On further inspection he made out another man lying under the thwarts.

The American worked through the scenario in his head: a mother ship pursuing them with no lights while maintaining radio silence, a souped-up launch ideally matched to the speed of a yacht and an "injured" crew member providing a convenient reason for requiring assistance.

As the skiff covered the last few yards, its occupants made a play of waving and calling for help in broken English, but the nervousness in their eyes spoke for them. Noting each man had a hessian sack at his feet, Hans had seen enough and put on a show of his own, gesturing he was heaving to and steering *Future* into the wind.

With the engine cut, the skiff glided to within a few feet of the yacht, and the bowman prepared to throw a mooring line. In one fluid movement Hans climbed up on the cockpit cushions, placed a foot on the coaming and emptied the bucket of gas over the visitors. Then he stood there motionless, staring into the eyes of the obvious leader while aiming the flare gun at his head.

For a moment the pirates were utterly bewildered, mouthing words as they looked alternatively at Hans and each other before the bowman screamed, "Gazolin!" and dived over the side. The injured man made a remarkable recovery and scrambled after him, as did the helmsman, but the leader held fast, whipping an AK-47 out from under his sack and swinging the barrel toward Hans.

Whoomph!

A streaking white rocket smashed into the man's chest, knocking him overboard as an orange-and-yellow fireball engulfed the wooden craft. In the same instant Hans lobbed the firecrackers and ducked back into the cockpit, his hair singeing in the intense heat. He reached for the engine starter button, and as fire tore across the water, creeping up *Future*'s hull, her two-liter diesel spurred into life. Hans shoved the throttle forward, and the yacht roared away from the danger zone, a cacophony of bangs, thumps and whizzes resulting from the firecrackers and ammunition lying in the pool of burning fuel in the skiff.

Hans wrenched a fire extinguisher from its bracket and turned to survey the blaze, just as the pirate leader attempted to drag himself over the guardrail, bloody melted skin dripping from his face, arms and torso. The American swung the hefty red canister in a high arc and brought it down with a crunch on the man's head, sending him reeling into *Future*'s wake. To the sound of ever-more-distant confusion, he set about dousing the remaining flames.

Later that morning Penny emerged from the cabin, the effects of the extra-strong sleeping pill obvious, to find Hans and Jessica barbequing the leftover tuna, along with thick strips of bacon and fat pork-and-apple butcher's sausages.

"Morning, sleeping beauty. You look as though you still have ninety-nine years left to snooze."

"Aw, you can say that again. I had the most bizarre dream . . ."

She caught sight of the scorch marks on the cockpit cushions.

"Hans, *what* happened?"

"Oh, I got a bit overzealous with the lighter fluid. Had a bit of a flameout."

"Had a bit of a flameout." Jessica concentrated on flipping a tuna steak.

46

In Alfonso's birthplace long outrigged canoes with mighty engines took preference over yachts, but as the Filipino sat in his crane forty meters above the dock in Yokohama, both pleasure craft and homeland were far from his mind. Instead, Alfonso concentrated on swinging a twelve-ton container toward the already packed deck of the *Tokyo Pride*.

Longer than the *Titanic*, almost twice as wide and two hundred and thirty thousand tons fully loaded, the cargo ship lived up to her name, but with the depth of her keel restricted to allow passage through some of the world's shallower waterways, safety concerns had been raised.

Alfonso did not need to know the contents of the forty-foot-long metal boxes, only how heavy each one was, information radioed through by the chief rigger on the dockside to allow for weight considerations and counter balancing. He wasn't keen on stacking the containers six high – not out of concern the additional stress on the lashings could see cargo spill overboard in heavy seas, but because getting them lined up so their lugs interlocked involved painstaking effort.

Alfonso was determined to get away on time to play in a card game on the other side of town. Poker was his only real vice – at times too much of a vice, the surplus of his hard-earned salary not always finding its way back to his wife and children in the village of Jimenez on the island of Mindanao. However, when loading and off-loading thousands of television sets and other high-value goods onto ships every day, and with contacts in customs and dockyard security, there were other ways for the crane operator to supplement his minimal wage.

On this occasion Alfonso was too eager to shut down his crane, for he had not informed the deck crew of several containers high up in the stack far exceeding their declared weight. Unbeknown to him, four of them housed industrial-sized diesel engines on pallets that were not properly secured. Two other containers suffered from structural fatigue, and due to an error in communication a number of missing twistlocks had gone unnoticed.

One of the last containers Alfonso lowered into place, SIDU307007-9, carried high-definition Hitachi television sets destined for the United States via the Suez Canal and Europe.

- 47 -

"That's it . . . Back this way . . . A bit more . . . Good job, funny face!"

Under Hans' patient tuition, Jessica reversed *Future* into a berth in Cape Verde's Porto Grande Marina on the island of São Vicente.

"I have *not* gotta funny face, Papa!"

"Oh yes you have! And you've got spaghetti legs and a mushroom nose!"

"Naughty Papa!"

Summoning all her strength she smacked his backside, Hans dropping to the cockpit floor as if hit by a linebacker from the Chicago Bears.

As far as bonding with his daughter was concerned and coming to terms with the loss of Mom and JJ, Hans felt the trip had beaten all his expectations. He knew he would support this delightful and intelligent creature until the end of his days. Although she was too young to understand the events in full, Hans was proud of her remarkable maturity and handling of the situation. Obviously she was confused and threw the occasional tantrum, but unlike most kids her age, yet to develop empathy and self-reflection, Jessica was always forthcoming with an apology, giving Hans the opportunity to talk things through and come to an understanding. What Jessica didn't know was that ten

213

months earlier, when Hans had pulled his Beretta out of the drawer, having downed a bottle of bourbon, she had been his reason for living then.

"Come on, shipmate. Let's tie this baby up and go exploring."

"Aye aye, naughty Papa!"

While Penny went to check her email and use the laundry, Hans and Jessica took a boat tour around a collection of vintage sailing ships sitting at anchor in the harbor. Immaculately restored, the tall riggers were the oceangoing greyhounds of their day, capable of crossing the Atlantic full to brimming with trade goods in record time. With their monstrous size, miles of rigging and striking black-and-white-painted timbers, the century-old schooners and brigantines were the stuff of literary and movie legend.

"See the spars right at the top, honey?"

"Uh-huh." Jessica stared upwards, dwarfed by the towering mast carved, unbeknown to them, from native Maine spruce.

"In the olden days the sailors would have to climb up there, even in real bad storms, to unfurl the topsails."

"What if they fell off, Papa?"

"Oh . . . if they fell off . . ." Hans paused, catching the vacant look in his daughter's eyes.

The slightest suggestion of death sent Jessica into a trancelike state, her traumatized mind attempting to make sense of something most adults struggle to understand. He wondered how to explain to a damaged seven-year-old the consequences of falling onto the deck from such a height or, equally as bad, into the sea. Back then the majority of sailors couldn't swim, and it was not as if these gargantuan sailboats could turn on a dime to pick them up if they did stay afloat.

"I guess they made sure not to fall, sweet pea."

Penny joined them back aboard, smiling with a sparkle in her eyes.

"Hans, are you and Jessie still looking for a crew member to help you cross the Atlantic?"

"Pretty sure we still are." Hans gave a sideways look.

"Then I'd like to offer my services. The Parisian millionaire's stock just took a downturn, and he's put the French Guiana crossing on hold."

Hans could hardly contain his joy. "What do you think, Jess? Would you like it if Penny sails back to Portland with us?"

"Yay!"

"Yeeeeeee-hah-hah-hah!"

Hans hopped up onto the cockpit cushions and, hanging one hand over his head and scratching his chest with the other, began to sing. "*Oh, ooh-be-doo, I wanna be like you-ooh-ooh!*"

"*I wanna walk like you, talk like you toooo!*" the girls chorused.

As the three of them goofed around the cockpit doing the monkey dance from Jessica's *Jungle Book* DVD, Hans wondered if the trip could get any better.

On the commuter train to Oyama, Kuro took up his manga comic, but read less than a page before stopping to stare out of the window, daydreaming as apartment buildings and industrial complexes whizzed by.

Kuro had started to question recently whether something might be amiss in his life, since fixating on the mundane backdrop while listening to the hypnotic beat of the tracks was actually more enjoyable than standing on the production line at Hitachi endlessly plugging components into TV motherboards. He felt an overwhelming urge to exit the train at the next stop and go and experience pastures new, but if he committed such a rebellious act his future with the electronics giant would not be a long one.

The young man had aspirations, though. Minakuchi-san had worked his way up from warehouse assistant to become operations manager. Last year he flew his family to Mexico for a vacation – Cancún no less, the epitome of the good life – where they swam with dolphins and saw Koichi Domyato, Japan's J-pop sensation, strolling hand in hand along the beach with Atsuko Morigachi from the hit soap opera *Love Exists*.

Kuro had never been abroad, as his mother and father were not adventurous types. His grandfather, Sukiyabashi-san, who lived with the family, had traveled to faraway places, although it was not something he talked about. Known respectfully as *Itamae* – "Chef" – he had been Japan's leading sushi master before the Second World War. Following the attack on Pearl Harbor, the Japanese army commissioned Sukiyabashi-san, who, rising to the rank of major, found himself in Burma overseeing construction of the infamous Death Railway.

One time Kuro sneaked into his grandfather's room to peek at the contents of an aging ammunition canister kept with the modest possessions in his closet. There were sepia-toned photographs of a determined young man and a demure young woman dressed in kimonos and staring solemnly into the lens – the latter, Kuro's grandmother, killed during an American bombing raid shortly before the war ended, the sortie leveling the restaurant and two square miles of the surrounding area. A set of gold-lacquered *hashi* – chopsticks – pinned to a base made from cherry tree were the only reminder of Sukiyabashi-san's glory days as chef supreme, this particular award bestowed upon him by the Fishmongers Guild in 1932.

Particularly moving were hundreds of letters, bunched and tied with brittle string dyed orange using wilted lawn clippings to symbolize romance, each impeccably written in daintily inked characters and with a dried blossom included in its folds. Kuro had thought of the beautiful Aiko, his coworker at the factory.

Yet the most pertinent keepsake in his grandfather's collection was a yellowing page from *Stars and Stripes* featuring a photograph taken in the Burmese jungle. A phalanx of Allied soldiers stood to attention in a dusty clearing as a Japanese officer saluted a victorious British colonel, the latter looking down at an exquisite sword held in his upturned hands. A captain from the US Marine Corps stood next to the general, flown in from an aircraft carrier in the Andaman Sea to organize the repatriation of American prisoners of war.

Despite the sword's military scabbard and remodeled hilt, Kuro knew the *katana* blade had been in his family for generations, forged from the purest carbon-tempered steel by Yoshi the Sword Maker in 1804.

To the stern-faced general in the photograph, the sword represented humility in defeat, but to Kuro's grandfather it signified the death of a samurai and eternal shame and dishonor. Beneath the aging snapshot, the caption read, "Following the Japanese surrender in Burma, Major Sukiyabashi, Imperial Army, offers his sword to Colonel J. C. Douglas, 14th Army, as Captain J. J. Larsson, US Marine Corps, looks on."

- 49 -

Penny stoked the embers and threw more driftwood on the fire. The flames twisted and curled, leaping like sprites into the night, ravishing the tinder-dry logs, which crackled, popped and wheezed as the ocean crashed on the beach. Jessica lay asleep on a blanket unfurled on the powdery yellow sand, the amber glow dancing across her face, emphasizing the child's perfect form.

"Look at her, Hans," Penny whispered. "She's so beautiful."

"Exhausted too."

Hans took a gulp of rum from the bottle and washed it down with beer.

"That was probably the skinny-dipping." Penny elbowed him in the ribs. "If there's such a thing as utopia, this must be it."

"Agreed." Hans kissed the top of her head as she lay against him. "But with a fire like that, I think it's *you* Tarzan, *me* Jane."

"A girl's gotta know her stuff, Jane."

"I loved those movies as a kid. You're probably too young to remember."

"I think we just got the cartoon."

"Saturday mornings . . . in black and white." Hans smiled in the darkness. "Johnny Weissmuller. Hell, he was my hero."

"Johnny . . . ?"

"Weissmuller – a German immigrant. Real good swimmer. Won five Olympic golds, so MGM signed him to play the part. Man!"

"What?"

"Ah, he was just the greatest role model a kid could have – handsome, muscular, fearless and loyal, and *boy* could he swim! Used to do these underwater sequences in crystal-clear African rivers. So beautiful – the scenery, sunken logs and weeds and gigantic fish. Tarzan and Jane would swim along holding their breath like they didn't have a care in the world. And there'd always be a crocodile attack. Tarzan loved all the animals except crocodiles. Used to stab them with his bush knife – especially when they tried to eat Jane."

"He kind of reminds me of someone." Penny wriggled against Hans' chest.

"I'm serious."

"I know you are."

"No, I'm serious when I say I developed a love of the water from this guy. When I snorkeled off Maine looking for lobster and crab and spearing fish, I *was* Tarzan. I wanted to live like him."

"Hans, I don't think a girl's ever told you this, but you do live like him! Don't you see it? You got a daughter who thinks you can do no wrong – you'd fight crocodiles for her. Anybody can see that."

"It's funny, because you know the best thing about this guy?"

"He . . . cooked a wicked jungle omelet?" Penny noticed a slight slur in Hans' speech.

"Ha, no. He had an adopted son, called him Boy. Tarzan loved this kid – would do anything for him – and the kid loved Tarzan. It was like the meaning of life playing out before your eyes. Hell, I woulda named my son Tarzan."

"Why didn't y—?" Penny froze.

Hans kissed her cheek. "He was named after his great grandpa. Jacob Johan Larsson. If there was ever a real-life Tarzan, he was it."

"Go on." Penny felt like reaching for another beer but didn't want to ruin the moment.

"He was an officer in the Marine Corps. Fought in the Far East campaign and Korea. Real character. Always up at five and out running along the shore. Swam in the sea every day without fail. I asked him why once and he said, 'It makes me feel good, son.'"

"Sounds more of a father figure."

"And the rest, Penny. I stayed with him a lot as a kid – kinda beat being at home. He lived to eighty-three. Doctors said he woulda lasted longer if it wasn't for the liquor."

"He liked a drink?"

"Up at dawn and the first thing he did was take a shot of rum." Hans lifted the bottle and swirled the inch of amber liquid around. "He was old school. *Marine* Corps! No such thing as an alcohol problem. Nothing you can't fix with jogging pants and a good ol' sweat session."

"Did he want you to join the military?"

"No, just the opposite. He'd have these reunions. Like every year his old Marine buddies would turn up at the house. They'd spoil me rotten, tell me stories about my grandpa's heroics, like the time he carried one of his injured corporals twelve miles back to base at the Chosin Reservoir."

"Bet he got a medal for that."

"He had medals all right."

Hans stopped talking and took a swig of rum.

"You okay?"

"Yeah, fine."

They listened to the sound of waves raking the beach and spits coming from the fire.

"The reunions," Hans continued, "always started the same. Busting out the beers and 'Hey, what about the time we took that ridge?' or such and such a place. And loads of 'Oorah!' Then as the evening went on it would be 'Do you remember Hanson . . . and Kowolski . . . and Bradsell?' and the tears would start."

That's so sad." Penny locked fingers with his.

"Grown men crying like babies."

"Hans, it's . . . just awful."

"One time, after his buddies left I heard my grandpa weeping, so I went into his room. He just hugged me – like *really* hugged me. Then he pulled an old trunk full of military paraphernalia from under his bed and handed me this sword – a Japanese sword. I remember it like yesterday: seeing my reflection in the buffed steel, little clouds scrolling down it, so sharp after forty years my grandpa made sure I didn't touch the blade. He asked me what I saw. I said, 'A sword, Grandpa.' He said, 'I watched Colonel Douglas take this from a Jap at a camp in Burma – men suffering all kind of hideous diseases, festering wounds, animal bites and malnutrition so bad you could circle their thighs with your thumb and forefinger.'"

Penny shuddered. Her late grandfather served in the war as a civil engineer on the London docks, but other than stepping over the body of a dead firefighter during the Blitz, he certainly hadn't experienced such trauma.

"He said, 'That sword is every life ever ruined by war, son. Souls so haunted they can't never be repaired. Old men seeing faces of dead comrades in their sleep, laughing and acting the fool, then blown to smithereens, guts wrapped around trees. That Jap officer, he was this sword. Losing it was worse than losing his legs – and for what, son?"

"Wow, heavy stuff for a kid."

"Yeah, but the crazy thing is, somewhere over there in Japan there's probably a grandson telling the other side of the story."

When they met Al Mohzerer outside Old Man Ali's carpet shop, the majority of the hashish still sat under the tarp on the pickup's cargo bed. Driving through the city's hectic traffic, Al Mohzerer gripped the steering wheel like a maniac, hunching forward and scowling at the other road users. Unusually stressed, he maintained his normal silence and let the truck's horn do the talking.

Without warning the boss wrenched the wheel over, leaving the thoroughfare to shoot up a slip road marked "Harbor."

A feeling of dread descended on the boys.

Al Mohzerer must have a contact in the port authority.

Their exploits were about to be exposed.

Ahmed pictured the scene in his mind: the Grower bundling them into an office, men in uniform sat around leering. "Yes, these are the boys, *sayyid*. They've been coming here every month to learn about sailing and making a damn nuisance of themselves."

The young Moroccan racked his brain trying to remember if either of them had mentioned their escape plan to any of the yacht crews they had met. He felt sure he hadn't but couldn't be certain about Mohamed. *You idiot!* he cursed silently, his mind in turmoil, not for a moment considering Mohamed was thinking the same thing.

In the small of his back, Ahmed could feel his sheath knife. The second Al Mohzerer tried to get smart with them he would whip it out and stab it into the Grower's neck as fast as humanly possible and not stop stabbing until the life drained from the evil pig's eyes.

He began nudging Mohamed, but his friend did not acknowledge him, and Ahmed worried the little fool was oblivious to their predicament.

Unbeknown to Ahmed, Mohamed was all too aware their lives might be about to end. He was just petrified their hawklike boss would spot any signal passed between them and remained frozen in his seat.

Approaching the harbor office, they both felt certain this was it, but Al Mohzerer drove right past without so much as a glance, his eyes fixed on the far end of the T-shaped dock. He pulled to a stop a foot from the edge of the concrete, yanked the parking brake and cut the engine. Then the Grower got out, lit a cigarette and began staring out to sea.

The boys breathed a small sigh of relief.

"What's going on?" Mohamed whispered.

"I don't know. He must be waiting for a boat."

Sure enough a yacht approached the harbor wall the likes of which the boys had never seen, timbers shining like the setting sun and sails the color of emeralds – and then it hit them!

- 51 -

Hans carried a sleeping Jessica aboard *Future*, careful not to lose his footing as the yacht bobbed under his weight in the floodlit marina's powder-blue water. He would love to have remained on the beach with Penny, sipping beer and talking about anything and everything, but both knew foreign shorelines are not safe places for tourists at night. He tucked the little girl into her bunk and returned to the yacht's spacious lounge to flop down on the maroon leather seating at the dining table.

"Here." Penny handed him a steaming mug of hot chocolate laced with scotch. "Is she okay?"

"Land of Nod." He smiled. "You really have a way with her, Penny. It's appreciated."

"The pleasure's all mine, Hans."

"There's not something you're hiding from me, is there? Ten kids stashed away on a boat in England."

Penny stared into her nightcap for a moment. "Actually, there is . . ."

Unable to tell if Penny was joking, a feeling of unease churned in Hans' stomach.

"I was pregnant once." She picked at a fingernail. "You remember the guy I told you about? The one I crewed for in the Caribbean?"

"Mr. Family Man."

Penny nodded and bit her lip. "I only found out after

226

we parted company. It was awful. I was stuck in Miami waiting to meet my next client for a five-month trip to Polynesia. I didn't know what to do – couldn't exactly go to sea with morning sickness and knew I wouldn't get any support from Mr. Cheater."

"Couldn't your parents help?"

"Mum and Dad would have supported me no matter what, but they'd already downsized their beloved yacht to put me through uni and then gracefully accepted me going back to sea. How was I supposed to tell them I'd messed it all up?"

"You terminated the pregnancy?"

Penny buried her face in her hands and began to cry.

"Oh, honey, I'm sorry." Hans pulled Penny close and pressed his cheek against her hair.

"It's okay. I wanted to tell you before, but there was never a right time. I found a clinic in Florida, handed over a load of my savings, told myself I wouldn't look back."

"Penny, you made a decision all by yourself in tough circumstances. You did what you had to do."

"I thought I was fine, Hans. You know, big tough girl. But . . ."

"Let me get you a tissue."

Hans got up and rummaged in the galley drawers. He returned with a pack of Kleenex.

"Thank you." Penny dabbed at her eyes. "I went on a hen night in London with a load of old mates – you know, a hen night?"

"Bachelorette party."

"Ah, that figures. Well, the head bridesmaid arranged for us to visit a fortune-teller – before we hit a club and got hammered." Penny forced a smile. "I thought, why not? Never believed in that kind of thing, but what harm could it do? The woman stares into her crystal ball and says, 'I see water,' so my attention picks up. She says a few more things that make sense and then drops a bombshell. 'I see a baby . . . a baby girl . . . and she's telling me to tell you it's all right and not to worry because she'll always be with you.'"

"You're kidding me! I thought they weren't supposed to tell you bad stuff?"

"So did I. For the first time it really hit me – that there was a tiny human being destined to be born into the world that I should have been attached to for life."

Hans kissed the top of her head and poured another shot into their mugs.

"Penny, she shouldn't have said that. She was taking advantage and stabbing in the dark."

"I know, Hans, but it dug up something I thought I'd dealt with. *Mean* old witch!" Penny managed another smile.

"Listen, we've all made tough choices in the past – you know, the best we could at the time. But I don't ever wanna hear you question yourself again, because . . ." Hans paused, his eyes welling up. "You're so goddamn good with my daughter."

"Oh, Hans, you're being—"

"No!" He cupped Penny's wet cheeks. "You came to us when the only reason I still lived was for her. And she didn't know which way was up or down, and I could only do so much to help. You've changed that, Penny. If you hadn't been through what you did, we would never have met, and you sure as hell might not be such an angel."

Penny appreciated Hans' honesty, relieved she no longer held a secret from him, but there was still an elephant in the room.

Hans checked on Jessica, then filled the kettle for another drink. His back to Penny, but sensing her thoughts, "The Concern," he said quietly.

"Huh?"

"You asked if what happened was to do with my work." He poured boiling water over the cocoa powder. "Some of my work is for a syndicate called the Concern."

"Is it a charity or something?"

"In a roundabout way." Hans set the mugs down on *Welcome to Plymouth!* coasters but remained standing. "You know if I tell you this stuff I might have to kill you?"

"We've all got to die sometime," Penny joked, feeling relieved the mood had lightened.

"No, seriously, nothing we do is untoward. We might bend the rules on occasions, but that's what rules are for, right?"

"Really, Mr. Larsson? I would never have guessed that about you."

"Ha!" Hans smiled somewhat bashfully and tugged his earlobe. "You know about the Masons, right?"

"Of course."

"It's a similar setup, but without the rituals, superstition and nepotism. Do you remember about five years ago Amy Falmer's disappearance in Colombia?"

"Wasn't she kidnapped while backpacking on a gap year? Got rescued by American special forces from some degenerate bandit group."

"FARC guerrillas. Her father was a big name on Wall

Street and agreed to pay the ransom, but the FARC have a record of accepting payoffs and executing the hostage anyway – or keeping them in a cage in the jungle until they die of some godforsaken disease. They shot the intermediary dead and retreated deep into the interior, and then a week later Amy turns up at the American embassy in Bogota, claiming to have been rescued by US military – least that's what was reported on CNN. No one questioned it publically because the Colombian government couldn't confess to having no clue about it, and Washington wouldn't risk an international incident by admitting the mission had been carried out by a civilian group. Besides, politically speaking it was a good result all round."

"And you're saying it was . . . ?"

"The Concern."

"Hans, how did you get involved in this?" Penny realized she had stopped yawning.

"I'd solved a few high-profile cases in Maine – missing persons, a bank heist the police drew a blank on – and some stuff abroad. Media went all out with 'ex–Navy SEAL, blah, blah, blah,' and I received a phone call."

"From who?"

"My proposer, who later became my control."

"Jeez, Hans, sounds like blue pill, red pill."

Hans smiled. "It would take ages to explain."

"Good!" Penny jumped up. "We've got all night, so start from the beginning." She grabbed Hans' arm and steered him to the seat, then pulled two beers from the fridge.

"The voice on the line says, 'Remember Tromans,

Glazebrook and Munroe' – three of my team who drowned in Sierra Leone – 'then meet me tomorrow in Boston.' How could I not meet him? So we're sitting on a park bench like Cold War spies, and Muttley says—"

"Muttley?"

"Yeah. Depending on your role in the organization, you're allocated an identifier. The controls are named after movie or TV sidekicks – Sundance, Robin, Boo-Boo, you know – the operatives, figures in Greek mythology."

"And you are?"

"Orion."

"Why does that not surprise me?"

"So anyway, this suited white-haired guy says he works for some kind of benevolent organization funded by stinking-rich businesspeople. Says they employ ex-service personnel, and my name had been put forward. When I asked about Sierra Leone, he said it was insider knowledge and gave me a few days to think about it."

"So if you accepted the role you would find out what happened to your team."

"Seemed that way, only I clocked a copy of *Metro* in his briefcase – the free subway newspaper. So I boxed around to the nearest station and, sure enough, he appeared and I tailed him home."

"You really are Jason Bourne."

"The next evening I'm sat in his apartment waiting to welcome him through the door and knowing he was Innes Edridge, an investment banker with Sachs. Naturally, I demanded some answers. He said that after Vietnam there were a lot of upset folks who had put their lives and reputations on the line for America, while others exploited the war effort – CIA operatives importing heroin, companies profiting from both sides, politicians playing the war game to suit their own aims. Turns out some of these unhappy people used their business connections and military skills to expose a few of the bad guys. Others were invited to join the cause, and things grew from there."

"What kind of others?"

"Good people with a track record of getting things done. Could be a doctor in Malawi or an airline owner willing to fly a team around the world at short notice. Passports, visas, a safe house in Europe – there's always someone in the Concern with either the means or the connection. You just never know who they are until you need to."

"Sounds real Illuminati."

"No, it's not about power, control or a new world order, just a global network defending the rights of those who aren't in a position to do it themselves. People like me get to put our skill sets to use out in the field and feel like we do some good in the world. The fat cats get to donate some of their ridiculous profits while playing John Wayne cum Mother Teresa from the comfort of their office chairs."

"I would have thought the fat cats were part of the problem."

"Every now and again there's a clash of interest or someone needs bringing into line, but it gets sorted."

"And Sierra Leone?"

"It was common knowledge the conflict was fueled by blood diamonds. Muttley said it went all the way to the Washington, someone the Concern had had their sights on for some time. That person saw to it we were delayed getting off the choppers, attempting to make us abort the mission so the West Side Boys could escape into the forest and continue to make them and their cronies rich – or richer. Wasn't it Chomsky who said, to find the motivation behind conflict you follow the money trail?"

"And where did it lead?"

"It led to a guy . . . I can't say more."

"And?" Penny took a sip of beer.

"How do my wife and son fit into this?"

"Hans . . . I . . ."

"If you work for the Concern, you get to deal with some pretty sick people in god-awful places around the world. Life can be cheap, and there are no limit to the lengths some of these folks will go to protect their slice of the pie. Every once in a while it goes horribly wrong." Hans' face darkened.

"It's getting late." Penny downed her drink. "Let's continue this tomorrow."

Container SIDU307007-9 had been drifting in the North Atlantic for months, along with its charge of high-tech televisions. Floating flush with the sea's surface, it was every sailor's worst nightmare, one resulting in many a crew evacuating to a life raft.

A lengthy hearing exonerated the captain of the *Tokyo Pride* on charges of sailing with improperly secured cargo. In truth, many large vessels put to sea with serious safety issues. To penalize every company would effectively render global trade untenable, so chalking up such incidents to within a generous margin of error had become the norm. Besides, how often did a force ten gale whip up the North Atlantic in April?

The majority of the trip went without a hitch, the container ship docking in Singapore and Yemen before negotiating the Suez Canal to stop again in Gibraltar. A few of the mostly Filipino crew took advantage of the docking to have their photographs taken with the Rock's infamous apes and buy cheap liquor and cigarettes, but the majority crashed in their bunks, catching up on sleep and saving their hard-earned cash to send home to loved ones.

It was in the North Atlantic en route from Le Havre to Boston that the ship ran into difficulties. An unpredicted low swung in from the Arctic, colliding with weather moving up from the Azores. With her shallow keel, the

Tokyo Pride took on a frightening roll, plunging to starboard like a demented beast. Plates, cutlery and food flew sideways across the galley, seasickness running rife as waves towered above the bridge.

The stresses resulting from a badly loaded manifest proved too much for the weaker containers, three of them crumpling like tin cans and causing the stack to lurch sideways, shearing off fittings designed to withstand forty-ton strains.

Had the storm abated, the *Pride* could have limped into port with all her goods, but it was not to be. Despite the captain's best efforts, a final pitch sent containers spilling into the ocean and SIDU307007-9 on its lonely voyage.

- 53 -

The next day, as Penny made final preparations for her change of plan, Hans and Jessica replaced *Future*'s worn fittings and took her for a sea trial.

A strong northeasterly carried them ten miles offshore in little over an hour, the genoa billowing up front like a huge white kite. The sun lowering to the horizon, Hans brought *Future* about, the impending darkness not the only reason he looked forward to reaching port.

Jessica sat on the cabin roof whittling a piece of driftwood into a point with her pocketknife, the gift from Old Bill.

"What's the number one rule when using a knife, First Mate?"

"You must never hold the blade toward you, Papa."

"Good! Now get ready for bed." Hans took the knife and put it in his pocket, lowering the junior officer into the cockpit and smiling as she scampered inside.

On Cape Verde, Penny called her parents from a telephone in the yacht club and checked her email and online bank statement. She stocked up on toiletries from the marina's convenience store, then headed for a nearby bazaar, delighted to find a pair of leather sandals with soles fashioned from used car tires for Hans – with his pragmatic nature, he would love them – and a wine-red sarong printed with gold seahorses for Jessica.

With time to kill, she took a seat in Salgadeiras, a café bar overlooking the marina, ordered a coffee and took up her book. Unable to concentrate, she scanned the horizon every few seconds, a pleasant tingling sensation rushing around her body.

Jessica played with Bear in the cabin, opening the emergency ditch kit and pretending the teddy was lost at sea.

"In you go, Bear." She popped him in a locker. "And you have to take these so you can be rescued and make some water."

She placed the EPIRB beacon, VHF radio and water desalinator next to him, along with a packet of fishing hooks and a bundle of energy bars, letting out a healthy yawn as she did.

Hans ducked into the cabin – "Bedtime for you, young girl" – dashing back out as *Future* made impressive headway.

Jessica sighed and dragged the heavy bag back to the companionway. Clutching Bear, she climbed into her bunk, the emergency equipment in the locker no longer a concern in her tired mind. She tugged off her sandals and pulled a blanket over the two of them.

"And Bear, you *always* gotta clip on your safety line."

She fastened the aluminum G-clip to the bunk's rail and drifted off to sleep.

Hans prided himself on *Future*'s progress, her replacement gear holding fast as she skimmed across the wave tops at eight knots.

Container SIDU307007-9 floated at 16° 15' north, 25° 40' west, directly in the path of the yacht.

The Drift

At 1831 hours, Hans felt relaxed, content with the direction his boat and life were heading, all the time looking forward to their reunion with Penny.

At 1832 hours, with a sickening crunch Hans' boat and life ripped apart. Slammed face-first into the control panel, he knew instinctively *Future* was about to sink.

- 54 -

"**Y**ou're late, cousin!" Al Mohzerer snapped, as the leader of the four pirates staggered from the beautiful boat and climbed the dockside ladder.

"What is an hour?" the man replied, spitting on the concrete.

In cutoff denim shorts and a dirty New York Yankees vest, he was clearly drunk and unused to receiving lectures.

"Did you find the money?"

"Just the timepiece." The pirate flashed the thirty-thousand-dollar watch, which looked completely out of place on his skinny brown wrist. "We searched the boat thoroughly and cannot find the cash."

"Give!" Al Mohzerer took the Cartier. "We load, and we will look again in the morning."

On the Grower's command, the boys sprung from the vehicle and, with a cruel mix of relief and bitter disappointment, began peeling back the tarpaulin. A second man passed a rope and bucket up the ladder, and they commenced the soul-destroying task of transferring the golden blocks to the beautiful wooden yacht.

"Now we drink," announced the leader. "For we have business and family to discuss."

He barked an order at the youngest bandit, who would stay on board to guard the product.

Now that the hashish was secure, Al Mohzerer

lightened up, becoming almost jovial as the prospect of looming wealth intoxicated him. There would be no problem from the port authority, whose officials would all get a cut, and, returning early the next day with crowbars, the gang would rip apart the cabin's exquisite cherrywood paneling and find the cash. Although with half a ton of prime merchandise sold for top whack in the Canaries, a few thousand euros going undiscovered was not a major issue.

- 55 -

Sitting in Salgadeiras, Penny no longer nursed a coffee – her fourth cup empty bar frothy brown dregs – but a double vodka and Coke. The previous shivers of anticipation had turned to waves of stone-cold dread. It was dark, and Hans and Jessica were four hours overdue.

She had been to the marina office twice to see if Hans had radioed in to report a delay. He had not, only a brief transmission on departure giving an approximate route and anticipated return time, and another providing coordinates as *Future* swung about and headed for port. It simply wasn't like him. He and Jessica only took the yacht out for a short trip to test her new fittings, and if there was one man in the world that arrived at a specified time, that man was Hans Larsson.

Penny visited the marina office a third time, demanding they alert the coastguard to initiate a search. Baba, the Senegalese manager, looked relaxed in smart knee-length white chinos and a dark-blue polo shirt with the marina's tall ships logo on the breast. "Miss Penny" he said softly, placing a gentle brown hand on her arm. "I have spoken to the coastguard, and both he and I have alerted all the vessels in the area. But they will not commence a search unless a Mayday has been broadcast or an EPIRB signal picked up."

"May I speak with the coastguard . . . please?"

Baba tapped a number into a roamer telephone and, after a brief discussion with a coastguard official, handed it to her, the ensuing conversation only reiterating the futility of her request.

Damn!

Penny hit the "Call End" key, feeling the way concerned family members must do when, completely out of character, a loved one goes missing and the police refuse to take action before forty-eight hours have elapsed.

"Baba, may I use your Internet?"

"Of course, Miss Penny. Take all the time you need."

He rolled back a chair at an empty desk looking out over the yachts.

Penny flashed up Google and typed "Innes Edridge," "Goldman Sachs," and "Boston" into the search bar, the inverted commas refining the results.

Several hundred pages returned, many detailing Edridge's staff profile, achievements and accolades but none giving a direct telephone number, only one for head office.

Penny opened her purse and pulled out a calling card, wishing she had bought more credit or owned a cell phone, something she previously prided herself on avoiding.

"Miss Penny, you wish to make a call?" Baba asked softly.

"Um."

"Please, please." Baba handed her the phone once more. "Just type this account number followed by the hash key first."

Penny could have hugged this sensitive man but instead dialed the number in Boston.

"Goldman Sachs, Carole speaking. How may I help?"

"My name is Penny Masters. May I speak to Innes Edridge please?"

"I'm sorry, Penny. Innes doesn't take outside calls. Would you like to leave a message or request he call you back?"

"Please, this is *really* important. Could you tell him it's a matter of . . . *Concern?*"

Seconds passed, and Penny worried if she was doing the right thing. *To hell with it!*

"Innes Edridge." The voice sounded courteous and British with a refined Scots burr. "How may I be of assistance?"

Penny hesitated for a second, fixating on the small red diamond in the Lexmark badge on the marina's gray plastic printer before playing what she hoped was her trump card.

"Muttley, Orion is missing."

"Oh dear me! Now *that's* not good news. Listen, Penny, I'm going to ask you some questions. I need you to answer as accurately as you can – no guessing. Do you understand?"

"Of course."

Penny was impressed. In quick-fire succession Muttley ascertained her personal details, including national insurance, passport and driving license numbers, her possessions and funds and contacts on Cape Verde. He then made a record of places, timings, communications, yacht specifications and onboard equipment, Hans and Jessica's moods, their last meal and drinks, any medication or drugs they may have consumed, and recent events of interest, such as disagreements with other sailors or unusual financial transactions.

"Listen, my dear Penny, we will be arriving at . . ." Penny could hear Edridge typing while listening to a voice giving instructions via loudspeaker on another line. "0800 hours at São Pedro airport. You can meet us there, or we will come to you."

"B-b-but, how will you know where I am?"

"My dear Penny, we know who you are and where you are. Don't worry yourself about that. Go back to Salgadeiras and wait for instructions, and we'll come and find Orion."

Back to Salgadeiras?

As Penny thanked Baba, who held out a reserved hand that immediately morphed into a bear hug, she wondered how Muttley knew about the café.

A double vodka and coke awaited her on the bar. "Er . . ." She fumbled in her daypack for her purse.

"It's okay, Miss Penny." The barman's eyes glinted. "It's taken care of. And a car will pick you up in twenty minutes."

"A car?"

"Your hotel."

"Oh."

56

Traveling back to the mountain in the rear of the truck, Mohamed kept quiet, knowing better than to bother Ahmed, who stared at his feet, trying to come up with a plan. Instead he leaned against the rear window, attempting to eavesdrop on the conversation inside.

As the city's urban sprawl gave way to lush green countryside and the Rif's distant rock faces glowed pink in the sunset, the first police checkpoint came into view, the officers searching for contraband coming from Europe. Used to the police waving them through, the boys were surprised when the Grower pulled over and struck up a conversation with the senior rank. Mohamed saw a fist-sized nugget of hashish change hands, two junior officers running over to place a box of Red Label whiskey in the back of the pickup, along with a crate of beer and five cartons of Marlboro.

Naseem continued a quarter of a mile down the road and stopped the truck again.

"Give." He jerked his head at the box of whiskey.

Mohamed slid it across the cargo bed. Naseem ripped open the cardboard and retrieved a bottle.

"Boy, he's in a good mood," Mohamed muttered, Ahmed still lost in thought.

Halfway up the mountain, the men polished off another bottle and opened a third. Laughter filled the cab as Al Mohzerer blasted around the brutal bends, the boys grimacing and clinging on for dear life. On the final left-hander it was obvious the boss was going too fast. The pickup's six-liter diesel revved ever higher, the cargo bed shuddering as the tires kicked up gravel.

Misjudging the angle, Al Mohzerer attempted to compensate by throwing the wheel over, which swung the back end out, sending the pickup into a terrifying slide toward the cliff edge. Mohamed screamed and grabbed Ahmed's arm, both instinctively ducking and bracing for the roll down the mountainside.

At the last second the drunken Naseem wrenched the wheel to the right. For an eternity a tire hung thousands of feet above the valley floor before digging into the shoulder as the pickup straightened and Naseem regained control.

Arriving at the farm, Ahmed and Mohamed clambered down from the truck, both fearing their legs would give way.

"I'm going to be sick." Mohamed clung to his friend.

Ahmed did not reply. He too had a metallic taste in his mouth.

Never so pleased to see the hut, Ahmed slammed the door behind them, muffling the sound of laughter echoing around the courtyard. Mohamed lay down and was about to say something but drifted off to sleep.

57

Penny sat in Salgadeiras sipping her drink, peering at the ocean's darkened horizon as the dulcet tones of Cesária Évora crooned from speakers above the bar. A sleek-lined Mercedes pulled up, the café's rainbow lighting reflecting off the vehicle's polished black paintwork. A young and smartly suited mestizo stepped out and made a beeline for her.

"Good evening, madam. I am Paulo, and your transport is here."

He led her to the car and ushered her into the backseat.

Lying back against sumptuous leather with the air conditioning sobering her thoughts but leaving them confused, Penny wondered what part the driver played in the global shenanigans.

After a while, "Are you with the Concern?" she tendered.

"Concern, madam?" The driver's greeny-brown eyes squinted in the rearview mirror. "I'm with the chauffeur company."

Penny felt stupid and wished she hadn't asked.

They drove north along the coast road for a quarter of a mile. Penny screwed her hands together, craning over her shoulder every few seconds to scan the blackened seascape.

"Er, are we going far?" She sensed her element of control sapping with every yard and wished she were back at the café bar.

"We are here, madam." The chauffeur tapped the windshield, pointing out an impressive pastel-cream-stone building jazzed up with stainless steel and glass. Set apart from far less striking contenders by tropical trees and scrub, it was tiered back against the hillside like an Aztec pyramid. "The Grande Verde."

After turning off the highway, Paulo headed up a palm-lined boulevard, the improvement in road surface immediately apparent as the Mercedes' tires purred against the smooth tarmac. He pulled up by an impressive floodlit fountain in front of the hotel. A woman wearing a dark-blue dress suit and jade cravat and heels stepped forward and opened the car door, introducing herself as Branca, the concierge. From Branca's olive complexion and nasal tones, Penny guessed she was of Portuguese descent. A porter approached, but Penny held up her small daypack containing the toiletries she had bought at the marina's convenience store, and Hans' sandals and Jessica's sarong, then smiled and politely waved her hand.

Branca led her under a gold chrome surround and through a smoked-glass revolving door into what had to be the most magnificent lobby she had ever seen – a white marble floor inlaid with black, purple and blue Arabic-pattern mosaics, natural stone walls, an abundance of mahogany, and burnished-leather seating surrounding a gently bubbling pool of brightly colored koi.

Penny's passport was aboard *Future*, not an issue as

Branca chaperoned her toward a futuristic elevator that spoke better English than she did. As they ascended, Branca engaged her in polite chitchat, letting slip enough information to reassure Penny she knew of the yacht's disappearance and that moves were in place to set a search in motion.

Penny assumed she would be ushered into a single room with a view out over scrub and rocks. When the elevator's digital readout climbed through one to twelve and rolled over onto "P," the electronic female voice announcing "Penthouse suite," Penny shot Branca a look.

"Penthouse? Am I really in the penthouse?"

"Oh, Miss Mast— Sorry, *Penny*. Your friends have booked out the penthouse and half of the floor below."

"Er . . ." Penny struggled to find words. Everything suddenly seemed surreal, and she had to remind herself this was about Hans and Jessica and not some exotic vacation she had won in a competition.

Sensing Penny's distress, Branca took her hand and, with a sincere smile of her perfectly painted lips, said, "Don't worry. We look after our special accounts."

To take Penny's mind off the situation, Branca gave her a tour of the suite. Palatial would be an understatement. They passed through a vast lounge furnished in chesterfield leather, Persian rugs covering a rich wooden floor, a seventy-inch television and vividly painted abstracts by Figueira hanging on walls papered in Jean-Paul Charles, to enter a kitchen fitted with state-of-the-art equipment, two fully stocked refrigerators and a touch screen for ordering specific items or ingredients.

"So much technology!" Branca joked as she

demonstrated how to scroll through the electronic menu.

Beneath a crystal chandelier, the dining room's French-polished table was large enough to entertain twenty people, and, as if this were not decadence enough, Branca led her past a bar circuited by optics, wines and snacks and into a cinema, complete with reclining chairs and a popcorn machine. Penny's mind flicked to the opera they'd enjoyed in Plymouth. She shuddered at the thought of watching a movie alone.

"Feeling fit?"

Branca attempted to keep the mood light as she showed Penny a gymnasium packed with fitness apparatus and a virtual running machine. Penny managed a half smile, exercise the last thing on her mind.

A swish office and computer station fronted a conference room with video linkups and interactive presentation board. A poolroom offered additional options of game consoles, roulette, a cards table and darts. Four spacious bedrooms enjoyed spectacular ocean views, one of which accessed a glittering master bathroom tiled in gold-flecked charcoal, with an adjoining wet room and sauna, and a hot tub nestled amongst tropical flora on its veranda.

"Fit for King Midas," Penny murmured.

"Ah yes." Branca thought for a moment. "But – how you say? *Gilt* plate, no?" Stepping back into the bedroom, "Penny, I took the liberty of ordering you some essentials." Branca nodded to an emperor-size bed on which lay a neatly arranged spread of toiletries, pajamas, flip-flops and a prepaid cell phone. "And if you come down to the boutique in the morning you can pick out some fresh clothes. I've asked our on-call doctor to pop up in case you need something to help you sleep. I'll leave you to settle in, and if there is anything else you require – or even just to chat to someone – dial reception and Michelle, our night manager, will be happy to assist. You'll like Michelle. I've informed her of the situation."

"B-b-but, I-I . . ." Penny burst into tears and collapsed on the huge mattress.

"*Calma, amiga.* You're in good hands and everything's going to be fine."

The hug couldn't have come at a better time.

When Branca left, Penny attempted to pull herself together, once again reminding herself this was about Hans and Jessica and that she needed to be on the ball. First, in a symbolic gesture, she hung Jessica's sarong up on a hanger in the warehouse-sized wardrobe, placing Hans' sandals on the rack below. Then, realizing she hadn't eaten a thing since breakfast, she went to the refrigerator, but just the thought of her last meal with Hans and Jessica saw her dissolve into tears once more. Spying shelves packed with smoked meats, caviar, foie gras and other delicacies, she slammed the door and went to the bar. She grabbed an ice-cold bottle of beer, then slid open the doors to the balcony and stepped outside.

The warm air provided a welcome break from the hotel's sterile air-conditioned atmosphere, and as Penny gazed out over the uninterrupted view of the ocean, she prayed that one of the many lights bobbing upon it belonged to *Future*. Unbeknown to her, the red, white and green navigation lights soaring out low over the sea were those of the coastguard's Dornier light aircraft as it raced toward *Future*'s last known coordinates.

To the far left of the vista, the marina edged into view, and on a whim Penny went back inside with the intention of calling reception to ask if, perchance, they had a set of binoculars. As her hand closed around the receiver, the telephone rang, giving her a start. It was the coastguard's office informing her they had received permission from a higher authority to initiate a search. A plane was in the air and liaising with the *Tatiania* – Cape Verde's patrol ship – as well as a Lynx helicopter from the British warship HMS *Fortitude*. In Creole tones, the woman on the line added that they had established communications with the United States Africa Command, based in Stuttgart, Germany, and moves were in place to coordinate NATO ships in the area to join in the pattern.

Penny put the phone down, breathed a sigh of relief and then downed the remaining beer. Her mind flicked to the conversation she had with Muttley little over an hour and a half ago.

Boy, these people work fast.

- 58 -

Hans stared at Mickey Mouse's smiling face. Jessica's souvenir beaker was one of the items that had floated to the surface as the yacht went down. Remembering better days, he bailed out the life raft and used his T-shirt to mop up the remaining brine.

Leaning out of the entrance, Hans screamed across the blue void, "We are a lively society that happens to be on this island!"

Zerbinetta's line from Strauss' *Ariadne auf Naxos*, one of his late wife's favorite operas, had become something of a family mantra, starting as a joke when they vacationed on Hawaii. Why he was shouting it now, Hans had no idea.

The raft consisted of two inflatable rubber tubes, one on top of the other, with a third narrower tube arching overhead to support the nylon canopy. Glued to the bottom of these was a rubberized groundsheet that undulated with the movement of sea like a seventies-kitsch waterbed. Around the inside of the tubes ran a canvas webbing strap to hold on to in bad weather and a series of nylon-mesh pockets to store equipment.

Hans was glad he had packed lightweight sleeping bags in the ditch kit. They now lay on top of the canopy, drying in the already intense morning rays. He hoped they would not need them again, that a local fishing vessel would pick them up before the morning was out, seeing them sleeping in clean and pressed hotel linen that night.

In reality, with the EPIRB and radio missing, the likelihood of a swift rescue was slim. They were already far from Cape Verde, and the trade winds blew them further out into the Atlantic every passing second. Their best hope lay in reaching the New York-to-South Africa shipping lanes far to the west, where a passing freighter might intercept their drift.

Hans made a mental inventory of their equipment and supplies. Water was a priority – moreover, the means to produce it. The raft came stocked with ten plastic-capped cans, a pint in each, and they had a gas can containing an additional gallon in the ditch kit. This should have been more than enough to last them until rescue had the goalposts not shifted. Now they would have to ration their reserve and rely upon the raft's solar power still to supplement it. Decanting a quarter of a pint of the precious commodity into the Disney mug, Hans wondered what had become of the hand-cranked desalinator and other items.

Sitting at *Future*'s helm during night watches, he'd run through the abandoning ship drill countless times in his mind. Unlike many sailors, who paid lip service to safety considerations, he knew from experience to prepare for every eventuality down to the last detail and that the best laid plans can still go awry – as had been the case when the yacht went down.

A calm and controlled evacuation was simply not possible when the hull ripped apart and several tons of seawater flooded the cabin. The idea of firing flares, broadcasting a Mayday, launching the life raft and then having time to load it with both crew and supplies would now have been laughable if the situation were not dire. Still stowed in the yacht's forepeak were their survival suits and a large Perspex box containing additional food, water, clothing and a comprehensive first aid kit. As for the expensive flare gun, it sat in a cupboard just inside the companionway, along with the cartridges. They would have to make do with what was in the ditch kit and equipment bag, along with the few bits and pieces from *Future* that had surfaced close enough to the raft for Hans to retrieve – the box containing Penny's jewelry-making kit and the cockpit's foam cushions among them.

The cushions proved invaluable. In his haste to board the raft, Hans had landed on the ditch kit, forcing a razor-edged filleting knife through its plastic scabbard and piercing several holes in the rubberized floor. Although not immediately life threatening, the punctures resulted in a permanent state of wetness, and the cushions kept him and Jessica above the worst of this.

"Etch A Sketch?" she whispered.

"No, no Etch A Sketch."

"Bleeding."

"Huh?"

Fingering his temple, Hans felt a deep gash, one requiring stitches – one not even superglue could fix. They had neither. His thoughts flicked to the vials of penicillin, syringes and sutures in the first aid kit lying on the ocean floor. In the tropics, seawater teamed with bacteria, and even the slightest cut turned septic within hours. He put this out of his mind, opened the ditch kit and returned to the inventory.

Assorted cordage of varying thicknesses, fishing gear, diving mask and snorkel, sea survival handbook, whistle, a week's worth of energy bars and snacks, the gallon can of water, a strobe light, duct tape, Silva compass, notepad and pens, ziplock plastic bags, chopping board, filleting knife, cigarette lighter and a few other essentials. In the equipment bag a basic first aid kit, seasickness tablets, hand pump, underwater drogue, ten-pint cans of water, miniature can opener, wooden paddle, signaling flares, sponge, foldout radar reflector, solar still, collapsible basin, hundred foot of rope, maritime charts, pencils, dividing compass, rudimentary directional compass, flashlight, signaling mirror, fishing line and single hook, and the raft's repair kit.

Basic navigation would be possible, though the thought depressed Hans. "Navigation" suggested control over one's destiny, something circumstance denied. He wished there had been enough time to grab the handheld GPS from the chart table drawer. He wished for many things.

"They're dead."

"I know."

"Are we gonna die too?"

"No, we're not."

Hans opened the repair kit and pondered how to fix the leaks in the floor. The rubber glue and patches would be no good, what with the punctures constantly hemorrhaging seawater.

Perhaps the quarter-inch-diameter screw-in aluminum plugs?

But that would mean boring out the holes in the groundsheet with a knife to ensure a snug fit, and if the plugs got the slightest knock – highly likely with all the movement aboard – they would rip out and unleash an even bigger flow. He resorted to placing the sponge over of the seeping slits and weighing it down with six cans of water lashed together with cord. It meant having to wring the sponge out every few minutes, but it was better than marinating in brine.

- 59 -

The Learjet came in fast and low on half flaps, just the tiniest puff of tire smoke as it made contact with the runway at São Pedro. Penny stood on the viewing balcony in the airport's other terminal, one reserved for VIPs, military and, in recent times, top-secret transit flights. She watched as the first four passengers disembarked – burly males dressed in black T-shirts, desert boots and beige fatigue pants, the kind of garb worn by private military contractors the world over – followed by a male and female in their thirties wearing smart causal clothes, and a white-haired man in a suit and an overcoat, despite the high heat. The group climbed into a people carrier with tinted glass, which, having been loaded with a large amount of luggage and plastic containers, made its way toward the arrivals area. She hurried down the stairs to greet them, wondering if life could get any crazier or this was all a dream.

The elderly gent spoke a few words to the immigration official, who waved them all through without so much a check of their passports.

Penny brazened herself and walked forward.

"My dear Penny." The man held out a bony hand blemished with liver spots. "I'm Innes. How are the sleeping arrangements?"

"Oh, you know. We all need to rough it now and

again."

"Exactly!"

Their laughter broke the tension.

In front of the terminal they transferred some of the gear to the hotel's Mercedes to make room in the people carrier for Penny, Edridge wishing to make use of every second of her presence to add to the intelligence portfolio.

"Oh, before I forget." Muttley reached inside his jacket. "This is for you." He handed her a crisp new passport. "Courtesy of the consulate general in Boston."

Although impressed with the speed and thoroughness of the operation, Penny worried this meant the Concern believed the yacht had gone down, taking her belongings with it.

Sensing her thoughts: "Don't worry, Penny. We're just covering our bases should we need to move somewhere fast."

As Penny stowed the travel document in her daypack, it occurred to her she hadn't provided and signed the required paperwork. The UK Passport Office must have authorized its issue immediately, supplying her signature and photograph held on file.

On the ensuing journey Penny learned that four of the men were former Navy SEALs, two of them having served with Hans, and that the nondescript man and woman were a surgeon and a medic. Between them the group spoke a number of languages, including Arabic, Portuguese and French.

"Nothing to be concerned about, my dear." Edridge could tell the personnel and equipment took Penny aback. He pulled on his shirt cuffs to square them. "But as we used to say in the Boy Scouts back in Scotland, it's best to be prepared."

Penny nodded vaguely.

"Don't worry, honey." One of the former SEALS, Phipps, gripped her shoulder with a gorilla-sized black hand. "If they're out there, we *will* find them."

Penny smiled and said thank you, her thoughts lingering on the latter statement.

Upon arrival at the Grande Verde, the team wasted no time in setting up laptops and other communication equipment to serve as a command center. What with the modern décor and bank of computer screens, Penny had a brief vision of the Starship *Enterprise*.

Edridge – "Muttley" – spent time on the telephone talking to the United States Africa Command. Clearly frustrated, he held his head down and gripped the folds in his immaculately pressed suit pants with a veiny hand. Having terminated the call, he whispered something to Phipps, who pursed his lips, shook his head and went back to scanning the grainy satellite images on his screen, downloaded at considerable expense from a private French company.

"Code Purple," Muttley muttered as he led Penny into another room for a second debrief.

"Purple?" She wondered if this was a good thing.

"Yes . . ." For the first time since they'd met, Muttley didn't look her in the eye. "Someone's putting pressure on the Pentagon to block our request for US military intervention. Code Purple means that for reasons of national security, no explanation need be offered."

Penny thought back to her conversation with Hans on

board *Future* two nights previous following their fire on the beach. Hadn't he said something about an undesirable in Washington? She kept quiet and was sure she heard Muttley swear under his breath.

By midafternoon the team had established communications with all the necessary agencies. They arranged for the printing of flyers and their distribution to yacht crews throughout the island group and shipping entering and leaving port, offering a reward of two hundred fifty thousand dollars for any information leading to the rescue of *Future*'s crew. Skippers of small craft joining the search would receive a thousand dollars an hour, five thousand for commercial vessels and the pilots of private aircraft.

Not surprisingly a veritable flotilla headed for the search area, along with a flight of twenty-plus planes, all coordinated by Phipps and his men over the radio and plotted on charts pasted to the command center's walls. The coastguard's plane now refueled a fourth time in preparation for another sortie, their patrol vessel continuing to sail a crisscross pattern. The British Lynx helicopter was down for routine maintenance but would be up flying again within the hour.

A website and Facebook page were set up to draw attention to, and share information about, the missing yacht, aimed at crews and shipping in the area and amateur radio enthusiasts. One such operator had already made contact to say he picked up a brief transmission of coordinates he believed to be from *Future* – quickly ruled out by the team, since the position was too far out into the Atlantic to correspond with the yacht's top speed.

Over the coming days messages offering well wishes and support bombarded the website. A psychic in Ireland saw the yacht knocked down by a rogue wave and its crew taking refuge on a tiny atoll. In view of there being no reefs remotely near *Future*'s last known position, and attempting to keep things in perspective, Muttley reminded her to be realistic, but it was yet another niggle in her overtired mind.

A leading public relations consultant in the US – "One of our own," Muttley said, winking – initiated a media campaign to raise the profile of the search, specifically targeting Cape Verde's news outlets and those in the Caribbean. Penny's jaw dropped when later in the day a report from RTC – Cape Verde's primary TV station – flashed up photographs of the missing crew that, although bearing a resemblance, were not the father and daughter she knew.

"You don't think we're going to show the face of one of our foremost agents to the world, do you, Penny?' said Muttley. 'It's a yacht or a life raft we're encouraging people to look out for. The identity of the crew is irrelevant."

An anonymous contributor to the website reported seeing Hans and Jessica in a restaurant in Guinea-Bissau. Phipps was right on the case, tracking the user's IP address to find it scrambled via a proxy server. It initiated yet another grave and hushed discussion between him and Muttley.

When *Yachting Life* ran a column detailing how a local fishing boat witnessed *Future*'s gas tank exploding, but was unable to provide a source for the information, Muttley took Penny to one side.

"Penny, it could well be that someone is attempting to sabotage our efforts. There's no logical explanation for a gas leak leading to an explosion in the galley. Hans doesn't smoke, and it's not as if he would be cooking a meal while single-handedly sailing the yacht, especially when they were due back in port in two hours. As for the sighting in Guinea Bissau, if Hans decided to disappear off into the sunset without informing anyone – which there is no evidence to suggest – then it would be for good reason. A reason known only to Orion."

"But, but . . ." Penny felt as though she had a million counter explanations, though attempting to formulate a coherent argument she realized they just weren't there.

Penny offered to undergo the harrowing task of contacting Hans' younger brother, Carl, in the States. They had not spoken before, bar friendly hellos yelled in the background of the brothers' cell phone conversations, but she figured such awful news better come from her rather than a complete stranger.

Carl remained surprisingly upbeat, thanking Penny profusely and stating firmly that "nothing will happen to *my* brother!" He offered to fly out right away, but Muttley suggested it was better Carl stayed in the US should either a rescued Hans or a concerned other party attempt to make contact.

"We've got weather!"

Clayton, one of the former SEALS, fixated on his laptop screen. A sophisticated map from an online company used by aircraft and shipping showed a full-color satellite image of the North Atlantic and, in particular, a ruddy-brown whirl indicating an area of low pressure sweeping in from Central Africa.

"Looks like a Cape Verde hurricane."

Penny ended the call and looked out of the window to see the palm fronds lining the Grande's immaculate boulevard swaying in the building gusts, the sky darkening and a metallic aura imbuing the atmosphere as lightning threatened and rain began to fall. She saw Muttley on another line at the far end of the room. Again, he shook his head, drumming his fingers on the tabletop, until all movement stopped and he sat looking at the floor.

He replaced the receiver slowly and, his stare unwavering, said, "Penny, shall we go for a walk?"

A banshee's wail built in the pit of her stomach. "Wh-wh-why . . . ?" she stammered.

"Oh, dear Penny! So sorry. I just thought you could do with some fresh air."

He picked up his overcoat and umbrella and, with one of his ever-gracious smiles, ushered her toward the door.

A wave slammed into the back of the raft, tilting it forward and sending its occupants tumbling across the floor.

Grabbing the webbing strap for support, Hans looked out to see black clouds building above an increasingly angry sea. Worse still, the raft had spun around, and the doorway now faced the approaching swell.

"It's okay!"

He attempted to zip up the entrance but was too late. The next wave surged up over the tubes to send gallons of water flooding into their recently dried home.

"No!"

Hans lunged for his daughter as the exiting sea attempted to suck her and their equipment bags into the cauldron. As the raft righted itself, stemming the outpour, he drew up the zippers to prevent further deluge.

Jessica stayed remarkably calm, floating around in what was now a foot-deep paddling pool. Ironically, the additional ballast gave the raft more stability, but the increased resistance meant the next wave crashing down on them would likely rip its seams apart. Fighting panic, Hans retrieved the drogue from one of the mesh compartments. When streamed underwater on its fifty-foot line, the device would create drag and reduce the risk of capsize.

The problem was he needed to secure it to the back of the raft to keep the entrance away from the oncoming sea. He considered dropping into the water and working his way aft while holding on to the exterior handline, but that could lead to catastrophe. The next big wave might wrench the raft from his grasp, sending it spinning away across the churning ocean.

What about the portal?

An air vent in the rear of the canopy doubled as an observation port. It had a drooping drawstring neck like an upturned duffel bag. Hans released the cord lock and pried the opening apart. He managed to force his head and one arm through, only to see another foaming behemoth bear down on the struggling craft.

Rather than withdraw inside, leaving a gaping hole for the ocean to exploit, Hans drew a deep breath. The seething mass broke upon them, collapsing the canopy and crushing Hans' torso into the top tube. Air spilled from his lungs, his head plunging underwater, until the muffled hiss of the raft's safety valves drowned out the noise of the building storm.

Silence.

Despite being seconds from unconsciousness, Hans felt his anxiety evaporating, leaving him with a surreal feeling of calm. He was tempted to suck in a lungful of the Atlantic, to reunite with his wife and son, but the image of his daughter alone in the raft spurred him on.

When the raft broke the surface, Hans wriggled back inside and, having checked Jessica was okay, undid the Velcro fastener on the neatly folded drogue and shoved it through the opening, making sure to keep a hold of the tether. Hans thrust both arms out of the portal, his bodyweight crumpling the canopy, and lashed a hitch around the exterior handline. With his face pressed up against the nylon, blocking his vision, it may not have been the neatest knot ever tied but it would do for now. With a sigh of relief, he slid the quick fastener up the portal's drawcord, gathering the material and shutting out the elements.

The raft had an arched entrance, with two zippers meeting at its apex like a dome camping tent. Hans pulled them down a few inches to create a football-shaped gap and set about bailing out the raft with the Disney mug. He considered emptying the flares from their Poly Bottle container and using it to speed up the process, but even though the pyrotechnics were supposedly waterproof, he did not want to risk them getting wet. Remembering the foldout basin, he retrieved it from the equipment bag and began heaving out the unwelcome liquid a gallon at a time – no easy task, the ocean buffeting them incessantly.

"Fishing time?"

"Not now."

"Painting?"

"Later."

Finally, the tether paid out to full length and the drogue flared, its function as a sea anchor preventing the raft from surfing down the face of the waves at breakneck speed. Yet it did nothing to lessen the impact of the rogue breakers slamming into tubes every few seconds, buckling them inwards and catapulting the two of them across the floor.

In the murky interior, the stench of rubber, talc and glue combined with body odor and salt to create a miasma of suffocating proportions, nausea worsened by the relentless motion of the raft. Had Hans the energy, he would have thrown up. Instead he retrieved two seasickness pills from the equipment bag and held them out to Jessica. She stared at them, void of emotion, as they dissolved in his clammy palm.

All day and night Mother Nature ran her course, testing a resolve that waned by the second. Howling gusts slammed sheeting rain and spray against the irrelevant orange pod, as deafening as a fusillade of machine guns in the thirty-foot swell.

Clinging to the webbing strap, Hans did not know what was worse – anticipating the thunder of the next roller to bury them, or the chaos ensuing when it did. He desperately worried the raft's adhesive would split and its seams come apart. Should that happen they stood no chance without survival suits and life jackets. If the surface spray didn't suffocate them, the resulting fatigue, combined with eventual hypothermia, would dull the will to live in no time at all, leaving apathy and indifference in its place.

Often the sets hit in close succession, seeing Hans fight for their lives as he redistributed his weight, bailed out the raft and reassured Jessica. Other times minutes would pass, the action exchanged for growing dread as he contemplated the enormity of their situation. Never did he allow himself to consider the storm might be abating – it was too much of a blow to morale when the next monster reared its unwelcome head and attempted to devour them.

A random wave broke under the raft, flipping it up on its edge and leaving them suspended in purgatory, until the drogue line tightened and yanked the inflatable back down. It seemed no matter what the conditions threw at the faithful craft, it buoyed triumphant every time. Only now did Hans yield to a glimmer of optimism, one burning brighter as dawn's long-awaited fingers clawed across the saturnine sky. Truly biblical, a gemstone sparkled through the dissipating cloud bank, unfurling a citrine carpet across the ocean toward them. Tumult morphed into calm as hope replaced fear.

- 61 -

As the growing morning warmth massaged his exhausted soul, Hans resisted the urge to lie down on his sodden sleeping bag, a luxury that would come later. From here on in every second counted. He needed to make a plan and take action. He had to think laterally, maximizing the potential of their equipment and supplies and exploiting all the environment had to offer. That way they might just live through this nightmare. Soon Hans would start a log – dates, times, conditions, position and drift of the raft – something to at least give the illusion of control rather than relinquish all influence to the sea's wet grip.

He hung the bedding out to dry and began the monotonous chore of bailing out their waterlogged home. Each time he lifted an arm, a searing pain spread from his temple to his jaw. Jessica lay asleep on the equipment bag. Even considering the traumatic events, Hans could see she was not herself.

He winced.

Figuring they were thirty days from the shipping lines – perhaps twenty-five if the breeze kept up – he pulled in the drogue chute to hasten their progress, folding it neatly and stowing it in its designated mesh holder ready for immediate deployment. Beneath the raft were four ballast pockets that automatically filled with water to give the raft stability. They certainly served their purpose in last night's storm, but now Hans wished there was some way to collapse them, reducing the drag and seeing them skim across the sea toward rescue.

Taking a seventy-foot length of cord, he tied one end to *Future*'s horseshoe buoy, one of the items salvaged when the yacht went down, and the other to the external handline. It acted as a man-overboard measure should either of them become separated from the raft, and as the orange life preserver dragged across the sea's surface, its bow wave created a disturbance, increasing their visibility to search-and-rescue aircraft. A ninetieth of a nautical mile between raft and buoy meant Hans was able to record the time it took for a piece of weed or other flotsam to travel the distance and work out their speed.

Next he contemplated their rations, making rough mental calculations as he did. If he could get by on half a pint of water a day and Jessica a third, the eighteen pints on board would last them twenty-four days – not long enough to reach the shipping lanes. With luck they might be able to supplement their meager intake, even build up a reserve, using the solar still and any rain they could collect.

Luck?

Reflecting on events, Hans allowed himself a moment of self-pity.

Food he was not too worried about, although kicking himself for assuming he would simply grab the emergency box should the yacht go down. Stocked with cans of meat, fish and soups, water and other vital supplies, it would have guaranteed their survival as long as the raft held out.

Tinned fish?

Although far from judging eyes, Hans felt foolish for packing the one fare that now swam beneath them in abundance.

Something that did go in their favor was Hans' knowledge of survival, as all SEALs passed through the navy's Survival, Evasion, Resistance, and Escape (SERE) school during training. One of his often-told anecdotes was of an exercise he underwent as a young frogman. In pairs, and wearing blindfolds, they had been bundled onto the back of a truck and dropped off a hundred miles from camp, their mission – with no money, map or food – to make it back in the fastest time possible. Standing there in the dark on a dirt track in the back of beyond, Hans looked at his buddy and knew immediately they had the same idea – scrambling up the vehicle's tarpaulin to stow away on the roof. As the truck neared the camp on the return journey, they dived off and rolled into the bushes on the side of the road, spending the evening in their local bar, beer and food on the house, before strolling back into base, fighting the urge to smile, early the next morning.

Hans' love and thirst for adventure began at a young age. An introverted kid, he was never happier than having his nose in a book loaned from the town library, most often a Willard Price novel detailing the escapades of Long Island teenagers Hal and Roger, whose father, a respected animal collector, sent them on exciting missions around the world in search of exotic species for his zoo. *Amazon Adventure, Africa Adventure, Underwater Adventure, South Sea Adventure* – the list went on, and Hans could not soak up the storylines fast enough.

For Hans' tenth birthday his grandfather presented him with a book titled *The Kon-Tiki Expedition*, the story of how in 1947 five Scandinavians under the leadership of Thor Heyerdahl sailed across the Pacific Ocean on a balsawood raft to prove a theory that settlers drifting across the sea from South America inhabited Polynesia. *Kon-Tiki*, named after the Inca sun king, proved a resounding success, the men able to collect a plentiful supply of rainwater and catch enough fish to supplement their fresh provisions of coconuts, sweet potatoes and fruit and see their dried rations redundant. During the crossing an ecosystem flourished beneath the raft attracting larger marine life, the men feasting on all manner of sea fare, including sharks they hauled on board and flying fish that bombarded their bamboo cabin at night. After her hundred and one days at sea, having crossed four thousand miles of ocean, huge breakers smashed *Kon-Tiki* onto a reef surrounding the Raroia atoll in the Tuamotu Islands, the crew making it safely ashore.

However, in Hans' opinion the ultimate story of endurance adrift had to be that of Poon Lim, who in 1942 worked as a steward on the British merchant ship SS *Ben Lomond*. A German U-boat sunk the cargo carrier en route from Cape Town to Suriname, seven hundred miles east of the Amazon. Lim grabbed his life jacket and jumped overboard, just in time to hear the ship's boilers explode. After several hours in the sea he located a wooden life raft, crawling aboard to find it stocked with the bare minimum of supplies – a few cans of crackers, a forty-liter jar of water, some flares and a

The Drift

flashlight. When food and water ran out, Lim took to catching raindrops in his life jacket, making fishing hooks out of the metal springs in the flashlight and nails from the raft's wooden decking, and tying them to a line braided using fibers plucked from the raft's hemp painter. With a knife fashioned from a sliver of can, he was able to slice up the fish he caught and hang the excess meat out to dry. When rain failed to materialize, he sucked blood from birds he snared and gorged on the juicy livers of hand-caught sharks. Finally, after Lim's one hundred and thirty-three days at sea, Brazilian fishermen picked him up, forty pounds lighter, just a few miles from land.

If there was one lesson Hans learned from reading these accounts, it was that the will to live and human resourcefulness far supersede available equipment and supplies, and if he kept the faith, Mother Nature would provide – though none of his heroes had a three-inch gash in their head to contend with.

Careful not to wake Jessica, Hans took the yellow Poly Bottle from the equipment bag and unscrewed its chunky red lid. Inside were six parachute flares, two handheld flares and a smoke flare. He added the signaling mirror and whistle and stored the container in a webbing pocket alongside the drogue chute and strobe light, ready to grab at a moment's notice.

The radar reflector consisted of flat-packed aluminum fins that slotted together to form an octahedron and sat on a mount that came in three interconnecting fiberglass sections like a fishing pole. When assembled, it looked like a prop from a Flash Gordon movie. With no practical way of securing the pole to the raft, Hans lashed the reflector itself to the outside of the canopy using a length of cord, which he looped through two of the utility ties stitched to the orange fabric. He did not hold out much hope. *Future* had a similar device at its masthead. Even at that height it proved ineffective more often than not.

Taking up a pen and notepad, he began a log. On the cover he wrote the name of the yacht, their personal details and a contact number and email address for his brother in the States. Should the worst case unfold, at least their bodies would be identifiable . . . if the raft stayed afloat.

Inside he recorded dates and a summary of events.

> *Day 1. Collided with foreign object (cargo container, whale?) Time: 1831 hrs. Approximate position: 16° 18' N, 25° 36' W. Both crew evacuated to life raft. Captain sustained severe contusion to side of the face. EPIRB and radio not on board. 7 days' food. 24 days' water.*

> *Day 2. Battered by storm day and night. Raft flooded. Bailed and drogue streamed. Desperately need sleep. Captain's facial contusion likely to become infected. Jessica appears healthy but withdrawn. No sign of rescue craft. Morale OK. 6 days' food. 23 days' water.*

Hans ripped a page from the rear of the notepad,

screwed it into a ball and soaked it in seawater. On his wrist was a Rolex Oyster diving watch, a present to himself after his first combat mission in the military. Now he used it to time how long the paper took to travel the length of the man-overboard line and reach the horseshoe float seventy feet away – forty-five seconds to cover one-ninetieth of a nautical mile, which meant they were drifting at half a knot and had covered approximately twenty-four miles. He divided off the previous day's tally and logged both distances accordingly.

Only now did Hans feel he could rest. Pangs of hunger and thirst racked his overtired self, but he resisted the urge to eat and drink, figuring if they fasted for forty-eight hours their stomachs would shrink and their bodies get used to fluid deprivation. He knew Jessica would understand. She still lay motionless on the equipment bag.

She's a good kid.

After making sure the sleeping bags were secure, Hans left them drying in the sun. Curled up against the tubes, he drifted into fractured sleep and a repeating nightmare. He dreamt he was clad in combat gear on a chopper with Jessica. They were heading to an island to rescue Penny, who lay sunbathing on the beach with his late wife. Every time they drew close to the shore, Jessica fell out of the door and plummeted into the ocean. He would jump to her rescue, the vision flicking to them being in a life raft and the helicopter returning but flying right past.

Wamp wamp wamp wamp wamp . . .

Hans awoke feeling confused. Having dreamt of a

helicopter, he could now hear one. It took him a few seconds to put the pieces together. *Search and rescue!*

Wrenching the Poly Bottle from the webbing pocket, hands shaking, Hans unscrewed the lid and took out a parachute flare. The noise of the chopper grew louder, until it passed directly overhead. As he struggled with the zippers, the infamous command wielded by military instructors the world over came into his head.

Move your fingers!

He fought to stay calm.

"Are you going to leave me?"

"No."

"You left them."

"No, I didn't."

"And you left her."

Hans peeled back the door. His spirit plummeted.

Dark-gray cloud blotted out the sky, the ceiling so low it would take a miracle for the aircraft to spot them. The sound of rotor blades drew nearer once more . . . and gradually faded away.

- 62 -

Ahmed sat upright, legs astride his mattress, staring at the lamplight dancing on the hessian and listening to the Grower and his piratical flunkies partying late into the night. He felt disenchanted and depressed but forced himself to contemplate their options, dismissing all but the most drastic one – entering the farmhouse while the men slept, shooting them dead with Naseem's shotgun and likewise the guard on the boat.

The guffaws quietened and grew further apart, eventually ceasing as the cocktail of booze and hashish induced slumber. Ahmed pumped up their small brass kerosene burner and made coffee. Sitting back down, he sipped his hot, sweet drink, willing the pick-me-up to give him the answer.

There *had* to be a way.

There was always a way.

. . . and there it was!

"Brother, get up!"

By the time Mohamed woke, Ahmed had their savings out from under the floorboards. "We go!"

"Wha—?"

"Don't ask. Just get yourself ready."

He lifted the door latch.

"Where are you going?"

"Where do you think?"

Mohamed recognized the look in Ahmed's eyes. "Me

too."

He whipped out his blade, and Ahmed knew it was pointless arguing.

They left the hut and crossed the yard. Music played in the farmhouse, covering the sound of their footsteps. Light shone from the window, Ahmed figuring the men had been too drunk to extinguish the lamps. He peeked around the frame to see Al Mohzerer sprawled in a chair, his guests comatose on the floor amidst empty bottles and a hookah pipe.

"Okay, wait here."

Ahmed eased open the solid wooden door and slipped inside, the stench of unwashed bodies and liquor fumes taking him back to the sewer. The bandits snored like swine, but Al Mohzerer looked as if he might wake at any moment, the wicked scar giving the impression he was grinning in his sleep. It was easy to see why he was so bitter. With yellowing paint peeling from the damp walls and the furniture sparse and shabby, it was not what you would expect of a man once revered as the biggest drug producer in the land.

Worried the floorboards would creak, Ahmed stepped onto the rug, its weave, faded and threadbare, offering little cushioning for his carefully placed feet. He crouched at the burnt-out fireplace, grabbed a handful of charcoal and dropped it inside his T-shirt. The music came from a cheap cassette player sat on an oak dresser at the far end of the room. Ahmed stepped over the prone figures and began searching through the drawers for the keys to the pickup.

Damn! They *had* to be somewhere.

He looked at Naseem, wondering if they were in his

djellaba. The thought of going near the man filled him with dread, but with a nervous check of his knife, he tiptoed over and dipped his fingers into the Grower's chest pocket.

"Urrh!" Naseem shifted position.

Ahmed froze. Seconds passed, but when Naseem snoozed on, his facial expression unchanging, Ahmed threw caution to the wind and slipped his hand all the way in.

Bingo!

His fingers made contact with cold metal. Pinching it between thumb and forefinger, he withdrew his hand . . . to find a gold watch with "Cartier" printed on its face in tiny black letters. He shoved it in his jeans and went back to the search, breathing an inner sigh of relief when he pulled out the keys.

His body trembling and mind on autopilot, Ahmed turned to creep out of the room, not realizing someone stood behind him with a shotgun.

"Uh!"

"Peeow-peeow!" Mohamed grinned.

"Fool!" Ahmed whispered, his body returning to earth.

- 63 -

The patter of rain replaced the thump of the chopper, the sky growing darker still. Hans leaned out of the doorway, flare in hand, wired on adrenaline and denial. Anticipating the chopper's return, he craned for an age, until the prospect of a wet sleeping bag forced him to accept the awful truth: it was not coming back.

The canopy's emergency light cast an ever more feeble glow around the miserable damp cave. Lying on his back, Hans stared up at the flickering bulb as it sapped the remaining life from the battery pack. It was tempting to wallow in despair. Often the occupants of life rafts died within a few days of abandoning ship, even before their supplies ran out, losing either their minds or the will to live.

Shaking himself, Hans set about collecting rainwater, Jessica's welfare foremost in his mind. Leaning over the canopy, he untied the cord securing the radar reflector and then removed its horizontal stabilizing plates. The remaining fins now formed an X-shape like the tail fin of a bomb.

Hans rammed the device into the observation port to act as a gutter, channeling the lifesaving drops into its drooping neck. Inside the raft, he tucked the Disney mug into the webbing pocket below the opening and trailed the drawstring down into it. As Hans explained the process, Jessica watched, looking mesmerized.

After a few minutes the drawstring started to glisten, and a puddle accumulated in the mug. Within half an hour droplets were spiraling down and the reservoir deepening. Hans giggled at first, until the stress of previous days evaporated into whoops of joy. "We've done it!"

Jessica gave him a toothy grin and shoved her arms in the air, her tiny biceps smothering her ears.

"Yaay!"

It took the best part of two hours to fill the beaker. Hans stuck to his resolve not to drink for two days. Instead he topped up the gas can to replace their first night's consumption. The beaker half filled a third time as the rain petered off.

Jessica eyed the all-important resource.

"Okay, just a little." Hans held up the cup and let her take a couple of sips, then as an afterthought took one himself to check its saltiness.

"Tphuh!" He spat it out.

It tasted vile, like bitter almonds. The chemical impregnation in the canopy's fabric must have contaminated the collection, and not just the water in the Disney mug but now the gas can too.

It was yet another crushing blow.

However, Hans was no stranger to disillusionment, developing immunity from a young age. No one ever said life was fair. That had been his experience, his creed, and now was no different. Rather than indulge in regret, he assessed the situation with a clinical detachment – a requisite quality in his former profession. He once watched an army ranger use a comrade's dead body as a windbreaker for his field stove. "You gotta roll with reality, brother," the soldier had said, casually stirring his chow. That same ranger made a satphone call to his wife a month later when insurgents surrounded his recon patrol in Afghanistan. "You better cancel Christmas dinner, honey" he told her.

As far as Hans was concerned, death was not something to fear, just something to delay if possible. He had to keep his head for the girl. The dilemma facing him was whether the water in the gas can was drinkable, despite its awful taste. Jessica looked okay, but she'd only had a sip or two. He doubted it was poisonous but worried it might make them vomit, leading to further dehydration.

A second rain shower compelled him to act. He emptied the gas can overboard and, using the filleting knife, sliced the bottoms off three ziplock plastic bags. With one of them turned inside out, Hans was able to connect it to another by pressing their nylon zippers together, thus forming a protective chute. After lengthening it using duct tape to stick on the third bag, he wrapped one end of the makeshift liner around the radar fins and draped the other down through the neck of the portal. The plastic now formed a barrier between the canopy's foul chemical treatment and the incoming flow. With the drops growing heavier, it looked as if their worries were over, but as the Disney mug slowly filled . . . the rain ceased.

- 64 -

According to the instruction booklet, the US military had used this type of solar-power still since the Second World War, and it could yield up to three pints of water a day. Two feet in diameter, the device consisted of an inflatable see-through plastic dome with a black cloth wick covering its base to create a distillation chamber. Floating on the sea like an enormous jellyfish, the unlikely contraption utilized the sun's rays to vaporize salt water into fresh, which then condensed and trickled down the sides of the dome to collect in a bag dangling in the ocean on a length of tube. Hans blew the still up and filled it with the recommended amount of brine, streaming it alongside the raft on its fifteen-foot tether.

Despite his reservations, their survival might soon depend on it. The area they drifted in, the Sahelian Belt, received minimal rainfall, as the dry wind blowing off the North African desert didn't have sufficient time over the sea for precipitation to occur. The rogue weather battering the raft previously was likely a Cape Verde hurricane, a twice-yearly phenomenon in which humid air sweeping upwards across the Central African savannah meets warm offshore water to create a tropical storm. It was unlikely they would experience such ferocious conditions again, nor the lifesaving commodity accompanying it.

Hans took up the pump and began replacing lost air

from the tubes. They leaked more and more as the days passed, leaving the raft flaccid and slow in the water. The pump itself was inappropriately suited to the task, the type of foot-operated device you might inflate a rubber dingy with on solid ground – the terra firma desperately lacking in this scenario. In the end Hans resorted to squeezing it like an accordion, its tedious wheeze not a composition any self-respecting musician would play.

The gash in Hans' head showed signs of infection, with swollen red lips surrounding the scab as it attempted to heal. His right eyelid was permanently half-closed. Every time he tried to open it, yellow fluid trickled down his cheek and pain shot the length of his arm. Sores had broken out all over his body – but not on Jessica, who appeared to weather the conditions better. Particularly bad were his knees, hips, and ankles, the joints in regular contact with the raft's wet floor. He put some serious thought into how to repair the punctures in the rubberized groundsheet, the ones made by the filleting knife when abandoning ship.

Again he rejected the repair kit's aluminum plugs, knowing he would have to widen the slits to accommodate them. The risk being if anything caught on the fatheaded screws, they might rip out and create an even bigger leak. Instead he rummaged through the rest of the equipment.

Pulling eight Bic ballpoints wrapped in an elastic band from the ditch kit gave Hans an idea. He removed a lid from one of the pens and, using the chopping board and filleting knife, cut notches in the shirt pocket clip to form an arrowhead. Having snipped the clip from the lid, he used the cigarette lighter to melt and flatten its end, the result a black plastic tack with a self-anchoring shank. He eased the improvised plug into one of the slits.

Damn!

It was a fraction too long, which meant it would ride up and create a snag. Hans repeated the process using another pen lid, this time paying attention to the finer detail. Squeezing it into place, he felt the little jaws grip the underside of the raft as the head of the tack came flush with the rubber deck.

Perfect!

He did the same for the other leaks, the gratification of something going favorably for once seeing him take a celebratory swig from their limited water reserve.

"Oh . . . *ooh-be-doo* . . . *I wanna be like you-ooh-ooh!*"

"*I wanna walk like you!*"

"*Talk like you toooo!*"

Singing aloud, Hans hugged his baby girl with all the strength he could muster.

The ballpoints reminded Hans of something he had read in Steven Callahan's account of his seventy-six days in a life raft. Using elastic bands, Hans lashed three of the pens together to form a right-angled triangle. He now had a crude sextant. When pointing one pen at the horizon and another at Polaris, the North Star, the V-shaped angle it created equaled their latitude. He could measure the angle using the degrees printed on the Silva compass. What with paying out the horseshoe float to give an idea of speed, Hans was able to estimate and chart their progress.

Kneeling in the doorway, he stared out across the endless undulating mass. By now the ocean's rise and fall had become a part of him, like a second pulse. He wondered if the sensation would continue after rescue – if rescue ever came. If not, Neptune's mocking embrace would be with them to the grave, continuing well into the afterlife until the raft succumbed to the waves, sinking to the seabed and taking their bleached bones with it.

At their current rate of drift, it would take almost a month to reach the shipping lanes, six hundred miles away across the desperate watery flat. With supplies running low, it was imperative to source food and water soon.

Despite them being in the tropics, as night fell there was a distinct drop in temperature. Hans shivered, stroking his daughter's cheek as she lay on her sleeping bag staring into space. Not once had the little girl complained. He felt as proud as ever to be her father. He pulled in the leash to retrieve the solar still, delighted to find a good half pint in the collection bag hanging down in the sea. Raising it to his cracked lips, he took a sip . . . and promptly spat it out. Somehow salt water had contaminated the distillation process. It was another blow to morale.

His little companion girl gave him a look. It said everything but nothing.

"There's one, Papa!"

The small fish darted for the foil attractor but veered off at the last moment. Jessica watched, excited.

Beneath the raft, barnacles, algae and seaweed had begun to form, initiating a traveling ecosystem in which these innocent minnows seemingly spawned from nowhere. Having no bait at hand, Hans had wrapped silver wrapper from an energy bar around a hook to form a lure, the sets in the fishing kit far too big for the mouths of these tiny creatures.

"I see it. Damn!"

Even with the smallest hook tied to the handline, it proved impossible to impale one of the tiddlers. To add to the frustration, every so often a shoal of flying fish burst through the surface, their tail fins powering from side to side to get them airborne, followed by a graceful hundred-yard glide to evade the ocean's predators. During the night a rogue fish had slammed into the canopy, shaking Hans from slumber but rolling off again to deprive them of a meal. Now desperately low on food, they needed to catch something soon.

That night searing pain kept Hans awake, denying him respite from the constant fear and doubt. Never in his life had he felt so desperate, so powerless and vulnerable. He pictured their home life in Portland, images so vivid he could almost reach out and touch them . . .

"Good efening, sir, madam. Nice to see you again,"
announced Aldo in his Latino tones, leading Hans and
his wife to a table overlooking the harbor, the
navigation lights on passing craft rebounding off the
jet-black water to add a jazzy aura to this treasured
seafood hideaway, Aldo's pristine white shirt open to
the navel to expose a hefty gold medallion bouncing
against the thick mat of hair sprouting from his olive-
skinned chest . . . Hans ordering a bourbon and a beer,
his partner – as always – a dry white wine and a
starter of house chowder . . . Cracking open fiddly
lobster shells before going on to the opera. Ahhh, the
opera! Arriving at the Merrill Auditorium's nondescript
building, its retro-style marquee more fitting of a movie
theater than the world-renowned acoustical experience
lying behind its blocky gray façade. Passing through
the foyer to enter a sea of red velvet and sit beneath an
impressive art deco ceiling with similarly exquisite
cream-and-gold flair surrounding them, his wife as
ever stunning in lilac silk and the beads he bought her
for their anniversary. Then a libretto to savor as Bizet's
Carmen *unfolded. Carmen's mezzo soprano trill*
fluttering around the hall, holding the audience in awe
and complemented by José's robust tenor pleading for
her to return to him from the arms of Escamillo the
Toreador. The knife plunging into her breast as
Escamillo receives applause from the bull pit's
bloodthirsty crowd . . .

Simple daily events, such as making coffee, watching
a ball game on TV or chatting to a neighbor, now seemed
such unbelievable luxuries, so taken for granted at the

time. How he yearned to be there now. He would appreciate every moment. Forget faxes, emails and telephone calls. Forget healthy living, adventurous vacations and improving his marathon time. Forget bills, mortgages and saving for the future. None of it was remotely relevant – pointless distractions to keep you from appreciating and enjoying the essence of life and the wonderful gift of just being, which cost nothing. He would willingly relinquish it all in exchange for rescue, for the chance to sit in the sand with Jessica on East End Beach tossing pebbles into the sea, content to never venture further than knee-deep in the waves lapping against the shore.

Upon their return to Maine, he would sell up and buy an RV so they could travel the United States and experience some of the unparalleled beauty the country had to offer, meeting interesting individuals along the way, all with their own stories to tell. Black, white, Hispanic, Jew, Muslim, Asian, Native American, young, old, rich, poor . . .

They would visit sites of historical importance – Little Bighorn in Montana, where Custer's cavalry bit off more than they could chew by taking on Sitting Bull and his nation of braves . . .

Man, I've never been there!

The Great Lakes, the Hoover Dam . . .

Ah!

The list would be endless.

Of course, Jessica would be in charge of the itinerary. He would even let her drive, sitting on his lap along the dirt tracks in the desert. They would make campfires, grill the fish they caught and gaze at the stars. It would be her trip, her future, her fulfillment. Content with having his feet on dry land, safe and secure with the sun on his face and fresh air in his lungs, Hans would want for nothing, his needs met, the trauma of being held hostage by a merciless ocean a far-distant memory.

The sense of not being alone interrupted Hans' muse, and, although irrational, he got up off his sleeping bag to check it out. When he crawled into the doorway to scan the horizon for the umpteenth time that evening, the scabs on his knees ripped off, seeing him wince in further agony. In this damp environment the sores never got a chance to heal and the red raw patches had turned into ulcers that oozed pus and grew larger by the day.

In the blackness he could just make out the contrast between sea and sky. No ships lay ahead or to the right of the opening. He kicked himself for his pathetic false hope, for acting like a child who keeps sneaking out of bed on Christmas Eve in the hope it will make the big day arrive sooner.

Out of bitterness and frustration he considered ignoring the left-hand side of the vista, but the obsessive-compulsive regime of raft life saw him unable to resist. He leant out around the canopy and, after a cursory glance, was about to retreat inside when a red dot caught his eye.

A ship! Definitely a ship!

It was heading straight for them.

Flustered, heart pounding, Hans fought to compose himself, the pain racking his body for days miraculously disappearing. He paddled the raft around so the doorway faced their rescuers and then retrieved the strobe light from its mesh holder. Fingers trembling, he switched it on and, after clipping it to the outside of the canopy, fumbled with the lid of the Poly Bottle containing the flares.

"Rescue, Jessie! We're being rescued!"

"Can we play Bop Rabbit again with Penny, Papa?" She looked at him in earnest.

"We can play Bop Rabbit, sweet pea, and . . ."

Hans grabbed a pint can of water and peeled off its plastic lid. He reached into his pocket, pulled out Jessica's clasp knife and spiked it through the top of the can twice. After placing it in her lap, he grabbed a parachute flare.

Whoomph!

The fiery red ball soared skyward and turned in a graceful arc before beginning its illuminating descent back to earth.

The vessel drew nearer.

Hans judged it was not approaching them directly but would pass at an angle some distance away. He reconciled himself with the notion the skipper had obviously spotted their plight but decided to intercept the raft's drift from downwind to avoid any last-minute complications. To acknowledge the unspoken yet understood arrangement, he fired off another flare.

By now the deep rumbling of the ship's engines eclipsed all other sounds, engulfing the tiny raft in an atmosphere of exhilaration. A thousand thoughts ran through Hans' mind, his soul enraptured by the prospect of closure. In addition to the red navigation light, he could now make out a green and a white one too, as well as the sodium-yellow glow of the bridge lighting as it radiated salvation from the block-shaped superstructure on deck. To celebrate, he spiked the lid of another pint can, guzzling its contents in homage to emancipation from the ocean's cruel grip and the further luxuries soon to be bestowed upon them by a welcoming crew.

As if to seal the deal, he let rip one more flare, reveling in its profligate flight and reassuring red blossom, feeling certain the vessel would slow at any second.

It thundered right on by.

In horror Hans witnessed the unmanned bridge, like that of a ghost ship, passing just fifty yards away, with no welcoming committee lining the decks ready to receive them. He fired off another flare and then another and another in hopes a crew member might be smoking a cigarette on the quarterdeck and raise the alarm.

Oblivious to Hans and Jessica's plight, their best chance of rescue slipped into the conspiring night.

Hans slumped back in the raft, his whole being telling him to scream aloud, to purge his anguish and not stop screaming until the vestiges of life drained from his useless body. Instead sheer shock and confusion saw him sit in silence, staring into the Poly Bottle to see all of the parachute flares gone. The pint can of water had spilled in Jessica's lap.

- 66 -

Once outside the farmhouse the boys headed straight for the truck. Ahmed took the shotgun and climbed in the driver's side.

"Push!" he ordered, shoving the key into the ignition.

With bandoliers of Naseem's ammunition wrapped around him like Rambo, Mohamed heaved at the tailgate and then scrambled into the cab as the pickup started rolling.

"We keep the lights and engine off until we get out of here," said Ahmed, whose driving experience was limited to a one-off joyride.

"Good idea," Mohamed agreed.

"Oh . . . oh . . . oh!"

"What is it?"

"It . . . won't steer!"

The truck picked up speed, and Ahmed, unfamiliar with steering locks, began to panic.

"Look out!" Mohamed shrieked. "Ghost!"

A white-haired figure in a white robe loomed in the darkness.

"*Noooo!*" Ahmed stomped hard on the brake. "It's Saleem!"

Without engine power to the servo, the pickup took an age to stop, the bumper inches from the old man.

"Lock the doors!"

Ahmed feared Al Mohzerer's trusted foreman would

put an end to their plan. He wound the window down a couple of inches.

"Going without saying good-bye?" Saleem asked softly, a smile clear in his tired eyes. "I thought you might need this." He poked a fat roll of dirhams through the gap. "It is all the savings I have, but you need it more than I."

"Errh . . . errh . . ." stammered Ahmed.

"And you must turn the key one click to be able to steer." Saleem chuckled, and, bidding, "*Vaarwel, mijn zonen,*" he disappeared.

Ahmed took his foot off the brake and freewheeled the truck far enough down the mountain to start the engine without fear of waking the men in the farmhouse. He soon had the driving under control, with only the occasional crash of gears.

"Drinky-drinky?" Mohamed pulled a bottle of whiskey from his waistband.

"Where did you . . . ?" Ahmed needn't have asked.

"Ha-ha!" Mohamed took a swig and handed it over.

"Now take off the shells."

Mohamed obliged, hiding the cartridges and shotgun under the pickup's bench seat.

"How did he know?"

"How did who know what?" Ahmed kept his eyes on the road.

"The old man. '*Vaarwel, mijn zonen.*' It means 'Farwell, my sons' in Dutch."

"He learnt it from the buyers, just like you did."

"No, I mean, how did he know we're going to Holland Land?"

Ahmed shook his head. "I don't think we'll ever know."

"A *big* one, Jessie! A *big* one!"

Out of the depths shot a monster fish, snapping its jaws to rip a minnow from the ecosystem burgeoning beneath the raft.

"Yellowfin, Papa?"

"No, this one's different."

Hans continued to jerk the silver-foil lure up and down, making it as tempting as possible, to no avail. He swapped to a trace of mackerel feathers from the fishing kit, but still luck evaded him. The huge fish retreated beneath a patch of sargassum weed trailing across the sea's surface, and the inquisitive tiddlers kept darting at the dyed-blue attractors but then rejecting them.

They needed to change tactics.

Gripping the filleting knife, Hans cut a mesh pocket from the inside of the raft, making sure not to damage the canopy and to leave enough excess material either side of the webbing seams to account for fraying. He took two sections of fiberglass radar pole and taped their ends together to form a V, adding a Bic pen casing as a cross member, the result a three-foot-long double prong onto the tips of which he bound the mesh pocket to form a crude shrimping net.

Taking great care, he lowered his creation into the water and waited for a minnow to drift away from the seaweed tendrils sprouting below. It was frustrating, since waves lapping against the tubes obscured his line of sight. In a moment of clarity he homed in on one, whipped up the net and . . .

"Ah!"

It was too quick for him.

Hans leant further out and began targeting the fish hiding under the raft itself. Despite several failed attempts, it soon became apparent the weed reduced the fish's vision – either that or it lulled them into a false sense of security. The next sweep saw one flashing white and silver as it tried to escape the net.

"Yes! We got one, honey! We *got* one!"

The minnow wriggling in his palm presented Hans with a conundrum. With their rations expended, it was tempting to simply gut the fish and share it raw with Jessica. Alternatively, he knew from survival training that placing the fish inside a piece of clothing and then wringing it out would produce a foul-tasting but drinkable liquid. However, he could also use the morsel as bait to try to catch the larger predator.

The decision made, Hans tied a size eight hook to the handline, its carbon-tempered point honed to such a sharp finish that a slight touch saw a bead of blood well from his thumb. To avoid catastrophe, he took great care not to let it contact the raft's exposed tubing. He guided the hook into the minnow's gullet and wove it through the flesh several times. Having cast it over the side, he sat in the doorway jigging the line up and down.

Hours passed and the light began to fade. Hans was about to give up when the big fish reappeared, shooting past the bait before turning on a dime and coming to a standstill just a few feet from it. Then it hovered in the swell, lining up on the offering as if contemplating its next move. Although intrinsically ugly, the creature projected a mystical quality, as if a throwback to the Jurassic period. A monstrous forehead towered over timid eyes and a comically downturned pout, which hid vicious triangular teeth like those of a piranha. A black dorsal fin tapered the length of its three-foot, green-and-yellow torso to meet a V-shaped tail evolved for power and agility. Hans believed it to be a dorado, or "dolphinfish," and knew it made good eating.

His hands shook.

Without warning the fish shot for the bait and in an iridescent blaze snatched it and shot downwards.

Hans couldn't believe it. In such dismal circumstances the possibility of landing a fish had felt beyond him, let alone a trophy such as this one. He let the spool run free, cradling it gently in his fingers, intent on letting the fish swallow the hook and then playing it for all it was worth.

His mind raced and he tried not to panic . . .

If I can land this beast, then I can catch more and more, and our food worries will be over.

But the excitement was short-lived. The line went slack, and he wound it in to find a frayed end where the fish had bitten it in two.

"Damn!"

When packing the fishing kit, Hans figured line with a twenty-pound breaking strain would be more than sufficient. He hadn't reckoned on these leviathans. Without a wire leader the nylon stood no chance against their razor-sharp bite.

- 68 -

The next day brought better luck. Hans worked out why salt water had been contaminating the distillate produced by the solar still. When a swell kicked up, the device drifted to the end of its tether and began jerking through the wave tops, splashing seawater in the evaporation chamber up against the still's domed sides, which then dripped down to mix with the condensate. Hans reckoned that by pulling in the tether every few minutes to keep it slack, he could prevent this from happening. By the end of the day this approach produced almost a pint of brackish but drinkable water.

As evening came the elusive dorado returned with three companions. Two looked distinctly different – smaller, with rounded and not jutting foreheads. Hans figured they were females. By now hunger took its toll. With weight dripping off him, Hans experienced a base ravenousness like never before, which emanated from the pit of his stomach and spread through every molecule of his being. His thoughts flicked to a documentary about polar bears he had watched on Discovery.

It must be the way a wild animal feels when food stocks are scarce.

He was sure Jessica felt the same, although she never complained.

With no other option, Hans picked up the makeshift

net and attempted to trap another minnow, donning the diving mask and snorkel to get a clearer picture below. He zeroed in on a two-inch-long fingerling with a turquoise-and-silver torso separated by a thick brown dorsal line. It looked like a cross between a young mackerel and a largemouth bass, its bulbous black eyes giving the impression of a permanent state of edginess.

Using the seaweed tendrils as camouflage, Hans gently raised the mesh and, with a deft scoop, ambushed the unwary fish, jamming the mouth of the net against the underside of the raft to prevent an escape. He drew the mesh toward him, delighted to find the tiddler flapping about in amongst the bottle-green strands of flora.

Hans caught a number of fry, perfecting his technique in the process, but when he baited up, the dorados took an age to strike and then bit through the line when hooked. There had to be another way.

During the day the larger fish disappeared to target prey in deeper hunting grounds. Hans took the opportunity to review the raft's inventory, going through their equipment piece by piece in hopes of finding something to substitute a wire trace. He racked his brain, thinking outside the box to consider all possibilities, such as removing the springs from the strobe's battery compartment, stretching them out and somehow linking them together. But that would jeopardize their chance of rescue, and without the proper tools his efforts would likely come to nothing.

Hans contemplated trimming a ribbon-like strip from an empty water can with the pocketknife. He would have to find a way to secure one end of it to the fishing line and pass the other end through the eye of a hook. Maybe he could heat it with the cigarette lighter and pound it into a smaller diameter using a can of water as a hammer and the chopping board as an anvil, like an oceanic blacksmith.

Just as he was about to put the plan into action, a thought struck him: *Penny's jewelry-making case.*

Didn't she make a bracelet for Jessica using the exact type of wire he needed? He popped the two tiny brass clasps and opened the wooden box to find a whole spool along with a pair of small pliers.

Yes!

Ignoring the pain, he picked Jessica up and held her above his head. "*Oh . . . ooh-be-doo . . . I wanna be like you-ooh-ooh!*"

"*I wanna walk like you!*"

"*Talk like you toooo!*"

Hans hugged his daughter tight and vowed to get her out of here. So long as they didn't give up hope, there would always be a way.

He cut a two-foot length of wire from the spool using the pliers' blades. Then, improvising with a pen as a form, he twisted one end into a loop to secure the fishing line to, and the other around the eye of one of the two remaining large hooks.

"Sometimes I got cross with him."

"Huh?"

"When he wouldn't share his toys."

"Oh."

"I told him Mommy said you gotta share your toys, or people won't like you."

"And did he?"

"He's dead."

"Yes. Yes, he is."

"And Mommy's dead."

"I know."

"If you don't share your toys, then you get dead!"

"No!"

"A boy at school told me JJ got dead because God was upset with him."

"He shouldn't have said that."

"I hit him . . . in the face."

"I know. I came into school, remember?"

"Uh-huh. To see Miss Potter because I was naughty."

"No! You weren't naughty. I told that old witch the only thing you did wrong was not hit that bully hard enough. Shoulda given him the old one-two like Daddy taught you."

"Penny said I was a good girl."

"You are a good girl."

"Penny kissed me and hugged me when I went to sleep."

"Penny's real nice – and she loves you, Jessie."

"She made me a bracelet."

Hans expected Jessica to hold the trinket up, but she stared at her feet. When he looked, her wrist was bare.

"Look, Jess." Hans waved the new fishing trace. "Penny's still making jewelry for us now."

"I miss Penny, Papa."

"We'll see her soon, sweat pea."

Right on cue, as the sun sunk to the horizon the dorados returned. Through the diving mask, Hans counted an additional fish in the ranks, making five in total. The dorado that had first shadowed the raft was instantly recognizable. It was considerably bigger than rest and, being male, had a massive forehead.

"Hello, Macheath!" Hans rasped – somewhat out of character for a man averse to anthropomorphizing animals.

Hans had started to do this of late, ascribing human characteristics to the ocean's wildlife and weaving an imaginary and colorful narrative into the unfolding picture. "All the world's a stage!" someone once said, and this is how he framed the situation. Moreover, it was an opera!

He saw himself as maestro, overseeing the arrangement from a lectern in the orchestra pit. The waves were the percussion section at work, no longer Wagner's stormy cymbals but brushes stroking the skin of a snare drum. The changing breeze represented the wind instruments. Whales, dolphins and seagulls, when called on stage, would be the strings. Flying fish skittering across the wave tops were punters rushing from the stalls for refreshments during the interval – or worse, fleeing a bad performance. The minnows were the stagehands and callboys working behind the scenes to change the seaweed and algae backdrops, altering the lighting and coordinating the performance. Obviously, Mother Nature took charge of the technical direction. Macheath was the notorious Mack the Knife, the charismatic underworld criminal who wielded a razor-edged blade and influence over his gang of deviants and misfits.

The latest addition to the somewhat mixed cast, a female, had an ugly cleft jaw, reminding Hans of the salmon he had seen as a teenager while working a summer job in a processing plant in Alaska. Standing by a conveyor belt, he'd trimmed excess fat and removed awkward bones from the prize sides of fish spewing out of the factory's industrial filleting machines. They would then be boxed, frozen and shipped to a warehouse in Tokyo ready to supply Japan's endless demand for sushi. Grown in enormous cages floating in the sea, the salmon were delivered to the plant in their thousands, a number of them sporting malformed jaws like this dorado, a consequence of the intensive farming method. He named the newcomer Cio-Cio after the lead in Puccini's Japanese tragedy *Madame Butterfly*.

Determined to try out the wire trace before sundown, Hans netted another minnow and prepared the hook. Dropping it over the side, he felt a pang of trepidation. If a dorado took the bait now, there would be no chance of it biting through the line, and the onus would be on him to play the fish until it tired and then pull it on board. Hans pondered this for a moment, shook his head and wound in the gear. He couldn't risk losing another hook, and this was not the right time to expand his repertoire of "the one that got away" anecdotes. He imagined holding his hands apart and shaking his head while telling Jessica, "Honestly, it was this big, honey! Oh, and I just lost some more of our precious tackle."

Instead Hans took the last size eight hook, and, using the wire and pliers, bound it tightly to the remaining section of radar pole to form a gaff. Then he wrapped the lashing around with duct tape for additional strength. As a safety measure he heated a Bic pen lid with the cigarette lighter and squeezed it flat. Snipping off the shirt pocket clip left him with a protective cap that slid snugly onto the gaff's unforgiving tip to prevent any mishaps.

Having recast the handline, he let it sink a few feet and was just wondering if a fish would take interest when a dorado hit the bait and line peeled from the spool.

Yes!

His first instinct was to wake Jessica and share his excitement, but he paused, figuring it better to focus on the task in hand and come up with the goods. He dropped the spool in his lap and began handling the line itself. There would be plenty of time to rewind it later – he just had to make sure not to let it tangle into a bird's nest. As the fish yanked the nylon in an effort to run deep, Hans let it slip through his grip, using his fingers and palms as a brake to deny the frantic creature any slack with which to break loose.

For ten minutes – to Hans it seemed like seconds – the dorado fought as if possessed, determined to free itself from this terrifying predicament. But the creature soon tired, and its attempts at diving reduced to tokenism. Hans kept his guard up, not taking his eye of the beautiful fish as it jackknifed on the surface, allowing him to draw it toward the raft. He reached behind, groped for the gaff and pulled off the protective cap with his teeth.

The dorado lay on its side, completely spent of energy with the exception of its piercing black eyes, which appeared to fixate on its captor. Hans lowered the gaff and, with a jerk, attempted to impale the exhausted prey behind one of its gill plates, only the wiry hook bounced off its armorlike scales.

In a quick change of plan, Hans went for the midriff, experiencing immense satisfaction when the barbed point pierced the dorado's soft white flesh and lodged in its underbelly. Hans expected the dorado to react to the pain and make a final break for freedom, but it did neither. So seizing the moment, he lunged, grabbing his prize by the tail to pull it aboard the raft.

The fish exploded into life, thrashing wildly, its two-foot length of sheer muscle spraying the raft's interior with blood, mucus and scales. Hans dived on his bounty, determined not to mess things up at this stage, the dorado's flailing torso smashing against his bony rib cage and knocking the wind out of him. Unable to reach for a knife, he resorted to pummeling the fish's head with his fist again and again until it finally lay still, with only the odd death throe as testament to the ordeal.

"Mullet fish, Papa?"

"No, not a mullet."

"Yellowfin?"

"No, sweet pea. Not a yellowfin. A dorado."

"Are we going on *Future* for a barbeque?"

"No. No barbeques at the opera, Jessie."

As the dorado passed into the next life, a strange thing occurred. Its spectacular iridescent sheen slowly changed from all the colors of the rainbow into a hideous dull green. Moments later it flickered through shades of black and gray, as a log does having turned to ash in a fireplace.

Hans watched in awe and sadness as this most marvelous of beings and determined adversary made the ultimate sacrifice so the two of them could live. He had never felt this way before. He had hunted and fished all his life. He had taken human life on more than one occasion. Yet it took this god-awful scenario for him to appreciate what life truly meant. It was as though the dorado represented his and Jessica's struggle to survive, a scene so powerful emotion overcame him.

"I'm sorry."

Tears rolled down Hans' emaciated cheeks. Not even Jessica lying against him could stop his outpouring of grief. Finally, he knew he had to give it up. By expending this precious energy, his soul was attempting to kill him, to run his body past the point of no return. Hans could not let that happen. He could never break his promise to his little girl.

Drifting into oblivion, he was far too tired to register the hefty thump on the bottom of the raft.

- 69 -

The young Moroccans stopped to collect their clothes and books from the locker at the ferry port before continuing on to the yacht. Ahmed pulled up at the harbor entrance.

"Are you happy with the plan?" He reached inside his shirt and retrieved the charcoal taken from the fireplace earlier.

"It's good," Mohamed replied, shoving out his chin.

Ahmed spat on one of the charred lumps and began rubbing it over his friend's face and clothes until he truly did look like Rambo. Lighting a match, "Close your eyes," he ordered, singeing Mohamed's fringe and eyebrows.

"Achk! Smells awful!"

"That's just what we want. Now do the same for me."

A blackened and scorched Ahmed drove along the quayside.

"Okay, look frantic!"

They leapt out and slammed the truck's doors, then scooted down the ladder to the exquisite wooden boat and jumped on deck making as much noise as possible. "Friend, friend!" Ahmed banged his fist on the cabin roof. "Wake up! Quick, quick!"

After a brief commotion, the young pirate appeared in the companionway, the fear of Shaitan evident in his rodent-like eyes.

"Mahour?"

"Come, come, come! There's been a fire at the farm!' Ahmed screamed. 'Your friends are hurt!"

The boy didn't argue, but climbing the ladder, he hesitated and looked back at the boat.

"Don't worry. My brother will stay and keep guard," said Ahmed.

They hopped into the truck, and Ahmed sped off down the dockside, continuing to spin the yarn as the terrified boy stared dead ahead.

Upon reaching the outskirts of the city, Ahmed turned into a deserted side street.

"Damn!"

A cluster of garbage cans blocked the route.

"Okay, we need to move them."

The boy jumped at the task.

Ahmed leant over and pulled the passenger door shut, then shoved the gear stick into reverse.

"So long, sucker!" he hollered, backing out with tires screeching.

70

Upon waking, Hans knew something monumental took place the previous evening. In his groggy state it took a moment to piece together events, and then it all came flooding back . . .

The fish! The glorious fish!

He pushed up onto his haunches, half expecting the dorado to have disappeared during the night. But there it was, and unbelievably its majestic color had returned from the dead.

Hans wasted no time setting about the fish with the filleting knife. He cut out its eyeballs and popped one in his mouth, crushing the chewy orb and reveling as fluid ran down his parched throat. He held out the other one for Jessica, but she wasn't keen to indulge. Hans downed it, figuring his daughter would fare better with the succulent fillets he intended to carve from this plentiful offering.

After rewinding the fishing line, Hans decapitated and gutted the dorado, delighted to find one of their lost hooks lodged in the fish's mouth. He briefly contemplated whether he could put the head and innards to good use, then dumped the lot over the side. A pool of blood, scales and slime had accumulated in the depression made by his knees in the rubber floor, so he mopped up the mess with the sponge and rinsed it in the sea.

The chopping board was only long enough to support half of the fish's body. Holding the fatter front end firmly against the wood, Hans was about to start cleaving meat from its bones when something struck the underside of the raft with a hefty whack.

He froze. *What the hell was that? Dorado? Turtle? Dolphin?*

The American placed the knife back in its scabbard, put on the diving mask and hung over the side. Nothing – only the wandering ecosystem of minnows, barnacles and weed growing ever bigger.

Hans was about to lift his head when a torpedo-shaped bulk glided past just feet away. He shot upright, his biggest fear confirmed.

Shark!

In that moment the minimal security the raft offered petered into insignificance. Hans suddenly felt utterly vulnerable. His hands trembled, and despite the morning warmth, a chill crept through him.

Sitting in silence, he contemplated the untold danger posed by the eleven-foot-long predator prowling below, knowing it be an oceanic whitetip, responsible for the most attacks on man, particularly shipwrecked sailors. Hans had read that, as a survival instinct, sharks initially bump potential prey to see if it puts up a defense. This was worrying enough . . .

But what if a great white appears?

At the top of the food chain, these impulsive brutes feared nothing, shooting up from the deep to attack without warning, even targeting small craft out of curiosity or anger. Just one brush of a man-eater's teeth against the raft would signal game over, the two of them treading water until exhaustion took hold or the shark closed in for the kill.

I can't let that happen.

Looking at Jessica and then at the filleting knife, Hans wondered if he had the courage to end it quickly for her if they ended up in the sea. He tried to put the thought out of his mind, but other dilemmas replaced it.

How will this affect the fishing?

He had strived so hard to set up the tackle and finally land a dorado. Would the shark's presence scare them away? Would it rip every fish he caught from the hook?

Hans decided not to mention the sighting to Jessica and strapped the mask back on. Scanning beneath, he could not see the giant fish, and after minutes elapsed he made the decision that, shark or no shark, life had to continue and he must focus on the here and now.

As a precaution Hans retrieved the carbon dioxide inflation cylinder. Redundant, it hung in the water in a plastic canvas holder, its red-painted steel covered in algae. He worried the raft's silhouette might be mistaken for a turtle from below, the cylinder and ballast pockets the creature's finning limbs, proving too tempting for their sharp-toothed visitor. Nothing could be done about the ballast pockets, but he was able to lash the cylinder out of harm's way using cord from the ditch kit.

Hans returned to filleting the dorado, wishing there was a way to get rid of the waste other than simply throwing it overboard. For the time being he sealed the fins and bones in the Poly Bottle, having placed the handheld flares and smoke flare in a ziplock bag. It was only to buy time while he mulled over how best to dispose of the fish's waste parts.

Isn't there a period when sharks don't feed?

Despite having to eat the dorado's flesh raw, Hans thought it was delicious. Moreover, as he crammed the juicy chunks into his mouth as fast as humanly possible, it satiated a hunger way past the point of starvation. Even when his shrunken stomach was full to the point of painful, Hans' mind and body craved for more. A drizzle of lime juice would not have gone amiss, but as it was, neither of them complained. It was quite simply the best meal ever.

Hans made sure to keep some of the fish back to eat later and for use as bait. As a test he cut fine slithers from the remaining fillet and strung them across the canopy to see if they would dry cure. He figured if he could catch two dorados a week, preserve some and keep the solar still working, they might well hold out long enough to reach the shipping lanes.

To eke out their limited water supply, Hans began adding a quarter ratio of seawater, knowing from reading survival stories it would do them no harm. He ripped his T-shirt in two and dunked both halves in the sea, then wrung them out and wrapped one piece around Jessica's head in a crude bandanna and the other around his own. He hoped that by keeping themselves cool, they wouldn't need to drink as much.

Before the afternoon was out, Hans made sure to ditch the dorado's inedible parts, believing sharks fed at dusk and dawn. To test the theory, he put on the mask and watched as the scraps sunk into the darkening blue. A couple of daring minnows ventured downwards to tug briefly at the unexpected feast before darting back to the security of the raft's seaweed skirt. The dorados had vanished, as had the whitetip.

Hans spent the rest of the day making sure there was slack in the solar still's leash and encouraging Jessica to read passages from the survival manual. She never complained of boredom, but he felt it best to keep her occupied nonetheless.

His efforts proved futile, though. After significant prompting to read a line, she would let the book fall into her lap. Hans wondered if this was her way of dealing with the situation and worried inner turmoil might be wreaking havoc behind her passive façade.

That evening a two-foot-high dorsal fin with trademark white tip sliced through the water just feet from where Hans sat staring out to sea. Despite his previous resolution to ignore the shark's presence, now darkness would soon reign the almighty fear returned. There was no telling how the creature could behave during the small hours.

Hans drifted off into a nightmare so vivid he began to wail aloud. Visions of the shark attacking the raft repeated in his mind, his efforts to fight it off with all manner of random objects failing each time. Every so often the shark did nudge the raft, waking Hans in fright. He would lie there in a cold sweat, his face ashen, taking an age to slip back into yet more tortured sleep.

As the sun began to rise, gruesome images continued to plague Hans' mind. In a moment of sheer terror he pictured the shark closing in on Jessica. "Papa!" he heard her scream, the beast wrenching its ferocious jaws from side to side, shredding rubber and canvas and ripping her tiny body apart.

Hans opened his good eye.

"*Noooo!*"

Blood splattered the raft.

"*No, no, no!*"

The shark had indeed taken his darling baby girl while he lazed useless in his sleeping bag, her lurid red life force running down the canopy in horrifying globules.

In the half world between sleep and consciousness, Hans fought to make sense of it all, unable to believe he had lost the one thing he held dear, left alone on an ocean he despised. Yet as his mind caught up, it slowly dawned on him the raft was intact – no gallons of ocean pouring in where the shark had left its mark.

In fact, there was no mark.

Hans peeled back Jessica's sleeping bag to find her lying there, eyes open but unhurt, the blood only rust-colored acid exploding from the strobe light's batteries following their prolonged exposure to seawater.

71

Days turned into weeks. A benevolent monotony took hold of raft life as routine set in and daily events became ever more predictable. None more so than daybreak, when the violet veil of the retreating night sky merged with Ra's ruddy halo, setting fire to the horizon as the sun god soared into the unfolding azure. The orange tent aglow, Hans paddled the raft round so the entrance faced east, remaining in his sleeping bag to rejoice in the spectacle and soak up the warmth tracking across the wave tops toward them.

What would I give for a coffee and a cigarette?

Hans had quit smoking years ago.

He unzipped his sleeping bag and began mopping up the water that somehow managed to find its way into their inflatable home. Having pumped up the tubes, noticing they needed more air each time, he streamed the solar still on its leash.

Most days the weather remained the same, the sun scorching down to bleach the raft's fading orange canvas, a gentle breeze producing a slight swell under a rich-blue sky. When the wind did pick up, Hans brought the solar still on board and lashed it to the right of the doorway, where it worked almost as well. Besides, from his rough calculations Hans reckoned that Eurus, the East Wind, had blown them to within seventy-two hours of the shipping lanes.

Jessica always slept much longer. Hans woke his little girl gently, offering her an inch of water in the Disney mug before checking her over for sores. She continued to fare well, though increasingly withdrawn. He made a mental note to trim her nails as they now looked more like claws.

Hans' own health was a constant worry. He must have lost four stone in weight, his ribs poking through the skin like a prisoner in a concentration camp. The gash in his temple was badly infected. For a while, after they had started to eat fish, the pain receded, and he hoped his body was healing itself. Only the agony now returned tenfold, searing through his entire right side, the open wound growing steadily bigger, along with a trench of putrid-smelling pus. Hans knew gangrene had set in.

More sharks arrived, the growing pack of dorados noticeably jittery and spending longer periods away from the raft. Catching them proved increasingly difficult. Several other species joined the roaming aquarium, including two pilot fish, who had switched allegiance from their white-tipped masters. Hans soon figured their place in the opera, for spectacular in shiny black-and-turquoise-striped costumes and unwavering in their attachment to the raft they were obviously talent scouts.

"There's a good deal of it down there," he cackled. "They're putting on quite a show!"

In white-on-black polka dots, the hilariously ugly triggerfish were a delight to watch, so graceful in the water, flapping up to the doorway, pirouetting, looping and swanning around one another like an act in a ballet.

"Ha-ha! *Swan Lake*!" Hans appreciated the display's

hidden sentiment.

The frequent knocks against the raft were less delightful. At daybreak the dorados would begin butting the floor or swimming alongside and smashing their tails into the tubing in an attempt to dislodge the gooseneck barnacles. Hans soon learned to distinguish between these opportunistic forays and the solid punches of a shark. The latter started at dusk and continued throughout the night. At first the knocks terrified Hans. In pain and discomfort, he would lie awake for hours anticipating the next blow, convinced it would sink them, their bodies shredded in a feeding frenzy. But after a time he realized that anxiety was sapping his remaining energy, and as the worst had yet to happen, he made a firm decision to compartmentalize his fear.

After this, nighttime became something Hans looked forward to, a welcome escape from the constant attentions of raft survival and the sweltering heat and lethargy accompanying it. When the sun dropped through the horizon, sucking in tangerine, magenta, crimson and cobalt sprays, he sought solace in the stars and moon, reassured in the knowledge the silver-studded backdrop was the exact same one experienced by all the sailors that had ever been in this predicament.

For several nights Hans chuckled to himself as he pictured Valkyries carrying the souls of slain Vikings skyward to Valhalla. The Norsemen would slash away at the moon's waning crescent with their battle-axes, only for "Máni" to retaliate, growing fatter in time-honored tradition, and all the while Wagner's "Ride" would blare across the starlit stage.

Hans often thought about food . . . *Herb-crusted filet*

mignon. New England lobster rolls. Chicken with lemon. Marmalade-glazed ham. Even dishes he never ate, like a crème brûlée dessert, always preferring the cheese board himself.

Reveling in unadulterated escapism, he ran through scenarios in his mind, such as trips to the store to buy ingredients for home-cooked treats . . .

Unhooking his car keys from the peg, rolling toward the mall, finding a parking space, strolling isle by isle with the shopping cart, selecting the necessary items – king prawns, coconut milk, coriander, cumin, ginger, lime leaves and a bottle of Cape red.

Each meal would be different, his imagination stretching to factor in every detail no matter how trivial, to make it even more real . . .

A bright summer's day, the smell of newly mown grass, the price of gas on the station's billboards, the food packaging, the store assistant's name badge, perfume or aftershave, announcements over the public address system, the balance of his bank account as he pulled his plastic card from the neat leather wallet JJ gave him for Christmas.

It got to the point where Hans became concerned about the effect his visualizing might be having on his health. Was he expending energy or risking a stomach ulcer by lying there night after night, mouth salivating, fixating on unobtainable delicacies?

He tried to train his thought to other scenarios – *playing softball with JJ in the park, teaching Jessica kickboxing, "tiggling" Mommy's ribs until she screamed aloud and punched him on the arm* – but the joy of reliving these treasured memories was not enough to turn his attention from food.

On the rare occasion Hans caught a dorado, he exploited the offering for all it was worth, no longer indulging in only its delicious flesh and juicy eyeballs but devouring internal organs – brains, kidneys, liver – without reservation. He began to crave offal and intestine as his body cried out for variation in a quest to absorb vitamins. One female he landed burst with rich golden eggs. Hans scooped them into his mouth without reservation, but Jessica remained indifferent, glassy eyed and dour.

Adapting to life as an aquatic cave dweller, Hans began to reflect on the fastidious nature of Western society and the decadent lifestyle choices that had become the norm. People no longer wanted to know how their meat came to be vacuum packed and sitting on a supermarket shelf – indeed it was de rigueur to shun the mere consideration of such repugnant nonsense. Folks refused to watch interesting wildlife documentaries in case they had to witness an animal's untimely but natural demise. Yet the exact same folks willingly shoved chicken burgers under the grill and watched mind-numbing game shows . . .

What has the world come to? Those indigenous communities – they had it all in perspective. Didn't Native Americans use every part of a slain buffalo, including its teeth? The skull as an altar, horns to make cups and spoons, brains to tan hides for teepee covers, clothes, shoes, bags, belts. Oh yes! Those folks had life in order. No pink carpet slippers and a cupboard full of cleaning products for them.

Hans would pick half-digested flying fish and

whitebait from the dorado's gut, rinse them in the sea and wolf them down. He cut the top and bottom off an empty water can and secured a sock to one end using Penny's wire. It was perfect for scooping krill and globules of plankton from the water, a ready-prepared seafood cocktail. When all other avenues were exhausted, Hans would pull in the man-overboard line and scrape off the gooseneck barnacles that had formed on it. He tried to tempt Jessica into eating one – to no avail.

Days passed, the action intermittent, like a record playing with music randomly inscribed in its grooves. By noon the heat became so oppressive it rendered Hans incapacitated. The breeze, when it arrived, provided welcome relief from the torture, allowing him to escape into visions of better days . . .

Playing in the yard with Kerry and the kids in the summer, swimwear on, pouring homemade lemonade from the big blue pitcher, ducking and jumping over the sprinkler as it sprayed life onto the yellowing grass. Lying in the path of the revolving jet and letting its revitalizing mist descend onto bare skin, providing sanctuary from the sun's relentless blister, or simply jumping in the pool for a game of Marco Polo.

How he longed for that time again, for happy smiles, for pitcher after pitcher of delicious concoctions and all the cool freshwater he could drink. He began to think about politics and current affairs, and how it was all so irrelevant . . .

The Democrats' second term, the greenhouse effect, send in the troops, bring the troops home, the Muslims, the Christians, the atheists, celebrity scandals, the rain forest, saturated fat, genetically modified crops, gun law, college fees, corporate fraud, hedge funds. Ha!

The next time a newspaper landed on his front lawn, he would throw it in the trash, the issues no longer important, incinerated along with all the other garbage polluting an idyllic existence.

Hans regretted the times he had argued with people, fallen out with friends just to make a stupid petty point, a point they were not ready to hear in the first place, one that did not matter anyway. What he would give to sit listening to one of those friends now, sharing a beer on the porch, letting them do all the talking while he lay back, reflecting on the wonder of diversity, the colorful characters it produced and the rich tapestry of life he was so lucky to be a part of.

Then there was the honking of car horns, the waving of fists, the shouts of "Hey *you*, buddy!," Fox News, live debates, online forums, keyboard morons, telephone polls, groupthink, dogmatism, and so on and on and on . . .

Everyone has an opinion. No need for education, study and research, hard-gained experience, reason, dialogue, understanding. Oh no! Just any fool with an Internet connection putting the whole world to rights with their acidic minds and a few comically misspelled words sans punctuation typed into a comments box, hit "Enter" and – hey presto! – you're a goddamn superstar!

He would quite happily let it all wash over him, remaining silent with a slight smile on his face and thinking, *Spend a month in a life raft, folks. Spend a month in a life raft.*

72

When Ahmed arrived back at the boat, Mohamed had the engine started. "Did the garbage can trick work?" he asked, handing his friend the whiskey.

"Does your mother look like a camel?"

"I don't remember my mother." Mohamed grinned.

Ahmed ran forward to untie the bow line from a cleat set into the harbor wall.

"Wait!" Mohamed scurried up the ladder to grab the shotgun and cartridges. Closing the door of the truck, he paused and let slip a mischievous chuckle, then unbuttoned his fly and left Al Mohzerer a good-bye present. With a grin, he flung the ignition key into the sea.

As Mohamed jumped back aboard, Ahmed levered the throttle forward, and the boys had their first taste of freedom.

"Bring in the fenders!" Ahmed ordered, looking down at the control panel to find the switches for the running lights.

In the warm night air, he steered the yacht out into open water, the sea perfectly calm, the sky alive with stars, which grew brighter as the lights of the city faded. Gripping the wheel, Ahmed leant back, laughing into the sparkling umbrella as a lifetime of servitude flowed from his being like the foam in their wake. Reaching for the whiskey bottle, he realized his friend hadn't returned from pulling in the fenders. "Fool, where are you?" he shouted, a touch panicky because neither of them could swim.

Mohamed reappeared, his face blank. He approached the cockpit like a zombie, clutching a foot-long nylon tube.

"Where did you get that?"

"Inside one of the fenders," Mohamed whispered, his expression deadpan.

"And?"

"You wanna see?"

"Of course."

Mohamed unscrewed the lid and poured thirty thousand euros into the cockpit.

"No!"

"And you know what else?"

While Ahmed gawped at the cash, Mohamed pulled a ziplock bag from his pocket and waved a hundred pink Mickey Mouse–faced tablets in the air.

"*Ec-sta-seeeee!*"

"Wha—?"

"A-hah-hah-haaaaaa!"

They danced around, hugging one another.

"Want one?" Mohamed cocked an eyebrow.

"I . . ." Ahmed always erred on the side of caution. "Are you gonna?"

"Oh, I took two already." The little fella grinned.

73

Hans attempted to wipe the splashes of rusty battery acid off the canopy with a damp sponge, to no avail. In the gloomy interior, the garish sprays added a haunting feel to the stinking cramped cave. Instead he set about putting everything in its place and sorting out the equipment bags. However, there was a problem. No sooner had he begun one task than his attention switched to another – checking the fishing kit to make sure the traces of lures were not tangled and the hooks had no rust setting in, finding himself engrossed in the survival manual, reading half a paragraph before checking there was slack in the solar still's leash. Unknowingly, he was having trouble focusing, and soon the raft was in a greater mess than before.

When the dorados returned, Hans knew he had to concentrate on fishing. Not having caught anything for days, they had no fresh or dry-cured rations, and starvation closed in once more. He netted a minnow and went to work.

Jigging the line up and down, he began to daydream, musing on the events in his life. It was as if everything – his family, the tragedy, his tough upbringing, his military experience, the investigation agency, the Concern, the yacht, Penny, the shipwreck, his love of opera, *everything* – had happened for a reason . . .

Is it all a test? Is this a challenge life has set for me, one I have to work out and come through? Are Kerry and JJ really dead? Did Future *sink? She was named* Future*! Is that because coming through this ordeal is part of my destiny? The Pilgrim Fathers sailed from Plymouth. Is this a pilgrimage? Of course! That's what my naval training was all about: surviving on the sea, preparation for this moment in time.*

Hans could see it as clear as day. This *was* a test! It had *all* been a test. His *entire* life! His experiences prepared him for the challenge of survival, the testing of his mettle to see if he truly deserved a place on this beautiful earth.

Why did I not see it before?

He kicked himself for being so stupid, so blinkered and dumb, for not realizing this whole damn shebang had been in play since birth, priming him to come good on the open ocean and prove to everyone his worth.

Jeez! I am an investigator for crying out loud!

It all fell into place and made perfect sense. He knew what to expect now . . .

A magnificent boat! Likely a paddleboat because this is all about letting off steam. It's gonna appear on the horizon and make straight for us. Lining the decks will be Mommy and JJ and Penny, my SEAL team, even old Jake, my next-door neighbor – the one who urged me to go on the trip. Marcel will be at the helm – the dark horse – guffawing in that endearing way of his, a huge doobie between his lips as he hands out tray after tray of mojitos. White rum from the White Knight. Yes!

They would *all* be on board, every person he had ever known, laughing and smiling and congratulating him on coming through this adventure and bringing Jessica with him. He felt deliriously happy, but as he scanned the far distance hoping to see the approaching vessel, there was a sharp tug, and nylon spilled into the deep.

He watched in confusion, before realizing . . .

The final test!

He knew that when he landed this king fish his worries would be over, his worth proved, the game in the bag – *Done. Dusted. Finito!* – the ship appearing out of nowhere to pluck them to safety. With the time difference, he pictured they would be in Orlando's for 10:00 p.m., Aldo serving Kerry a crab starter while he entertained old Jack Daniel's and the Allagash Brewing Company.

Hans concentrated on playing the fish, reckoning it was Shadowboxer, the largest of the dorados, so named after the opera based on the life of the legendary Joe Louis. It put up the biggest fight so far, wrenching line from his grip, thrashing its head from side to side in a bid to break free. Hans realized the giant was actually towing the raft, ironically in the direction of the shipping lanes.

"Ha!"

There would be no need to reach the fabled seaway when he landed this beauty. It would be the answer to all their prayers.

The dorado fought for hours, well into the dark. At one point the powerful fish stripped all but a few inches of line from the spool, and Hans thought he would lose it. He wondered which one of them was more exhausted and in the most pain. Blood dripped from his skinned palms and the deep cuts in his fingers.

Shark fins broke the black surface and began circling

the raft. He prayed the apex predators would not steal his glory in the last seconds. The arrival of the steam ship depended on him landing the goliath.

Finally, Hans was able to draw the fish toward him, expecting ferocious jaws to snatch his prize at any moment. He reached for the improvised gaff and attempted to spike Shadowboxer's powerful torso but only managed to nick his tough skin. The fighter snapped into life and shot under the raft. It was all Hans could do to keep hold of the gaff and prevent the fish ripping it from his grasp.

Hans teased Shadowboxer back to the entrance, but the mighty brute had one last trick up his sleeve. He flipped onto his back and dove with all the strength left in him. Both the gaff and fishing hook tore loose, and as the hunter lost his balance and toppled backwards he felt the gaff's merciless tip lodge in the raft's bottom tube.

Hans collapsed, drained of all energy, the pain now too much to bear.

His world folded in on itself.

Overcome with shock and shaking violently, he experienced a thirst like never before. He could not believe what just happened, going from hero to bust in a split second, not only losing the valuable catch but also destroying their chance of rescue and the raft in the process.

Mitch never did get to know what happened to the Hitachi 42-ES-1080, complete with HD, surround sound and VGA connector he had ordered off the Internet. It proved impossible to find a telephone number for Digital Direct's customer service department. When he finally received a reply to his emails, he learned that due to reasons beyond the company's control the shipment of television sets had not arrived, and they offered him an upgrade to the Hitachi 44-ES-1080 at no extra cost.

Mitch declined and asked for a refund.

He wasn't bothered about a new TV now. Bud had called from Portland to say sorry their trip to Vegas on Harleys never came off, but would he be interested a round-the-world yachting adventure? Jeanie had filed for divorce and they had sold the house. He'd invested his share in a secondhand cruiser and was in the process of fixing it up. He sure could do with another pair of hands, and it wouldn't cost Mitch a dime bar spending money.

Would I be interested? Mitch thought, taking two seconds to weigh up his options – namely, another year of twelve-hour shifts at the call center, coming home to microwave meals and *Gulf War III, or* sailing with his oldest pal to those exotic places he'd seen on Discovery.

The decision made, "Permission to come aboard, Captain Budmeister?"

"Permission granted, sir!" the skipper replied.

75

Hans dreamt water was coming into the raft, and despite his shattered mind yearning for sleep, something told him this was more than a nightmare. He opened his eyes to see the equipment bags afloat on the three-inch-deep pool sloshing around them.

No!

He had a vague recollection of attempting to land a mighty dorado the previous evening, but at the forefront of his mind was the moment the gaff pierced the raft's bottom tube. He looked out the door but could not see the object in question. It must have come unplugged and floated away during the night, resulting in even more air spilling from the damaged craft.

The raft now sat so low in the water its freeboard was only a couple of inches. Waves lapped over the entrance, sending gallons of seawater into the cabin. Realizing the danger, Hans zipped up the doorway and connected the foot pump to the bottom tube's inlet valve. He began inflating the chamber like a man possessed, beads of sweat running down his face and dripping into the swamped interior.

"Are we sinking again?"

"No, no, we're not."

"Can we go home now?"

"Soon, honey. Soon."

It took a superhuman effort to get the raft back to its

proper shape. Hans began bailing out, his mind in overdrive as he contemplated how to fix the leak. Finally, he was able to hang their bedding out to dry. He dropped back inside to see how quickly the raft deflated, praying for a slow puncture, meaning the tube only needed to be pumped up every few hours.

However, the speed with which the raft had collapsed overnight was worrying, and besides, any amount of time it took to operate the pump would detract from other important tasks, such as fishing and making sure the solar still produced enough water.

Within ten minutes the tube started to sag. Half an hour later the ocean threatened to surge on board once more. Hans began the laborious task of pumping and then donned the diving mask to view the extent of the problem.

What he saw terrified him. Air bubbles the size of peas spewed from the puncture in rapid succession, growing ever bigger as they shot to the surface. Had Hans not been so shocked and exhausted the night before, he would have strapped the gaff's handle to the raft, preventing it from doing further damage while still plugging the hole. As it was the viscous instrument must have flailed around in the waves, tearing at the rubber membrane until it finally worked free and fell away into the wake.

If there was ever a time to give up on life, it was now. The pain down the right-hand side of Hans' body was almost too much to bear. His right arm was semiparalyzed, and he had a splitting headache. The smell of necrotic flesh permeated the already rank air in the confined cabin. They had not eaten for two days, the chance of catching dorados thrown into jeopardy by the loss of the gaff. Their water reserves were at an all-time low, and with the raft sinking they had a crisis on their hands.

"Shall I read a page from the book, Papa?"

"Huh?"

"The survival book?"

"Oh, sure."

Hans took a deep breath and drew the equipment bag toward him. He handed the manual to Jessica and pulled out the repair kit. But before deciding on a course of action, he needed a closer inspection of the ruptured tube to ascertain the shape and size of the hole. He put on the diving mask, and after a check for sharks leant out of the raft as far as he could and plunged his head underwater.

Damn!

As Hans looked down on the damage, the bubbles interrupted his view, and from the side presented too obtuse an angle to get a clear picture. If he wanted to inspect the puncture properly, it meant reducing the pressure on the tube and viewing the hole straight on. There was only one option.

"Jessie, I need to climb in the water."

She looked at Hans but did not reply.

"Honey, I want you to stand here, and if you see a shark you gotta holler, okay?"

The little girl sat with her arms and legs out in front of her like a children's toy, the glassy look in her eyes permanent. Hans made sure she had an arm tucked around the webbing strap for support and then pulled the mask down over his face and eased over the side.

"Ouch!"

A stinging sensation spread across his skin like wildfire. Worried he had landed amongst jellyfish, he was about to hop back on board when it occurred to him it was only salt water invading the sores and boils covering his body.

"Okay, hun. Keep an eye out."

Hans dropped below the surface, pleased to see that without his weight in the raft the flow of bubbles reduced significantly. Further rewarding, he found the hole was nowhere near as big as he first thought. In fact, it was surprising how much air could pour out of such a tiny aperture. It was not much bigger than a pinprick but likely to expand threefold with pressure on the tube.

Hans was about to clamber back inside but instead decided to inspect the bottom of their home. The transformation amazed him. A mass of barnacles, large and small, covered the underneath, the black and white contrast giving the impression of a patch of whale's skin. Seaweed tendrils dangled up to five feet in length, in amongst them minnows of varying size and color and an abundance of krill-like creatures.

What part do these shrimpettes play in the Grand Old Opry? Or is it Ben-Hur?

Skirting the underwater jungle were the two pilot fish, the talent scouts, resplendent in their shiny blue-and-turquoise-striped regalia, tails gently swaying, completely at ease as they scoured the performance for up-and-coming stars.

Where are your shark bosses?

Hans reckoned the cutthroat controllers with their sleek gray suits and pointed white handkerchiefs to be the record executives.

The thought of sharks opened a window on reality. Hans felt a pang of fear as he remembered the danger lurking below. Wrapping his less-painful arm around the top tube, he tried to haul himself on board, but it was no good. He simply did not have enough strength, and slipped back underwater.

His anxiety increased. He grabbed hold of the raft with both arms and, despite the immense agony tearing through him, tried again. Still it was useless. Clinging to the deflating pod, he forced himself to take deep breaths, shaking out an arm at a time to relieve the fatigue.

Remember your training!

Kicking himself, Hans recalled the hundreds of times he had clambered into Zodiac speedboats following scuba dives in the SEALs. The easiest way was to bob up and down three times and then pull with all your might on the handline whilst finning hard. Steadying himself for the maneuver, Hans felt a bump against his leg and the rasp of sandpaper-like skin against his own.

Fear turned into panic.

He looked up but could not see his daughter.

Wasting no more time – "One . . . two . . . three . . . huht!" – he wrenched the raft downwards, kicking like a demon, amazed with the ease with which he reentered the flimsy craft.

Jessica lay star-shaped on the floor, completely uninterested. Hans let her be and sipped water from the gas can while gathering his thoughts.

Inside the repair kit were patches of varying sizes and a tube of adhesive. Fixing the puncture would be no different to mending a bicycle inner tube, only this tube was a foot underwater and surrounded by killer fish. A further challenge would be emptying all the air from the tube and drying it sufficiently to apply the rubber glue and patch. Hans doubted it was possible but had no choice but to try, because the alternative did not bear thinking about.

He briefly considered the screw-in aluminum plugs but then dismissed the idea. As with repairing the floor, it would mean widening the hole, and if the plug blew out it would spell certain death. The same went for using another cut-down Biro lid.

Once again Hans found himself systematically searching through their equipment, racking his exhausted brain for an answer.

The dividing compass!

Similar to the instrument kids draw circles with at school, the dividing compass had a second sharp point instead of a pencil holder. Hans had used it to work out their predicted arrival at the shipping lanes. However, it was by no means an essential piece of kit. Hans reckoned that if he removed one of the inch-long stainless-steel points from its wheeled clamp, he might be able to insert it into the hole and seal a good part, if not all, of the leak.

Leaning over the side, wearing the diving mask, Hans was acutely aware he only had two chances at this. With his body seizing up and cramps setting in, it was vital he did not drop the slippery little spike – all the more difficult as his wet and painful hands trembled. Holding the point between his thumb and forefinger, Hans drew it around the spot the bubbles spewed from, until finally he located the tiny indentation and eased the stopper home. The flow of air decreased immediately, reducing to a barely visible trickle.

Yes!

He made sure to leave a quarter of an inch standing proud in case he had to remove it for any reason.

"Yes! Yes! Yes!"

Hans giggled like a lunatic and thrust his fists in the air. Fingers crossed, he hoped the rubber tube would clamp the compass point in place, but as a precaution he smothered it with duct tape. With great care he began pumping, experiencing an immense sense of relief when the tube fattened to normal size.

Yes!

Now life could return to normal – whatever "normal" was atop this crazy fish tank.

76

"We are a lively society that happens to be on this island!"

Zerbinetta's line from Strauss' *Ariadne auf Naxos* scrolled in Japanese characters across the screens set into the backs of the blue velvet chairs in front of them. In the stunning setting of the Opera City Tower in Tokyo's ultramodern Shinjuku District, Kuro could not believe his luck, turning to see Aiko looking as radiant as ever by his side.

Aiko had her screen turned off. She did not need a translation to interpret the moving performance unfolding in front of her eyes.

They smiled.

Their hands met.

Kuro savored the moment he had waited a long time for.

In his new role as a test inspector in Hitachi's Oyama factory, Kuro was "product focused," "target driven" and saving every yen toward the day he would move out of his parents' poky apartment into an even smaller one of his own. Who knew? This time next year he and Aiko could be swimming with dolphins in Cancún.

Kuro had never been to an opera before but figured this might be the way to Aiko's heart, mulling over the idea for weeks before finally plucking up the courage to invite her. He was delighted when she had said yes.

Hans stared at the sagging tube, praying it was his mind playing tricks, but a cursory inspection confirmed that air bubbles signaled the raft's demise once more. The duct tape must have come unstuck and the tube had spat out the compass point. Now he would have to put all the tasks he had resumed on hold while attempting to save them from disaster *again*.

What about the other compass point?

If he attached a wire lanyard to the second compass point, he could reinsert it each time the pressure blew it out and maybe buy them enough time to reach the shipping lanes. They *must* be close now. He opened Penny's jewelry case and went to work with the pliers, not just twisting one loop of wire around the stainless-steel shaft but two to be on the safe side.

His endeavor was in vain. The raft deflated within the hour, ejecting the makeshift stopper as if it were a thorn in its side. Subsequent attempts also proved unsuccessful, Hans unable to pump the tube to half capacity before the dreaded flow of bubbles leeched life from the failing craft once more.

Hans' mind and body screamed at him to lie down, to close his eyes and take time out from this god-forsaken hell. But he knew if he did, lassitude would take over, seeing him slip from this world into the next and condemning his beautiful girl to a watery grave. Their survival rested on Hans patching the leak. Somehow he had to raise it out of the water and let the sun work its magic, drying the area around the hole so the adhesive would take.

Solid rubber anchor points secured the exterior handline to the top tube at three-foot intervals. Hans took a coil of nylon cord from the ditch kit and cut off a length. He lashed one end to the section of handline below the starboard side of the doorway and the other to a webbing strap at the rear of the raft, repeating the process for the port side, resulting in two guy ropes spanning the doughnut-shaped hull like thwarts in a rowing boat.

Hans inserted the raft's wooden paddle into a bight in the starboard cord and began twisting it slowly. The effect was immediate, the tubes bowing inwards like a pair of lopsided lips. He locked the paddle off against the rope with a length of string and repeated the process using the snorkel for leverage on the port line.

Although Hans was pleased with his effort, the floor hung low in the water and the bottom tube dipped below the surface every time he leant out of the doorway to inspect the leak. It was imperative to keep the damaged area out of the sea long enough to make the repair. The alternative meant hopping overboard and attempting to fix the problem while treading shark-infested water, and by the time the tube dried enough for him to patch it, he doubted he would have the strength left to climb back aboard.

Hans' stress increased, and the stabbing pain intensified. He took a few deep breaths, which only exacerbated the agony, and went to work untying all his knots. Adopting a different approach, he fed the remaining ten feet of cord through the section of handline directly below the doorway and pulled it back on itself to create two equal lengths. He knotted the doubled-up cord in the middle and lashed the two ends a yard apart to webbing straps on the opposite side of the raft, resulting in a Y-shaped arrangement. He hoped that when tensioned, the rope would divide the strain across the three points, and only the raft's damaged front section would rise up, like the prow of an inflatable speedboat.

Hans inserted the paddle into the doubled-up stem of the Y and began to wind, gradually letting air out of the top tube's valve as he did.

"Hee-hee-hee!"

Although far from perfect, the pulley system worked better than before, the punctured area slowly scrunching inwards as planned. Hans treated himself to a rest.

"What are you doing, Papa?"

"Well, I'm supposed to be conducting the orchestra, but the stagehands have gone on strike, so I'm doing *their* job too."

In the relatively calm conditions, the troublesome hole lifted clear of the water, with only the odd wave lapping up to foil Hans' plan. He found that by positioning their weight and equipment accordingly, the section of tube remained out of the water long enough for the sun's rays to take effect. In no time at all it was as dry as the day it came out of the factory.

Hans took a small square of sandpaper from the repair kit and, lying flat across the sagging floor, roughed up the area around the leak so the adhesive would take hold. He knew from countless times fixing bicycle punctures it was best to be generous with the glue, so he squeezed a large bead from the tube and wiped it around the hole. Hans' arm went into spasm, his face screwing up as he stifled a scream. When he opened his eyes, their only tube of adhesive had slipped from his grasp.

"No!"

Hans considered diving after it but knew it was too late. Instead he scrambled for the repair kit, pulling out the first patch he found. In his haste to lie back down, water surged up over the carefully prepared hole. Fighting to stay calm, Hans blew off the worst of the unwanted brine and, using his finger, dabbed at the adhesive in an attempt to spread it evenly. He removed the protective film from the back of the patch, but the situation did not look good. The minimal amount of glue adhering to the tube had turned milky in color, indicating contamination with salt water. Hans had no choice but to slap on the patch and hope for the best.

He clambered over the restraining cords and slumped against the tubes at the rear of the raft, trying to keep the repair aloft long enough for the adhesive to dry.

The Phantom of the Opera is here . . . inside my mind . . .

Hans could see it now. This whole experience had been a battle of good versus evil, and the phantom had struck again. The phantom was winning.

After half an hour Hans released the tension in the cords and pumped the top tube back up to capacity. Then he secured the connector to the bottom tube's valve. This was it. Everything rested on whether the patch held.

As he squeezed it in his hands, the pump wheezed like a forty-a-day smoker running for a bus. Hans was hesitant to inflate the chamber completely, happy to leave it slightly under pressure to give the repair the best chance of success. But just as he thought the battle was over, bubbles spilled out from under the patch with as much vigor as before.

Under a halo of cigarette smoke in a Filipino restaurant basement on the outskirts of Tokyo, Alfonso played the poker game of his life.

Sipping whiskey, the usual suspects crowding the baize, he reflected on what a tough week it had been sitting in his crane loading goods onto the endless stream of colossi pulling up at the dockside in Yokohama, a process made all the more difficult by stringent safety rules implemented in the wake of the *Tokyo Pride* incident. The subsequent inquiry into the loss of eighty-seven containers went on for months, yet Alfonso managed to come through it unscathed, the guilt assigned to the haulage company for supplying aging equipment. Besides, universally accepted was that no one could have anticipated a force ten gale wreaking havoc in the North Atlantic in May.

In the Philippine village of Jimenez on the island of Mindanao, life ticked over at a snail's pace compared to the bustling Japanese capital. Auto rickshaws and other mostly dilapidated modes of transport spewed noxious fumes as they chugged in a slow procession along the narrow high street, roadside entrepreneurs selling all manner of fast food, fruit and vegetables off barrows shaded from the sun by large parasols.

Alfonso's wife, Nichol, pulled a tissue from a cellophane pack and wiped the sweat from her brow before presenting her ID card to the woman in the post office. The worker smiled and barked an order to an elderly man in a sleeveless shirt, shorts and flip-flops, who sat dozing under a cooling fan. He disappeared into the backroom and returned seconds later hefting a large rectangular object wrapped in cardboard and plastered with airfreight stickers.

With the help of her two children, Alfonso Jr. and Lilibeth, Nichol lugged the surprise delivery back to their wooden shack, its brand-new corrugated-iron roof shining like silver foil in the midday rays. She cut through the packaging with a kitchen knife to reveal a Hitachi 42-ES-1080 widescreen TV – another luxury sent from Yokohama. As the children shrieked with joy, Nichol's devout Catholic mind didn't question how her husband afforded such gifts on his paltry salary.

That night, although utterly drained, Hans barely slept. He did not have the energy to inflate the leaking tube with the five hundred pumps an hour it required to keep its shape. As a result, the ocean splashed up over the canopy and seeped through the zippers, the excess drag working against Eurus' compassionate blow to reduce their progress to nothing.

The sagging floor enveloped Hans, and he feared they would drown. He attempted to lie at the edge of the raft but soon rolled back into its waterlogged folds. Raising himself took increasing effort, Hans' panic worsened by sharks knocking against his outlined figure. Being lighter, Jessica fared better and slept peacefully.

In the morning the little girl's gentle snores signaled obliviousness to her father's failure and broken promises. Hans watched his angel's chest rise and fall, happy memories floating up out of the insanity like compassionate ghosts . . .

Rescuing her mother in Sierra Leone. Waking up in the hospital after the car crash to find Kerry there by his side. Buying their first home in Maine and – ha! – painting over those ugly pink walls. Founding the Larsson Investigation Agency and holding his tiny baby seconds after she entered the world without so much as a whimper.

He thought about the night terrors she experienced as

a tot, knocking on their bedroom door with tears running down her cheeks, and the satisfying sense of family he experienced when she climbed under the covers between them.

Boy, did we make a fuss of her in the morning!

The time he taught her to ride her first bicycle – not that she needed teaching. Hans had steadied his child for all of ten seconds before she pulled away and pedaled up the street without so much as a backwards look.

When JJ arrived, Jessica doted on her sibling as if nothing else mattered. The two years between them could easily have been ten for all the love and attention she gave him. Their bond had been strong. She had been so brave since his death.

"She didn't deserve it." Hans burst into tears. "She didn't deserve it . . . She didn't deserve it!"

Anger engulfed him, like wildfire raging through a tinder-dry forest.

"*Nooooooo*! *God*! *Nooooooo*! She doesn't deserve this! She doesn't deserve this!"

He sobbed and sobbed, until apathy took hold, gradually pacified his ire. He was tired of struggling to survive, tired of fighting all his life.

"Damn you, phantom! *Damn* you! I don't care about your pathetic opera, your stupid scary games! I don't care . . . I *don't* ca . . . a . . . a . . . re . . . u-huht . . . huh . . . uh . . ."

Hans pulled Jessica's knife from his pocket and peeled open the blade. He paused, contemplating whether to slash at the raft's useless tubes, but decided to plunge it straight into his heart. He climbed into the doorway with the intention of letting his dying body fall overboard. Without his weight in the raft, Jessica stood a better chance of reaching the shipping lanes.

He held the knifepoint a foot from his chest with his good arm. It was all he could do to reach out and close his other palm around the handle, blanking the agony in the knowledge it would be over in a moment and he would reunite with his wife and son.

He thrust the blade toward him. "*Arrrrrrrh!*"

"Papa!"

The knifepoint stopped an inch from his rib cage.

Jessica was not impressed. "You must *never* hold the blade toward you! Naughty Papa!"

Fraught with pain and guilt, Hans let his daughter's words sink in. He stared at the knife, remembering the day Old Bill pressed it into Jessica's hand, her smile of appreciation – gratitude he felt tenfold, truly understanding the sentiment represented by . . . the silver anchor *screwed* to the ebony handle!

Hell!

Why had he not thought of this?

The screws!

Surely he could use one of them to seal the puncture.

Everything suddenly made sense.

Old Bill wasn't stupid. He knew dilemmas like this were the norm. He prepared us for the worst eventuality, not only with his kind words but also with this gift from afar.

Hans set to work, using the filleting knife's fine tip to locate the screw's slot and applying gentle pressure to turn it. Triumphant, he held the small stainless steel fixing aloft, knowing their troubles would soon be behind them. Leaning over the side, he pondered how to secure the screw in place, or at least get its thread to bite into the raft's rubber skirt. There was no way he could mess this up. No way would he would let their last chance at salvation end up in Davy Jones' locker.

Hans clamped the the screw between his thumb and forefinger, ignoring the pain to focus on locating the miserable little hole. He scraped the brass point over the carapace in ever-decreasing circles until he felt the point sink home. As he turned the screw, the thread bit into the rubber and its beveled head began to rip through his shriveled fingertips. It was a positive sign. The fit was snug. He switched to the filleting knife, delighted when the screwface finally countersunk in the rubber.

Hans had a good feeling about the repair, a perfect union in every sense. With no waiting for glue to dry, he began pumping up the tube, experiencing a degree of contempt and flagrant disregard for the seriousness of their predicament. The screw would either hold or it wouldn't, and there was not a lot he could do about it.

The tube plumped to near capacity, and despite feelings of recklessness, Hans was content to stop there. A wave of nostalgia swept over him as he remembered fixing the leaking planks in his daysailer as a teenager before putting to sea for a test.

He crawled into the doorway to inspect the repair, his body tingling with suspense.

Yes!

Not a single bubble.

Ahmed popped the ecstasy pill and washed it down with a gulp of whiskey.

"Right, I'll put up the sail. Stow the money inside."

Mohamed began gathering their windfall and shoving it into the nylon tube.

Ahmed cut the motor and went on deck to haul up the canvas. Doing exactly what the yacht crews had taught them in the harbor felt surreal. It was magical to see the rich-green sailcloth blossom in the breeze and feel the boat pick up speed.

He hopped down into the cockpit and adjusted the wheel, no need for a compass heading when the lights of Spain shimmered in the distance. With the ecstasy invoking a nostalgic caress, he reflected on the journey so far. The uric stench of the orphanage where he first met his beloved brother. The sewer where they overcame Rat Boy. The hut and the vicious beating Al Mohzerer gave Mohamed. The kind old man Saleem. The pirates. And their escape from the dock.

Never had Ahmed felt so happy and alive. Whatever challenges Europe conjured up, they would face them with pride. No one would mess with the boys, who intended to become the continent's biggest drug barons. He *knew* it!

"Jiggy, jiggy, jiggy!"

An idiot emerged from the cabin to the blare of the

Stoner Brothers' 'How Fast Can You Live?' Wearing his luminous-orange parker – pockets crammed with Golden Monkey and bottles of Havana Club – a string vest, cowboy boots and fake Ray-Bans, he had wrapped himself in ammunition belts and held the shotgun and an AK-47 aloft. On his head was a black baseball cap with "BOY" emblazoned across it in pink letters. In his mouth the fattest joint ever rolled.

"Girls, girls, girls!" He grinned.

Ahmed looked to the sky and laughed until he could laugh no more.

81

Hans stared at his reflection in the signaling mirror, unable to recognize the alien looking back at him.

Is this me?

Fish scales and blood caked tanned, wizened skin stretched taut over the contours of his skull. One was eye bloodshot, wild pupiled and sunk in its socket, the other swollen shut by the festering wound eating up his face. His unkempt hair and beard had turned white, and his scalp had bald bleeding patches where the raft rubbed against it, pulling clumps of roots out. Ugly boils and lesions covered his body, and he had lost the cap from a front tooth. The Rolex hung loose on his wrist. In too much pain, he could not adjust the bracelet if he tried.

Hans forced a half grin, knowing he was dying.

He had given up recording their progress and writing entries in the log. They were in the hands of Mother Nature now. He hoped she would be merciful and blow them to the shipping lanes. They must be close. Surely someone would spot their plight.

The sea around them now teemed with life. Schools of bonito and tunny joined in the ever-evolving chaos, whipped into frenzy by an abundance of plankton blooms. Hans watched a dorado zip along the surface, sending a school of flying fish airborne, their tormentor then wrenched from the chase by the jaws of a huge shark. A mass of fins appeared in an instant, the sea wolves' tails thrashing as they fought for a share of the prey, a crimson tinge infusing the boiling sea.

Erring on the side of caution, Hans retrieved the solar still. The last time he checked, there was a good pint in the collection bag, but he had decided to float the still a while longer to accumulate more of the priceless commodity. Now, as he pulled up the nylon tube, the bag felt a little light. In fact, there was no resistance at all.

Panic set in.

Something had gone wrong.

Hans inspected the empty bag, to see a minute bite mark in the plastic.

"Damn you, triggerfish!" He cursed the obvious culprits. "Why couldn't you leave us alone?"

Fixing the hole with duct tape was easy, but the lifesaving liquid that took a day to collect had been lost. Now that evening drew in and the sun's distilling rays took leave, it would be another twenty-four hours before they had anything to drink.

That night, consumed by pain, Hans slumped in the doorway watching an electric-blue light trail stream in their wake. In reality, the spectacular display was bioluminescence given off by single-cell organisms encountering the raft, a protective mechanism to ward off predators. This was of no concern to Hans, though. His vision blurred. Pain ricocheted around his skull whenever he moved his eyes, locking his jaw and making him nauseous. He was content simply to sit there, entranced by the beautiful phenomenon and absorbing its comforting aura.

A bulbous silhouette cut a swath through the light

show. In his hallucinating state, Hans checked himself, but, sure enough, there it was again, something monstrous yet majestic rising from the depths to scope the tiny craft. Hans stared into the heavenly color storm but could see nothing until the surface erupted with a *phhhhsssssskkkkk!* and two enormous black heads emerged – a humpback whale and her calf.

At any other time in Hans' life, the mammals' impromptu appearance would have taken him by surprise, but so close to death and with no energy left to expend, he resigned to the moment and let the experience wash over him.

The mother's eye stared at him knowingly, reassuringly.

"Hey Jessie! Come quick!"

She lay unstirring in the gloomy interior. Hans woke the little girl and, with his good arm, helped her into the doorway.

"Guess who's come to see us."

"Mommy and JJ, Papa?" she whispered, her eyes glinting in the dark.

"Yes, sweet pea. They've come to tell us everything's gonna be all right. It's gonna be okay."

Hans held Jessica out so she could stroke the nearest whale's rubbery skin.

"Don't worry, Mommy. Don't worry, JJ. Daddy will look after me. He promised."

With that the creatures sunk below the waves and disappeared into the abyss.

After tucking Jessica into her sleeping bag, Hans dozed off, drifting between dreams of hope and hellish nightmares.

Something disturbed Hans' slumber, a sound impossible to place at first. He awoke to the thunder of a powerful diesel engine. Through the doorway he saw a ship less than a hundred yards away, its lights blazing terror as it closed across the moonlit void.

Hans wrenched himself from torpor and lunged for the Poly Bottle containing the remaining handheld flares, but his efforts were in vain. Looking up, he could make out individual rivets on the ship's iron prow as its bow wave slammed into them. Their humble home flipped upside down, catapulting Hans out of the doorway and into wet darkness. He kicked for the surface, horrified to see the raft cartwheeling in the white water along the ship's rusty hull.

"Jessica!"

Hans could not believe what was happening, and as the unrelenting hulk ravaged the fragile pod, he prayed his baby girl was not still inside.

Using sidekick and his good arm to propel him through the water, Hans struck out for the raft, which lay on its roof, bobbing in the ship's churning wake. The perpetrator had fled the scene, careening into the night like a hit-and-run drunk.

Nearing the raft, a frantic Hans scoured the choppy surface. He hoped to God that the equipment bags had not smashed Jessica to a pulp as they tumbled around inside the canopy like rocks in a washing machine. Worse, that the ship's enormous screws hadn't sucked his little girl under and shredded her to ribbons.

"Jessica!"

Still no sight or sound of her, Hans heaved on the man-overboard rope to right the raft. As it splashed down, he grabbed the handline and clawed his way around to the entrance.

"Swimming time, Papa?"

"Jessie!"

She floated on her back in the flooded cabin.

Fueled on adrenaline, Hans pulled himself aboard, tears pouring down his face as he gathered the first mate in his arms.

"I got all wet!"

"I know, honey. I know."

"And the bag hit me on the head!"

"Oh, sweetheart . . . sweetheart."

82

In Cape Verde, Penny took up her usual spot in Salgadeiras, the café bar overlooking the marina, and in particular the berth *Future* should have occupied. She sat there every day, hoping the yacht would cruise into the harbor, Hans stoic at the helm while Jessica played with Bear in the cockpit, her nights tortured with visions of *Future* going up in flames.

As Penny cradled a coffee, a plethora of memories occupied her mind. She thought about the moment she first met Hans, so handsome, courteous and in control. It was a recollection she would treasure forever, knowing she fell in love with him the second he spoke. When tucking Jessica into bed that evening, she had to refrain from smothering the little girl in hugs and kisses. Her cuteness and intelligence made her instantly loveable and a joy to be around. Penny prayed for their safe return, willing to exchange a life at sea to be with them in Maine.

However, after three weeks the Concern had no choice but to scale down its expensive operation. If *Future* was adrift or her crew had taken to a life raft, they would be too far out into the Atlantic for rescue aircraft to continue flying an effective search pattern. No commercial flights or satellites had picked up an EPIRB signal, the coastguard concluding the device must have gone down with the yacht. At one point the crew of the *Monaghan* contacted the website to report sailing into a debris field, later adding, upon inspection, it was likely garbage cast overboard by a cargo ship en route from South Africa. Washington continued to block Muttley's requests for military intervention, something he promised Penny she had not heard the last of.

Phipps, Hans' former Navy SEAL buddy, would stay on Cape Verde another month and continue to liaise with commercial vessels and yacht crews, particularly those making the trip west to the Caribbean. "There are millions of miles of empty ocean out there, Penny, but there is still a chance if they can reach the shipping lanes."

Each passing second Penny contemplated possible explanations – a rogue wave taking down *Future*'s rigging and ruining communications, Hans smashing his head in a fall and Jessica struggling to take charge of the boat – until the scenarios became so implausible that not even she could believe them.

Every few seconds her eyes flicked to the restaurant's flat-screen TV. She hoped the looped CNN reports would be interrupted by a bulletin announcing that the occupants of a life raft had been picked up or that a ragtag pirate outfit had kidnapped an American and his daughter and were demanding a ransom.

Penny watched with dismay as *Growing Old Disgracefully* pulled into *Future*'s berth. Its crew, John and Margie Grenson, had pottered about the North African coast for years, John having retired from a successful dental practice in which Margie had been his assistant. A sprightly couple in their seventies, not an awful lot phased them – the open ocean or otherwise – but recently they had been forced to consider selling their cherished craft and moving back to Connecticut. Piracy was on the increase and proved a constant source of anxiety, and the ocean was full of all manner of floating foreign objects – or "space junk" as John referred to it – that could sink a yacht.

- 83 -

Morning broke, and Hans clutched Jessica as he surveyed the damage. Despite an ugly smearing of rust and algae following its slide along the ship's hull, the raft had come through the ordeal relatively intact. The screw stayed in place, and the pressure valves did their job, but the tubes would need a good few pumps to get them into shape. The Larssons still had the equipment bag and the items stowed in the raft's mesh pockets, but the ditch kit was missing, along with the fishing gear, bait net and water can. The solar still was punctured and flattened beyond repair.

As far as survival was concerned, the situation could not have been much worse, but Hans was just glad they were both still alive. He retrieved the collapsible basin and began bailing out, reflecting on the irony that with no prospect of food or water they had retained the item doubling as a potty. Only one sleeping bag was present. Hans hung it out to dry and began inflating the tubes, stopping to rest every twenty pumps utterly exhausted.

It must feel like this to climb Mount Everest, inching up through the Death Zone a step at a time.

In truth, what with the fatigue, heat and deprivation – not to mention loneliness, fear and paralysis from gangrene – climbing Everest would have been an easier option.

Hans set about making an improvised still, tearing a

thin strip from one of the halves of T-shirt and taping it around the rim of the basin. Fortunately, he had stored the filleting knife in a mesh pocket prior to the collision. He used it to cut a square of black fabric from the equipment bag, placing it in the bottom of the basin to act as a heat sink and wick. He filled the contraption with a quarter of an inch of brine and sealed it in a plastic bag. Placing the still in the sun, he hoped the salt water would evaporate into fresh, condensing on the plastic bag to drip down and collect in the T-shirt material.

When darkness fell, Hans lay in the doorway, using the empty water can and attached sock to scoop up krill wriggling in the raft's stunning blue halo. He was beyond exhausted and about to give up when a triggerfish shot from the deep and butted his wrist. Taken by surprise, Hans took a moment to realize the luminescent dial on his Rolex had acted as an attractor.

An idea formed . . .

He cut a two-foot length of webbing strap from the interior of the raft and tied one end to his watch – not an easy task with little feeling in his right-hand side. Then he taped the filleting knife to the wooden paddle to use as a spear. Hans jigged the world's most expensive bait up and down until the fish struck again, but he was too slow. After several attempts, Hans managed to impale the triggerfish, gutted to see it wriggle off the blade as he drew it toward him. Although in desperate need of the juice the fish's flesh contained, the American drifted into sleep.

Hans awoke to find the raft caught up in a mesh of sargassum rolling around in the swell like a sea monster. In amongst the weed was a heap of trash, testament to a world of ignorance and greed Hans and Jessica had long since ceased to be a part of.

Something caught his eye . . . He found himself shaking.

It was a plastic bottle – a mineral water bottle – floating at an angle that suggested it was not empty.

Hans pulled the vegetation toward him, and another bottle popped up and then another. If there was ever a gift from the gods, then this must be it. Plucking them from the sea, he could hardly believe they contained varying amounts of freshwater, almost a pint in all. He unscrewed the top of one of the bottles and guzzled its contents.

"Jessie."

"Huh?"

"Drink, honey. Drink."

"Mojito?" She looked up at him with glassy black eyes.

"No, princess. Better than mojito."

He held the bottle to her mouth. There was no point rationing such a small amount, so they finished it off, though Jessica was uninterested and spilt a good deal.

With a newfound zest, Hans returned to spearfishing, but the revitalizing effect of the water did not last long, seeing him slump to the floor. He lay there with the stench of death invading his nostrils, tongue swollen beyond all proportion in his ulcerated mouth.

In the heat of the afternoon, he summoned up the energy to remove the T-shirt fabric from the improvised still and sucked out the few drops it held before collapsing in agony. He considered setting it up again but knew it was not worth the effort.

The next morning luck shone on them once more, for

during the night two flying fish had landed on board, the moisture in their tissue enough to see them through another day. Hans reached for the spear and . . .

Hans had no idea how long he had slept for, only that a swell kicked up under them for the first time in weeks.

Could it be . . . ?

He peeled back the door to see building heads of dense, dark cloud towering into an overcast sky. The raft slid headlong down ever-higher breakers as the rumble of distant thunder signaled an approaching storm. His first thought was to stream the drogue, but he got all confused, taking an age to find it and misplacing it when he did. When at last he threw the device overboard, it immediately ripped into shreds.

Hans couldn't miss this opportunity to collect water. He rummaged through the equipment bag and stuck all the empty cans to the outside of the canopy with duct tape. The raft looked like a woman's hair in rollers. Kicking himself, Hans realized he had fixed them on upside down.

When the weather hit, Hans was past caring, whooping aloud as the tired orange pod rode the waves like a roller coaster. Fork lightning electrified the sky, the downpour rinsing salt from his matted hair and beard.

Hans held out the collapsible basin. It filled in seconds, and with no other vessel at hand in which to decant it, he tipped it over his shoulder into the cabin. The torrent was such that Hans was able to pour basin after basin into the floating tub until the sheer weight of water threatened to sink them.

"*Drink*, Jessie! *Drink!*"

Chris Thrall

As he spoke, the sound of rotor blades drowned out the tempest, and a chopper emerged from the gloom. Hans fought to remain upright in the doorway as its downwash flattened the canopy and he gagged on aviation fumes.

Hans thought it was a rescue bird at first, expecting a crew member to descend on a winch and whisk them to safety, but when he looked again he saw that it was a single-seater, the kind used by forest rangers to report on wildfires.

He spotted a compartment behind the chopper's Perspex bubble.

We can squeeze in there!

He caught the pilot's attention and gesticulated wildly. The pilot shook his head and, risking life and limb, leant out of the cockpit, opening the cowling to show Hans it housed avionics. The pilot made a chopping gesture with his bladed hand, indicating Hans should look to the distance.

Sure enough, a light shone intermittently as the sea peaked and troughed. Hans saw another, then another and another as a convoy bore down upon them.

"Yes!"

Utterly ecstatic, Hans dove headlong into the pool of rainwater . . . *to find himself fixing a puncture on JJ's bicycle in their garage back home in Portland . . . The tire was made of chocolate, causing a big problem, for when he tried to ease it back onto the wheel rim it broke into chunks, which disintegrated into purple gunpowder. Hans resorted to wrapping it around with bands of licorice, but no sooner had he done so he realized the confectionery would be put to better use doubling up as putty to seal the leaks around his neighbors' windows, except that seagulls kept flying down to land on the window ledges and pluck out the sealant with their greedy bills before flying off again . . .*

Hans sensed their chance of rescue slipping from his grasp. He forced his mind back to the chopper . . . *to find the pilot had transferred to a glider as it was all about fuel economy and far more fun doing 360-degree rolls with his great aunt on board, the lights of the approaching convoy morphing into attractions at the Bangor State Fair, garishly colored cotton candy stalls, brightly striped tarpaulins, high-pitched screams coming from the Wheel of Death, the smell of hot dogs, candy apples and fried dough . . .*

It was too much for Hans. One moment he had been convinced they had all the water they would ever need and were on the verge of rescue, but he awoke to find the raft dry and stinking and their situation as desperate as before. He dragged himself into the doorway, thrust his head into the deceptively refreshing sea and drank until he could drink no more.

Passing in and out of consciousness, Hans heard the call of a seabird and the flutter of wings as it settled on the canopy. He stared at its silhouette, unsure if what he saw was even real. It took all the strength left in his broken body to raise himself up and thrust a hand out to grab the surprise visitor, feeling a waft of air as the bird bid for freedom. He collapsed back down, unable to reach for his daughter despite knowing the end was near.

Hans drifted between this life and the next, and for the first time since the collision, images of the sinking yacht flashed through his failing mind . . .

. . . He remembered sailing *Future* ten miles off Cape Verde with Jessica, priding himself on the yacht's progress, her replacement gear holding fast as she skimmed across the wave tops. He'd felt relaxed, content with the direction his boat and life were heading, all the time looking forward to their reunion with Penny, who had stayed ashore, taking care of last-minute business.

Then there was the sickening crunch as *Future* ripped apart.

"Jessie, get out! Get out now!" he'd screamed.

As the life raft's hydrostatic releases hissed and the bright-orange capsule deployed, Hans had dived inside the cabin, launching the ditch kit out of the companionway as a barrage of seawater washed him back into the cockpit.

Fighting to compose himself, Hans had sucked in a lungful of air and thrust his body into the downturned hull, frantically trying to reach his daughter as the boat descended into the depths. His chest felt as though it was about to implode, but he continued into the blackness, rewarded to see his little girl swimming up to meet him.

That's it, Jessie! That's it!

Their hands had clasped.

Hans had experienced immense relief.

Well done, kid!

Then he'd spotted his daughter's safety line still clipped to the bunk, the sinking yacht ripping the drowning girl from his grasp, Jessica's desperate eyes fixed on his as the ocean devoured her, leaving him to clamber into the life raft alone.

- 84 -

Death was close now for Hans, the stench of necrosis eclipsing all others in the rancid floating tomb. Paralyzed throughout most of his body, he breathed in shallow gasps, his eye weeping, an arm stretched toward what he thought was his little girl. He desperately wanted to hold her one last time.

As a lone gull mewed a pitiless soliloquy, memories of better days saw a light flicker in his fading eyes.

"Hey, Jessie . . . sometimes . . . when I feel the sun on my face, I close my eyes and imagine we are walking along a soft sandy beach by a beautiful blue sea. You, me, Mommy and JJ. And it's sunny and warm . . . and the seagulls are squawking . . . and the air tastes fresh and salty . . . and we're smiling, sweet pea. We'll always be together . . . and we're smiling, my darling. We're smiling . . ."

The teddy bear gave him a look. It said everything but nothing.

Chris Thrall is a former Royal Marines Commando and author of the bestselling memoir *Eating Smoke*. A qualified pilot and skydiver, with a degree in youth work, Chris has backpacked throughout all seven continents, worked with street children in Mozambique, driven aid workers from Norway to India and back by coach, and scuba dived with leopard seals in Antarctica. He lives in Plymouth, England, and plans to continue adventuring, charity work and writing.

www.christhrall.com

www.twitter.com/ChrisThrall

www.facebook.com/ christhrallauthor

Acknowledgments

To my Jenny for your encouragement and unconditional support. My loyal Eating Smoke readers, many of whom said, "Chris, you write it, we'll read it." My awesome delta team of Mike "Rosco" Ross, Carole Poke, Patrick Burke, Nikki Davenport, Sian Forsythe, Marc Grey, Nikki Densham, Fiona Jackson, Kenneth Fossaluzza and Marc Spender for volunteering to read the manuscript and feeding back with invaluable observations and advice. Andy Screen at Golden Rivet your amazing artwork and dedication has brought the Hans Larsson series to life. Marcus Trower, for polishing the final draft and being a great editor to work with. To fellow authors J.R. Sheridan, Nije Thorpe and Shannon Young. You are inspirational writers and I value our friendship. A special mention to Steven Callahan, author of *Adrift*, the ultimate story of real sea survival and the best book I have ever read. Thank you.

Books by Chris Thrall

The Hans Larsson series

1 - The Drift

2 - The Trade

Non fiction

Eating Smoke: One Man's Descent into Crystal Meth Psychosis in Hong Kong's Triad Heartland

Printed in Great Britain
by Amazon